PASSPORTS TO HELL

Terry L. Vinson

PASSPORTS TO HELL

DOUBLE DRAGON

Chapter One
Pandora's Box Personified

Strangely, it's the fresh air I miss the most. Not trees or green grass, or even a cloudless blue sky. Not a freshly cooked steak, a homemade apple pie or a chilled brew on a muggy summer day, but a single whiff of sweet, stale-free oxygen. Air that doesn't contain the faint scent of day-old farts, the coppery stench of burnt coffee or tar and nicotine breath.

Nine months inside a concrete tomb, that's basically what it comes down to, although this particular mausoleum does hold considerably more charm than our last extended rest stop, 'The Glow Motel', as Sergeant Rock had so aptly dubbed it. Don't believe any of us were ever quite comfortable spending two months in an abandoned nuke silo. Just didn't have that 'homey' feel, so to speak.

The 'Hive' isn't exactly the Hilton either, but at least it does contain a dozen separate walled sections, so there is a semblance of privacy anyway.

I found the unmarked, unlabeled DVD's at the bottom of a cardboard box in the rear of the supply room, buried beneath a pile of yellow pocket folders overstuffed with dry-rotted files from decades past. The entire room smelled of ancient rat droppings, despite the obvious impossibilities of such. The place is so spotless, so strangely sanitized, that it almost makes you lonely for the occasional roach or dead fly lying about. Not sure why I decided to take an impromptu inventory of the room after all this time, other than to chalk up such a fruitless task to extreme boredom. Despite the camaraderie of the unit, we all desire our moments of solitude, especially with the impending scenario looming like a dark storm cloud. Humans crave companionship, true, but are also a solitary creature at heart. As a species, we are...were walking, talking contradictions. I never dwelled upon such matters, never had a reason to actually. Scary how things change, like that guy from The Eagles once sang, in 'A New York Minute'.

I can hear Lieutenant Lava's shrieking rant through the thick concrete walls, no doubt railing on Private Brain Dog, who patiently waits, preparing his hip-hop themed, profanity-laced rebuttal to whatever she's moaning about. Those two seem to revel in the art of argument for argument's sake, complete opposites in terms of personality and general opinion.

Sergeant Rock is always telling them to 'jump between the sheets and get it over with', a suggestion that never fails to induce a cringe from Father Pete, despite the fact that everyone knows such a coupling between the two is old news.

Being the only two females within the unit, both Lieutenant Lava and Airman Legs willingly accept their unspoken responsibilities to the male troops, as well as the 'mother figure' roles they assume solely for Kid Cadet, the only child within our skeletal crew ranks. My admiration and respect for those two women (especially the good Lieutenant, but more on that later) goes even beyond that of the Chief, the man most responsible for keeping us alive the past year and a half.

As I begin to repack the box (a brief time filler at best) after setting the mystery DVD's aside, I hear the Chief chime in as if on cue, spouting the now nauseatingly familiar 'Stow it, clowns!" refrain in his deep, husky tone. Despite his best efforts, however, it's obvious his bark is decidedly worse than his bark of late. I would think it's rather easy to lose your authoritative edge when mortality is staring you dead in the face.

They are all gathered about the makeshift monitoring room, no doubt sipping lukewarm coffee and munching on MRE crackers that are less crisp than rubbery from decades old packaging. Everyone, save myself and Sergeant Rock, who I can hear thumping around in the exercise room. I don't have to glare into a monitor to know what awaits us. I don't have to see or hear them to know they're out there, swarming like bloated maggots on a rotting corpse. The ad campaign worked wonders, it seems. Better than we could ever have hoped. The ruthless hordes know we're here. Probably smell us, like roasted wienies propped over a blazing campfire. We are truly the life-source for their being, serving a double purpose to the future of their survival as a species while our own has been so cruelly, systemically eradicated. Not that we're one hundred percent positive that there aren't others like us still out there somewhere, living like moles instead of humans, but even so, it's a safe bet that the numbers are frighteningly low. The hordes seem increasingly frantic the past few months, decidedly more desperate. Hosts are becoming few and far between, and the air space they occupy is becoming thick with

7

anxiety.

As I depart the supply room for 'sleep bay', the largest of the Hives' compartments, I hear The Chief instruct Corporal Chatty to up the amps on the outside speakers. The vibrations are whipping them into a frenzy, like a dinner bell ringing from some unseen buffet hall.

I kneel onto my sleeping bag, lay back and remove the rubber band which serves to hold the coupled DVD's together. The discs are pitch black in color, the outside cases clear and without markings of any kind. I deduce they must consist of 'Top Secret' war contingencies or Op Plans, possibly even training films on how to survive a nuclear holocaust-ravaged earth. Regardless, the utter uselessness of such drivel strikes me as hilariously ironic as a wide smile creases my usually stoic visage. Laying back to further study the stone ceiling overhead, I realize how dramatically I've aged since the plague, especially in the psychological sense. A twenty-seven year old man housing a senior-citizen attitude; battle worn and constantly at odds with a level of mental fatigue he never previously thought possible.

Another loud thump from two rooms down, and I hear Sergeant Rock sigh loudly. A true creature of habit, is our Kenneth McKay. Pounds those weights for hours on end, like a man prepping for Mr. Universe honors. Hits the hard bag until his fists are raw and his knuckles bleed. I guess we've all developed our own unique technique to stave off the insanity boiling just below the surface of our skullcaps. Mine is to journal this maddening existence as the days drone on, despite the reality of never having such a dairy read by anyone of my own kind. Everyone's been asked to add something to the time capsule that Father Pete is putting together. He's packing the objects in a stainless steel tube he pulled from the silo. Doubtful it will survive the blast, but it's the symbolism of the deed that counts, not the eventual fate of the object itself.

Eighteen months of avoiding death's sharp-edged rapier can take their toll, both mentally and physically. I'm sure all nine of us would be a real study if such an occupation as psychiatrist still mattered. Incurable head cases with multiple phobias and remarkable tolerance levels for pain and anguish. We've all seen more death and destruction in these past several months than in every ultra-violent movie or TV show ever produced.

I reach over and pull the worn, leather bound journal from my duffel, careful not to tip over the small makeup stand sitting between my own sleeping bag and that of Airman Legs. Maintaining her looks is Pam Vincent's vice. I can't say I don't approve of the effort, however moot. Pam is what society used to label 'drop dead gorgeous, despite the added battle scars of recent times.

Flipping to the front of the book, I glance over the initial entries with an astonishingly diverse mix of feelings, the gist of which include both pinning nostalgia and gut-wrenching, primal fear.

Some of the names had long since departed our dwindling ranks, and the attached faces vanished just as quickly from my tattered mind.

The present line-up:

Yours truly, Barry Hooper, AKA 'Private Radar' (for my inexplicable talent for sensing impending danger. More curse than godsend, in my humble opinion, but even I cannot completely deny its usefulness in our plight).

Age: Twenty-seven (last October, when months, days and hours actually meant something)

Physical Description: White male. Five-eight, one-hundred sixty pounds. Prominent, beak-like nose (a mark of us Hoopers since my great, great grandad), pasty complexion (never could hold a tan. Skin would always turn rose red and proceed to roast).

Former occupation: UPS Route Driver, Austin, TX; part time writer of un-published fiction.

Family status: Wife (Denise) and five year old son Wallace missing, presumed deceased (taken three days after the nest was unearthed in Northern Alabama). You hold out hope for a while, then it slowly fades into reluctant acceptance. The sour feeling never leaves my gut, however, whenever their faces enter my dreams.

'Swarm Day' Location: When the city was besieged upon on that steamy hot Austin summer day, I had driven my route truck towards home like a doped up lunatic, only to discover the house (actually the entire street we lived on) ravaged and my loved ones gone. Looked like someone had rocked our house, as every window was shattered and every door bashed open. I had been on my way to my parent's place in Fort Worth, the interstates packed to overflowing and moving at a snail's pace, despite the shoulders on both sides being used as lanes. The hordes swept down on us from all directions. I saw several unfortunate individuals pulled from their vehicles and whisked away like confetti in a funnel cloud. The idling Greyhound was parked just to the left of my UPS van. Just as one (several?) of the swarm landed atop my vehicle, I leapt from the truck and sprinted to the bus. Inexplicably lost the pinkie finger of my right hand in the process. Hope they choked on it. The rest, as they say…will soon be history.

***

NCOIC In Charge: Kenneth McKay, AKA 'Sergeant Rock'. Age: Forty

Physical Description: White male, six-feet two, two-hundred twenty pounds. Strong as an ox and twice as ornery, his physique seemingly carved in stone from decades of hard work and a daily weight lifting regimen. Completely bald (riddled with recently obtained scars) from daily shaving, sports a Fu Manchu mustache that hangs from the corners of his granite jaw like twin caterpillars.

Disposition: A man of infinite jest, old Rock Jaw, although he'd never admit such under oath. The equivalent of a rabid wolverine during combat conditions.

Former Occupation: Warehouse Manager, Selma, Alabama. Served two decades in the National Guard, where he was once a member of his unit's boxing team.

Family status: Wife and three children (all high school age) missing and presumed dead (taken in initial attack on southern Alabama just two days after the unearthing in the northern part of the state).

11

Much like myself, Kenneth had raced home from work to find his rural, country home torn apart and his loved ones missing. Witnessed his elderly neighbors pulled from their home through a living room picture window and swept airborne, their screams muffled and weak as they were hauled into the clouds by their ankles. After a frantic but fruitless search of the besieged township, had immediately drove north to Birmingham, ditched his own vehicle and caught a Greyhound bound for his brother's home in Lawton, Oklahoma.

'Swarm Day' Location: Same stretch of interstate as yours truly, already taking up a seat in the aforementioned Greyhound.

***

Grunt #1: Pamela Vincent, AKA 'Airman Legs' (for obvious reasons. Those slick, impeccably toned bad boys seem to go on infinitely).

Age: Thirty-one

Physical Description: White female, five-feet nine, approximately one-hundred twenty-five pounds. Tanned complexion, lengthy straight brown hair, hazel eyes.

Toned, muscular build without being overly masculine. Legs of a dancer (see former occupation), face of a Victoria's Secret model. Basically, a woman who stood in the beauty line more than once when looks were being doled out.

Family Status: Twice divorced, no children.

Disposition: Relatively mild-mannered and even tempered unless alcohol happens to pass over those ruby, ever- pouting lips, resulting in her wildly uninhibited evil twin springing forth in a gusher of

12

howling laughter and booze induced shrieking. The shakiest of the crew when faced with imminent combat, she always seems on the verge of a complete meltdown.

Former Occupation: Exotic dancer, various locations. Hawthorne, California.

'Swarm Day' Location: Traveling interstate in late model Mustang GT, abandoned car as attack commenced. Practically dragged into the Greyhound by force, she continued to scream for at least a half-hour after the battle had waned. It was weeks before she completely snapped out of her hysterical daze to begin training as the serviceable (albeit a bit shaky) soldier she's become.

***

Grunt #2: Clarence Warren, Private Brain Dog (rap music aficionado with an IQ measured at around one-sixty. Mechanical, as well as electronics whiz).

Age: Twenty-two.

Physical Description: Black male, six-feet, one hundred seventy pounds. Sports a thick, uncombed Afro (cultivated over the past eighteen months) he comically refers to as his 'tribute to the lost bro's of the seventies'.

Family status: Single. Parents reside (d) in Tulsa, Ok.

Disposition: Comically sarcastic; loud and boisterous. Can be standoffish, but usually good-natured. Calm and collected within the combat zone, he is heavily counted on for his natural ability to problem solve.

Former Occupation: Student, ITT Technical

13

Institute. A self-taught electronics whiz. Worked part time stocking groceries.

'Swarm Day' Location: Within the Greyhound that eventually served as our safe haven, headed to his parents home in Tulsa from Little Rock, where he was attending ITT classes.

***

Grunt #3: Robert Gonzales, AKA 'Corporal Chatty' (For his less than vocal persona. A man of precious few words).

Age: Forty-eight.

Physical Description: Hispanic Male. Five-Five, One-sixty to one-sixty five (down at least thirty pounds in the last year). Thick wavy brown hair that is graying at the temples but hangs over his forehead like pasted shingles. Slowly transformed sagging, pudgy build into rock hard muscle by joining in on Sergeant Rock's daily work out routine.

Family Status: Watched in muted horror as his wife of twenty-six years was abducted from their Ford van as they drove south from Chicago to their son's home in Dallas.

The Chief (more info below) managed to pull Robert onto the bus as he stood with his back against the door, fighting one off with a tire iron as his wife was being air-lifted into the clouds just a few dozen feet in the distance. It took three of us, practically sitting on top of him for almost an hour, to calm him somewhat. He finally passed out from sheer exhaustion. I sincerely believe the man would have taken on the whole damn swarm without a moment's hesitation, armed with a can of Raid in one hand and a flyswatter in the other. Not sure I've ever, or ever will, love anyone that much, although that particular question has arisen of late (again, more later as this narrative drones on...)

Disposition: The textbook definition of low-key. Quiet, reserved, soft spoken. Says more with the least amount of words than anyone I've ever met.

Former Occupation: Owner, G & G Vending, Chicago, IL.

'Swarm Day' Location: See above.

***

Grunt#4: Tia Stephens, AKA 'Lieutenant Lava' (see disposition).

Age: Twenty-Three

Physical Description: Asian female. Five-feet, ninety-five pounds. Pitch-black straight hair that hangs in a tightly wound pony tail reaching to the pit of her back. Small, pug nose gracing a flawlessly sculpted face whose most striking feature are her piercing, dark-brown eyes. Lithe and wiry; easily the most agile of the unit. Unofficially second in command of the unit, solely due to her nerves, which seem welded from the purest of metal alloys.

Family: Legally separated from husband two years earlier.

Parents reside(d) in South Korea.

Disposition: Difficult to narrow down, depending on the minute. Mood seems to swing like a pendulum blade. Kind and accommodating at times; foul-tempered and moody the next, hence the nickname. Combat ready at the drop of an eyelash, Tia seems to invite the rage and harness it as pure adrenaline.

Personal Note: The woman exudes eroticism.

15

I'm literally a walking pile of moist putty within her intoxicating space. Airman Legs might score more points in the natural beauty category, but Tia's whimsical charms and raw sex appeal are off the charts. She's the ultimate temptress; a dragon-lady goddess in tight leather pants. As much as I despise myself for saying it, my wife didn't possess half the seductive drawing power as this woman. Of course, I might just be a tad biased (more on that later, as time permits).

Former Occupation: Telemarketer/Data Entry, Dayton, Oh.

'Swarm Day' Location: Driving home (the scenic route) from visiting a friend in Colorado Springs. The Honda Civic she navigated was stationed directly behind the Greyhound when the attack commenced. Sergeant Rock and I pulled her into the bus from a rear window (Slamming it shut just as one of the enemy landed where the relatively narrow opening had been). If Tia had been two inches taller or her torso a tad wider, this particular journal entry would not exist.

***

Grunt#5: Peter Wilkes, AKA 'Father Pete'.

Age: Forty-six.

Physical Description: White male. Five-nine, two-hundred twenty pounds (down twenty pounds since team inception). Mostly bald except for thick tufts of grayish-white hair around his jug-like ears. Pointy chin, red-tinted, bulbous nose (typically observed on heavy drinkers, which Father Pete readily confessed to being decades earlier). Reminds Sergeant Rock of the actor who played

Lumpy Rutherford's dad on 'Leave it to Beaver'.

Family Status: Divorced in late eighties. No children. Parents deceased.

Disposition: Predictably, Father Pete is kind and helpful. Unpredictably, he shows streaks of unabashed stubbornness and occasionally gets downright mean when his opinions are challenged. Does not push his religious beliefs, although he openly objects (but rarely verbally) to the relationship (agreement?) between the men and women of the unit regarding carnal activities.

Still, Father Pete provides a calming influence amongst the ever-present lunacy surrounding us. Former Occupation: Methodist Preacher, Lawton, Oklahoma. 'Swarm Day' Location: Within the Greyhound, returning from a weekend visit to his older sister in Fort Worth. Had debated for days before the trip on whether or not to take the chance of making the drive in his well-worn Chevy truck, which had been having transmission problems. Has since chalked up the decision to 'bus it' to the lord's overall plan for his place within our ranks. 'No squadron is complete without a divine messenger,' Father Pete was apt to repeat in those early, anxiety-fueled days. Despite his less than menacing outward appearance, has proven he can hold his own in a firefight.

***

Grunt#6: Jake Johannsen, AKA 'Kid Cadet'.

Age: Ten and a half (white Male).

Physical Description: Four-feet six, seventy pounds. Bushy blonde hair, blue eyes, pale complexion.

17

Family: Parents missing and presumed deceased.

Disposition: Despite the living hell his young eyes have witnessed since the age of nine, a very level headed and typically carefree kid. His youthful exuberance rubs off on all, just as the sincere innocence he displays reminds us of the reason we continue to persevere. Other than the mass extermination of the enemy, we have dedicated ourselves just as strongly to overseeing his survival.

Former Occupation: 3rd Grader, West Union Elementary, Fort Worth, Texas.

'Swarm Day' Location: Riding to Wichita Falls with his mother to visit his aunt. Vehicle was overturned beneath concrete underpass as the enemy descended in never-ending waves of humanity. Jake's mother had just enough time to shove him into the van's rear compartment before being pulled through the shattered remains of the driver's side window. Jake had been crawling from the rear door when the bus bounded by in a wavy lurch, searching for an off-ramp leading away from the onslaught. Private Brain Dog pulled him into the bus feet first while Sergeant Rock and I played sentry from the bus entrance.

***

Team Leader: Conrad Masterson, AKA 'The Chief' (see former occupation below).

Age: Fifty (Black Male).

Physical Description: Six-two, one-ninety-five. Four words: Lean, mean, fightin' machine.

Family: Lifelong bachelor. Parents deceased.

Disposition: Stern but caring. A disciplinarian

18

from the old school that follows a single, simple rule of thumb: expect no more from others than you're willing to contribute yourself.

Former Occupation: Police Officer, City of Houston (hence the 'Chief' label). Retired as Patrol Sergeant (served a total of twenty-six years). Had worked as home security advisor for a local Houston security firm for less than two months when attacks commenced.

'Swarm Day' location: Three vehicles behind Greyhound as assault began. Exited his Ford Explorer to assist a nearby elderly couple as their own vehicle fell under siege. Unable to foil their abduction, he fought his way to the bus entrance and assisted in loading others inside. Spearheaded our 'back roads' route to the first of many temporary safe havens. As days progressed and tensions built to a fever pitch, the Chief became our unofficial team leader by default. He inspired us to turn our pity into anger, our suicidal depression into motivation to live...live to kill. Kill to live. Simple but effective.

Personal Note: Without the Chief, our existence as a unit would have never materialized, much less made it this far. I'm fairly certain this opinion is unanimously shared within the ranks.

***

My eyes painstakingly scan additional names, all of which have been vanquished from our midst as the long months (and many moves) have transpired. I had began to mark out the names as they departed our ranks, but soon found the simple task of doing so depressing to the extreme, and discontinued the

19

practice. It was as if I was keeping a part of them alive and with us by refraining from marking through their names.

Jerome Weaver, a painfully thin, lanky, middle-aged black man from Memphis, taken from us during an enemy raid at Dyess Air Force Base in Abilene. He'd been stationed as a sentry as we departed the bus for the fenced-in confines of an abandoned Alert Facility just off the edge of the main flight line. There one minute, gone the next. They found his Super-Soaker rifle (filled with liquid pesticide) lying in the tall weeds near the sentry point, along with a single size twelve Reebok tennis shoe.

Catherine Wheeler, a twenty-something, pudgy white female, and her young daughter, whose name I never even learned, swept away in a lurch as the enemy penetrated our defenses within the aforementioned facility. (Excerpt from Journal):

From my crouched position behind an overturned dining table, I watched Airman Legs try to hold the woman back as her child was being enveloped less than a dozen feet away. Legs was flung back as Wheeler darted forward with squirt-guns blazing from each hand, like a 'stay-at-home-mom version of Clint Eastwood from an old spaghetti western. The twin-spray of chemicals did little but annoy the circle of opposition, two of whom whirled around and charged the woman, who was subsequently scooped up and hauled away through an already partially shattered glass wall. Her water pistols fell from her clinched fists just as she sailed from sight, followed by her equally hapless offspring, who I heard scream out one last time for her mother as she was flown through the same jagged opening.

Russell Cummings, an Hispanic teenager (eighteen maybe, nineteen at the most), quick-witted young man, always wearing a big, broad smile, no matter how dire the situation. We were bugging out of the National Guard Armory in El Paso, having just replenished supplies at a local Wal-Mart.

Russ was driving one of the supply jeeps and didn't notice the uninvited stowaway lurking in the back until it leaned into the front seat and sprayed him full in the face with cleaning fluid. That's our little definition of their 'gurg juice. They only use it when severely threatened, otherwise it has a way of spoiling a potential host. By the time the convoy stopped to check on his lagging vehicle, a full blown battle had ensued. Father Pete and Corporal Chatty supplied cover for Sergeant Rock and me as we attempted to recover the jeep. I've seen some grisly sights since this shit-storm began eighteen months ago, clipped scenes that play out in my mind like mini-horror films, especially on those (frequent) nights when sleep is fleeting. None compare to what we found slumped over in that driver's seat, a bubbling mass of quivering flesh that looked to have been dipped head first in battery acid, still audibly sizzling....like grilled beef. Sergeant Rock cleared away the mutilated remains as I ran to the back of the vehicle and dry-heaved until it felt like I had dislodged a lung.

Others suffered similar fates along the winding, back-roads trail that brought us to the mountains of

21

Colorado, dwindling our ranks from thirty-two to the present count.

I skim the names just as Tia strolls into the room, the end of her left pinkie finger (the lengthy nail of which is shaded dark crimson) lodged seductively between her loosely clinched teeth. She winks at me playfully while straddling my waist, bowing until our crotches gently meet in a warm caress. There are no doors within the shelter to ensure privacy, but I hear the echo of Private Brain Dog's boom box from the control room, the familiar echoes of Johnny Cash's 'Ring of Fire' cascading softly through the stale air surrounding us. The Man in Black's four-decade old classic is my and Tia's code, our personally devised 'Keep Out' sign. Every coupling is assigned one, a specific tune that conveys the same message to the others. Such devices are necessary since the Hive became home base. It was much simpler within the other stops. Just pick a room, shut and latch (or similarly barricade) the door...instant privacy.

Tia eyes the pile of DVD's curiously, then returns her attention to me without ever questioning their possible content. Her lips are moist and inviting, the slightest taste of strawberry assaulting my honed senses just as the tip of her luscious tongue greets my own. Our movements are growing increasingly frantic with each bout, inherently more passionate and animalistic.

Afterwards, Tia assures me that we will indeed couple several more times before the inevitable. Not sure if such comments do more to console or scare the living hell out of me. She dresses hastily and departs just as Johnny Cash's 'Boy Named Sue' fades to numbing silence.

My breathing starting to stabilize as the minutes pass since her departure back to the control room, I remain happily prone, unable or possibly unwilling to let the moment completely pass.

A moment later, just as Kid Cadet's high-pitched laughter ricochets through the halls like small-arms fire, my mind replays (as it will at least a half dozen times within a twenty-four hour period) a certain spring day some eighteen months earlier. A time when such everyday, commonplace trivialities as breathing clean air, sleeping in a warm, soft bed, and moving freely along the planet's surface were, rather sadly, taken for granted. Sure, we had wars in the Middle East, racial unrest, food and energy shortages ravaging Third World countries, and premeditated terrorist attacks on every corner of the damned globe. It was far from a perfect world, and growing increasingly unstable by the day. Serial killers had become as commonplace in the everyday scheme as crooked politicians while the media saturated the airwaves and internet with a lethal dose of negativity under the guise of necessary journalism. World leaders spoke of peace while prophets lectured on the hammer soon to fall. We rooted for the leaders but listened to the prophets. Good call, as it turned out. Good call, tragic consequences.

***

The man's name had been William Greene. A forty-eight year old white male from Galvan, Alabama, a tiny township of around one-thousand citizens, sixty miles east of Mobile. William, like his father before him, sold farm implements for a living, everything from tractors to backhoes to garden tillers. William had done quite well, providing three counties of farmers with all their cultivating needs for almost two decades, and had decided to share his success with his children and grandchildren by having an Olympic-sized pool constructed in his spacious backyard. Taking a friend's advice, he hired a small company from Mobile for the task.

The initial dig uncovered the strange alloy plate buried a dozen feet within the solid red clay. A plate no one present could readily identify, its surface as smooth as sanded ivory while maintaining the tinsel strength of iron.

Day two saw the plate accidentally penetrated by a backhoe operator sporting a hellish hangover. One can only imagine the exaggerated look of comical terror stretched across the man's face as his bleary eyes focused on the uninvited visitors that sprang forth.

Within a span of less than three hours, the small, tranquil southern burg of Galvan was the recipient of a swift, rather gruesome, extremely unpleasant makeover that would soon sweep over the surrounding landscape like a raging, surging virus of unparalleled magnitude.

Atlanta and Birmingham were taken by nightfall, even as the media tried desperately (and failed just as miserably) to warn and advise nearby cities and states of impending attacks, all the while attempting (invariably in vain) to maintain a semblance of journalistic integrity. From a viewers standpoint, it was not unlike hearing repeated playings of Orson Welle's famous 'War of The Worlds' transmission.

By the time scientific minds from half a dozen countries had figured out and conveyed what we were dealing with, it was already far too late to even slow its progression, much less halt the process altogether. Military intervention came a day late and several million lives short, actually contributing more to the carnage with ill-advised bombing raids and chemical weapon drops. Less than forty-eight hours after the initial unearthing, the skies above the nation's capitol grew dark from the slowly descending cloud of fluttering wings. Needless to say, a scheduled Presidential news conference never materialized. Seventy-two hours after a backhoe's blade had shattered the shell, the North American Continent as a whole ceased to exist.

It took less than three days for the rest of the plant to follow suit.

***

A multi-planetary team of highly regarded entomologists had labeled them 'Cyclortors', due to the physical resemblance to the Cyclorrhapha species of fly, although the majority agreed their origin to be alien in nature. A full grown adult measured three and a half to four feet in length, and some weighed in excess of seventy pounds. It was quickly established (by all unfortunate enough to witness the actual scenario) that the human body was their mammal of choice for two distinct (and equally grisly) reasons. Number one: it provided a protein-based host for their offspring. Number two:

in a word, nourishment. Upon capture, the Cyclortor instantly paralyzed its victim by penetrating the mouth and throat with a slimy, tube-shaped appendage which sprang forth from a horizontal slit beneath its saucer-sized eyes. The tentacle-like tube then emitted a numbing dose of fluids that worked quickly to shut down the victim's nervous system, thereby rendering them paralyzed while also keeping them at least semi-conscious. While incapacitated, the victim is then implanted (below the rib cage on both sides) with the Cyclor's eggs via a syringe-thin genitalia at the base of their thick, scaly torsos. The eggs gestated within the victim's adrenal glands (over each kidney), hatching a mere six hours later with as many as three offspring per gland. The adult Cyclor would then extract the now-obviously deceased victim's pituitary gland for feeding purposes. All told, less than twelve hours would pass between the implant and the young Cyclor's full growth.

The Cyclor's had no stinger, but instead utilized a pair of crap-like pinchers on either side of its upper body as the main weapon within its arsonal. The pinchers could either hold an opponent at bay while prepping for implantation, or effortlessly sever whatever fell between its razor-sharp edges. The 'slice 'n dice' technique was rarely used in lieu of the impregnation scenario, for obvious reasons (an active pulse was actually needed for the brief incubation period), although it wasn't uncommon when the Cyclor felt particularly threatened. On such occasions, the beings were known to utilize the deadliest self-defense measure of all, one gruesomely familiar to bug doctors everywhere. The acid spewed forth from their moist maw mouth in a fine mist, instantly turning human flesh and bone into a bubbling, boiling pile of throbbing, crimson oatmeal.

Upon landing, they crawled about the surface much like a housefly, taking off and landing in a similar mode as the Army's Blackhawk helicopter, requiring little room to maneuver within a restricted space. Their lower bodies were incased with a heavy armor plate that protected the exposed underside, while a multi-pointed layer of the same covered their bulbous heads like a spiked helmet made of iron.

There were filmed reports of citizens firing into the swarming masses with handguns, rifles, even crossbows and air rifles. One such report, filmed in the lower east side of Cleveland, displayed an elderly woman standing on her front porch, swinging a long-handled broom like a Louisville Slugger before being snatched airborne in a frenzied blur. It might have been amusing if filmed within the confines of some Hollywood Sci-Fi/Comedy. Within the realm of stark reality, however, it was nothing less than horrifying.

On day three of the onslaught, Air Force and Navy jets were armed with what the Chief of Staff refered to as 'Pissiles', missiles filled with large amounts of Pesticide, for scattered carpet bombings outside several major cities. Unfortunately, it was soon reported that the human population would suffer the majority of the casualties from the effort, having inhaled lethal amounts that had blown into several suburban areas.

27

Attempts to slay the species with artillery fire was equally ineffective, as for every handful of Cyclors that were fallen, there was no shortage of replacements to fill the unoccupied slot. It was similar to digging a handful of sand from the base of a large dune and watching haplessly as it instantly replenished itself.

The Greyhound had exited the interstate on day two of the takeover and found the back roads surprisingly abandoned for the most part. Cyclor sightings were few, as they seemed to be concentrating their attacks on Major cities and their connecting thoroughfares.

Thirty-two individuals, including the driver; a short, stocky, middle-aged Hispanic man named Ivan, packed into the front eight rows of seats, huddled together like survivors on a life raft.

The initial stopover had been on the outskirts of Synder, Texas, almost six hours after departing the madness and mayhem of Interstate 20. A list of essential supplies had been scribbled down by Sergeant Rock and the Chief, even though the majority of the group had not yet resigned themselves to the fact that there was indeed 'safety in numbers'. The Snyder Wal-Mart had been packed to overflowing with people of a similar mindset. The checkouts stood empty as people sprinted through the parking lot with armloads of unbagged items. The entire lot was layered in debris, everything from unrolled toilet paper to empty boxes once filled with shotgun shells covered whatever spaces weren't occupied with haphazardly parked vehicles.

The group had managed to secure the last full

28

box (a dozen cans) of Raid (Sgt Rock's idea) and Terminex Flying Insect Killer, along with two twelve-gauge shotguns and six boxes of shells (25 each). They also loaded up on the aforementioned toilet tissue and bottled water, plus as many canned goods as could be held within folded arms.

The plan to lay low was the only logical course. Options became severely limited with each passing moment, as reports of additional cities falling under siege filtered in through the sporadic waves of frenzied media reports.

Our driver was taken outside an abandoned BP gas station on the outskirts of Moreland, New Mexico on day six of what the media had begun to call 'The Deadly Invasion'. The group had exited to stretch and suck in some of the fresh, cool desert air. Some twenty minutes later, Ivan had not returned. The Chief (having already begun to establish the leadership role) had taken Sergeant Rock and began to search the station's pitch-dark perimeter. They had re-entered the bus a few moments later, each with expressions of shell-shocked weariness. Private Brain-Dog was immediately assigned as the new driver, and instructed to depart the area post-haste. Once a seemingly safe distance from the station had been reached, The Chief, Corporal Chatty, and Sergeant Rock quickly departed the parked vehicle and began the daily ritual of spraying down the outside with Raid and Flying Bug Killer. No one knew if such a measure actually served as a deterrence to the enemy, but if nothing else, it did seem to ease tensions a bit amongst the group.

By Day ten, all radio communications had

ceased and electrical power had become a luxury that most of the free world no longer enjoyed. By last reports, most major metropolitan cities within the US and Canadian borders were either burning or utterly abandoned, or a combination of both.

The group was held up in an abandoned County Jail a few miles east of Las Cruces; stone walls, thick metal door entrance and exit doors, and most importantly, it was located far from the beaten track. It also housed a fairly well stocked arsenal of firearms (thirty gauge pump actions/thirty eight and forty-four revolvers) along with an indoor firing range, small but well furnished gymnasium, and a Com center complete with multi-channel scanners and radios both citizen's banned and secure lined.

Six months passed, during which time, only a single supply run was executed (a nearby hardware store) for generator fuel. It was during this time that the rag-tag group of shell-shocked, downtrodden survivors began to slowly merge together as the tight-knit group they would eventually become. With the Chief comfortably at the helm, combat and weapons training became a daily ritual. Sergeant Rock held both morning and evening Tae Kwon Do classes (he had earned a first-degree black belt years earlier before knee surgery forced him from the sport), while the Chief supervised daily target sessions at the range. It was also during this time that the world's fate as a whole became horrifically apparent, as all radio transmissions ceased in lieu of static waves and dead air.

It was also during the latter portion of their stay at the 'Las Cruces Hilton' as Lieutenant Lava had labeled it upon their arrival, that inhibitions began to fade just as physical yearnings reemerged. Long-abandoned jail cell cots soon found a use besides housing the occasional drunk or pot smoker as various couplings ensued, most of which were never spoken of verbally amongst the team. Father Pete held his tongue, despite obvious objections. He began to spend inordinate amounts of time within the cool stone walls of the gym, along with Corporate Chatty and Sergeant Rock, who never seemed to tire as he willingly allowed frustration and rage to fuel his Olympian workouts.

The Unit, christened 'BUG STOMPERS INC' by Private Brain Dog during the mid-way point of the Las Cruces stay, decided to depart for possibly greener pastures just as the western skies chilled with winter's initial frosted huffs. The Chief had a spot picked out in western Colorado, and figured the cold air and winter conditions might actually have the same effect on the Cyclors as other flying insects. That being, they most probably were hidden away in warmer climes, no longer patrolling the skies as frequently or with the same enthusiasm as during the spring or summer months. The group had unanimously voted on the proposed move, weary of cowering and grimly determined to set into motion a mission of renewal for the human race.

The hardware store run had also provided several gallon cans of liquid pesticide that the group had drained into 'Super Soaker' water rifles obtained from the Wal-Mart in Synder, each of which guaranteed a firing range of up to thirty feet. Upon exiting the Jail for the Greyhound (which had been literally coated in several types of insect repellent the morning of), each team member would arm themselves with both a conventional weapon and a 'bug-canon' as Sergeant Rock so affectionately called the water rifles.

Four days later, the bus pulled onto a desolate, formerly fenced off two-lane roughly ten miles north of Monclave Air Force Base, which stood on the eastern edge of Denver's city limits.

All told, the relatively short trek from Las Cruces had seen the group's ranks dangerously depleted, and not without the psychological loss that accompanies such heavy loses. Twenty-one had either died or been taken in what was now referred to simply as the 'shit-storm', a frenzied battle royal that, in retrospect, lasted no longer than five minutes from inception to conclusion, although the survivors unanimously agreed that its duration seemed closer to an hour or possibly two. The hordes had descended in waves, pounding the bus from all sides, as well as from above and below, just as the occupants had settled in for the night's bivouac along an endless stretch of treeless dunes. Sergeant Rock's 'Off-Granades', basically water balloons filled with insect repellent, would later be given credit for the enemies eventual retreat, but not before the bus chugged away from the site dented, battered and housing only nine of it's original thirty passengers. Needless to say, the team's initial optimism had severely dissipated, replaced by a lethal mixture of shell-shocked disbelief and bitter, unyielding depression.

The "Hive", as isolated and coldly desolate as it

was, served as the perfectly situated safe-haven for the initial month of the group's stay, if solely for the surrounding mountain's thick, impenetrable walls. After the waking nightmare that had been the 'shit-storm', bruises both physical and mental had welcomed the surreal calmness with open arms while attempting an impromptu reload of optimism within the group's skeletal ranks.

The Chief had served a stint with the USAF in his late teens/early twenties, permanently stationed at Monclave while also being given access to the 'Hive' for occasional armed security duty. The fenced off, once-heavily guarded road was steep and winding, and just wide enough to allow the clear access to the mountaintop it lead up to. The Greyhound was left parked at the center of a wide, paved circle at trail's end, resembling a war-seasoned tank left to rust on an ancient battleground, having far surpassed expectations from the brigade it had so efficiently served.

Even after a quarter-century, the Chief recalled the 'Hives' sole entry point without a moment's doubt, a camouflaged stucco wall that mingled with the surrounding rock like a threatened Chameleon lying atop an oak leaf.

Once the control panel was accessed, it took Private Brian Dog less than a half-hour to analyze and subsequently break the code.

The emergency generator powered elevator whisked them into the belly of the beast (ten stories down) a few moments later. Never within the annuals of history had cold, unfeeling concrete and steel felt more undeniably homely.

Sergeant Rock, Corporal Chatty and Airman Legs join me in the Rec room as I prep the DVD player with the first of the mystery discs.

"Probably nothin' more than a trainin' film on how to properly panic following a Nuke attack," the Sarge quips after hopping into the cushioned confines of the leather sectional that fronts the large screen TV, his face and bare arms still moist with fresh sweat. His biceps and forearms are hideously pumped, veins the size of cable cord standing out on each. Man resembles the aged version of 'Hollywood Hulk Hogan' more every day, Fu Manchu 'stache and all.

"Yep, VD film maybe," Corporal Chatty agrees with a slight nod, wiping the wetness from his face with a small towel as he joins his workout partner on the spacious couch.

"Nah, probably porno. Soldier boys will be soldier boys, I'm guessing," Airman Legs adds, shooting me a playful wink before lounging in a nearby love seat, her combat boots propped atop a nearby end table littered with various magazines, all depressingly outdated. Her lips are freshly coated dark crimson and set in permanent pout as she stifles a yawn with the back of her left hand.

"Might be blanks. Found 'em in the back of storage closet number two. Can't believe we missed 'em the first time around," I say while powering up the state of art Panasonic DVD/VCR player/Fifty-two inch screen RCA 'Home Theater Unit', a task that hadn't been attempted since week one due to an obvious lack of reason (no discs...no tapes...no cable...etc..,) to do so.

Father Pete joins us just as I back away from the unit, the tiny, remarkably compact remote clutched tightly in my left hand resembling a 'Phaser' from Star Trek infamy.

"Movies after all this time? Was there a reason we were saving them?" he asks sheepishly, joining the Sarge and the Corporal on the wrap-around sectional. He eyeballs me with just a hint of disdain before turning to the static filled TV screen, obviously flashing a non-verbal reprimand my way for the recent tryst with the Lieutenant. Such trivial annoyances no longer register on the temper gauge, though. In fact, these days I find the good father's concern for my soul strangely comforting.

"Radar just discovered 'em, Father, like a gynecologist diggin' for Tyrannosaurus bones," Sergeant Rock states matter of factly and without a hint of humor, sending everyone into chest heaving, rib-throbbing, throat burning hysterics. All that is, save the Sarge himself, who is blissfully unaware of his Freudian slip, as is normally the case. The 'Yogi Berra' of the survivalist set, is our Ken McKay.

"What? What did I say this time?" he finally mumbles as the rest of us only begin to recover. Wiping the moist trail of melted mascara from her left cheek, Airman Legs is the first to regain the power of speech.

"Sarge, two things I'm fairly sure of. Number one; an OB-GYN doc you ain't. Number two; that the possibility of a Dinosaur bone being lodged between a woman's privates is definitely slim and none, although I'm fairly certain many similar expeditions have probably occurred."

As I power up the DVD/VCR with shaky hands, The Chief and Private Brain Dog join the festivities, obviously drawn by the echoes of jocularity.

"What's up, Father Pete fart the Stars 'n Stripes forever again?" Brain Dog asks while positioning himself behind Airman Legs and subsequently giving her a quick, forceful neck massage. Father Pete frowns, but not without an initial giggle escaping his tightly pursed lips. His nose holds a heavy tint of maroon from the recent outburst of guffaws.

"Sergeant Rock break out his Archie Bunker thesaurus again?" The Chief queries, his arms crossed loosely around his barrel-shaped chest.

"Fog-Horn Leg-Horn strikes again," Corporal Chatty manages while wiping fresh tears from the corners of his eyes. The Sarge smiles and claps Chatty on the upper back, his smile comically exaggerated.

"Ya almost surpassed your six-word sentence limit, Chat. Watch that shit, pal. Yer only allowed two-hundred a month, y'know, and you're ridin' on danger's edge as it is."

"You people planning on staring at static for a change of pace? Didn't we play this sad little game about nine months ago?" The Chief asks me while staring over at the Sarge as he and the Corporal trade playful jabs.

"Found some unlabled DVD's at the bottom of an unchecked crate, Chief. Just want to see what's on 'em. Maybe it's some old slapstick comedies. I'd give my right arm for a Three Stooges Marathon.

Anything to wipe away the dreariness," I answer as Lieutenant Lava practically leaps into the room while executing side and roundhouse kicks, one of which narrowly misses the back of the Sergeant's rapidly swaying head.

"Shiiiit…. Radar, with our luck, it'll be H.G. Well's 'Food of the Gods' or maybe one of the 'Fly' sequels," Private Brain Dog spouts, departing Private Leg's massage therapy in lieu of play-boxing Lieutenant Lava as they dance a wild jig to the back of the spacious, mostly furniture-free room.

"Stow that garbage, Private. By all means, Radar…engage that power button. At this point, I'll watch anything but a documentary on plant life," The Chief announces while taking a seat across from Airman Legs, who has stretched out in a lazy, napping pose.

"Kid Cadet on monitor?" the Sarge queries, wearing a deep frown.

"He never tires of it. Must be his video-game past. My eyes begin blearing after fifteen minutes of scanning those swirling masses," The Chief replies with a shrug.

"How…long we gonna wait for the Queen to show, Chief? I mean..," Airman Legs asks, leaning forward with her elbows balanced atop her knees.

"Airman, being that we're not even sure one exists, it's damned hard to say. From what I've observed, the swarm is building by the hour. Looks like a grouping of cumulus clouds around the mountain's tip. It's not like they're going anywhere as long as we're in here," The Chief answers stoically, eyeing each of us briefly as he speaks.

"Gotta be a Queen, Chief. Only thing that explains how quickly their numbers increased before using us as hosts. Even those egghead scientists we're convinced it was the only explanation that made sense. Whether they be alien or subterranean in origin, it's only logical that an egg-layin' bitch does exist," Private Brain Dog injects from the rear of the room, his breath labored from the playful sparing.

"Looks to me like the whole damned bug world is scurrying about just outside our window. We must be playing their song," Lieutenant Lava comments after a winded huff.

The Chief nods in agreement, then glances over at me wearing a taunt, tense smile.

"Speaking of playing, hit that 'P' button, Radar. Whatever's is on them, it has to beat staring at that monitor."

"Like Brain Dog said, with our luck it'll be one of those 1950's Sci-Fi 'giant bug' flicks," Airman Legs says sarcastically.

"I sincerely pray not," Father Pete answers with a wry grin.

As I initiate the remote's controls, Corporal Chatty exits the couch to dim the lights.

The screen quickly transforms as wavy static is initially replaced by pitch-black darkness, followed by a purplish tint as the wide-lettered words fade gradually into the picture...

Chapter Two
Purebred

As he cowered down onto his knobby knees in a rear corner of the dark, musty smelling barn, Bobby realized his own stupidity. He slapped his right palm forcefully against the side of his sweat-moistened head, repeating the same words over and over in a harsh whisper as the sound of slowly splintering wood intensified within the small space.

"Should'a known when he killed the cat...when he chewed up that damn cat."

He then gripped the pitchfork in both hands, holding the sharp end out like a man attempting to hold back oncoming floodwaters with a whiskbroom.

The growling noises were no longer canine in origin, of that he was damn certain.

Bobby swore if he got out of this situation (highly unlikely) with his skin intact, that Roy Akins would pay, and pay dearly. It had to be those damn chemicals the man had been stuffing inside his cattle that caused this hell on earth to transpire, he was almost certain. What else could explain it? Roy's loony 'alien pet abduction' theory?

One of the planks began to give away at the center as the thing outside worked itself into a raging frenzy, first backing away and then charging forward in a full-blown head butt.

Bobby's mind raced back to the specific day his wife had brought the creature home. That had been over a year ago to the day as he presently stood cringed against a barn wall, dangerously close to peeing his jeans.

"I wish she'd brought home one of them 'Taco Bell dogs', chew-wa-wah or whatever the hell they are," he spat nervously as the plank imploded inward, sending shards of wood flying past his crouched frame.

Bobby maintained his combat stance even as his hands shook uncontrollably, the pitchfork's handle oily-slick in his fevered grip. .

Behind the narrow opening the creature had made, only mini-funnels of dust were visible. He heard no further growling, canine, alien or otherwise.

The pause, obviously a ploy by the creature to toy with his already overwrought mind, irked him beyond the point of just simple rage.

"Come on, ya little shit heap.

Stop playin' games now. You may kill my ass, but by god, you'll know you was in a scrap!"

The pumpkin shaped, grotesquely bloated head shot through the opening in a blur, only to be subsequently halted as the space provided was not ample enough for the shoulders to squeeze through.

"Now I'll show ya who the true master is, you freaky SOMBITCH!" Bobby shrieked, sprinting forward with the pitchfork, the creature's eyes locked on his own, a searing, mutual hatred immediately recognized by both.

Bobby's warrior-like screams were only partly muffled by the creature's own.

SIXTEEN MONTHS EARLIER

"Oh heck, woman. I ain't got the time nor

40

patience to take care of a puppy. I thought we talked about this. We ain't got the yard space to start breeding 'em. I have to tear down that old barn first," he grumbled over a semi-soggy bowl of Fruit Flakes.

The woman snarled at him from behind the oak counter as she slowly chopped separate portions of onions and carrots.

"Bobby, we won't get this chance again. Sally and Spence are givin' away that dog. They sold the others from the litter for two-fifty apiece. We'd be pretty foolish to pass this up."

Shrugging, his back slumped like a man of fifty-five instead of forty, Bobby Drake tossed up his hands in apparent defeat.

"Okay, darlin', alright. You win. Go pick up the mutt. I'll fence off a small corner of the yard. Turning into Dr. Doolittle around here, I tell ya. Here we are already with a goat that does nothin' but eat the property and everythin' on it, and chickens whose only talents are crappin' and eatin'. Now we're getting into the dog breedin' business. I tell ya, the boss man has already told me I can't get any more overtime at the plant. How are we gonna feed.."

She put an end to his rant with the casual raising of a hand. A tight, rather grim smile that translated to 'better stop now dear, or I'll aim this frying pan at the back of your scrawny neck'. Bobby knew the drill all too well, and fell silent while filling his mouth with a large bite of cereal.

"I'll take care of it, Bobby. I can work a few more hours down at the market if I have to. We get a female to match this one up with and in a year we can be making three hundred apiece on the little ones."

Pushing away from the table, Bobby stood up with loudly creaking knees and pulled his cap, which read "Klaxon Steelworks" in smudged red lettering, snugly onto his balding head.

After a perilously shaky start which included all night whining bouts and massive collections of doggy doo sticking like dried cement to the bottom of his work boots, Bobby had to admit he took quite a shining to the mutt.

He had owned both a Bluetick and a Bloodhound as a youth (his dad had been an avid hunter), but had never had any dealings whatsoever with their smaller, evidently more stubborn cousin, the Basset.

They were slow moving, slow reacting, comically fleshy dogs that were sweet of disposition one minute and stubborn as the proverbial mule the next.

He gave his goat away to a neighboring family with small children, freeing up more yard space for the hound. His wife had fallen for its long eared, hang dog look right from the start, and he realized that whether he liked it or not, a new member of the family had arrived for the duration.

The dog had the natural instincts of a hunter, seemingly living just to sniff and pillage every square foot allowed within the backyard's confined spaces.

He and the wife had never had children due to her inability to, and various pets had always taken

42

up the void, but they hadn't dealt with dogs of any kind in the last decade of their twenty-year marriage. Bobby was finding it a challenge (equally frustrating and invigorating) just to properly maintain the needs of one, and tried not to dwell on how much attention and care the female basset they were currently searching for would need besides.

The wife greeted him at the dinner table a full seven months after they had taken the male basset, joyfully named "Butterball" the first moment she had laid eyes on him, and planted the classified ads almost directly on top of his fried chicken and potato salad.

"Read line six under dogs for sale, dear," she beamed.

He thumbed down to it and squinted after donning his reading spectacles.

"Female basset puppies, seven weeks old. All shots given. Two hundred per. HURRY, only three remain'!"

He peered back up at her and grimaced.

"Dear, I just got laid off, 'member? We're behind on the truck payment and your dental bills are due. How are we gonna swing the money without sellin' off our body parts to science?"

Her chest protruding proudly like that of a prize hen, her smile widened ever further (almost to the point of frightening him a bit. She was going to have to get that top plate worked on).

"Remember I worked last weekend and picked up ten hours of overtime? Well, besides that we also got that hundred-dollar check for switchin' our long distance carrier. I can buy the female today, Bobby."

43

He relented without argument, which was the norm since he had mysteriously, unexplainably 'misplaced' the pants in the family all those many moons ago.

***

The female basset was a bit livelier, had ears that didn't drag along the ground like the males, and was tri-colored instead of plain black and white, but was otherwise the spitting image when Butterball had been the same age.

Bobby had built a separate fenced in area for the female, and spent half his time away from work scooping poop and picking fleas and ticks from both of their big boned, flabby skinned bodies. He would walk away from such tasks covered in frothy goo, smelling like the inside of a soggy boot.

As maddening as the raising of the pups had been, he did feel surprisingly attached to both by the time that the female reached breeding age.

His wife would have taken a bullet for each of them by that time, all thoughts of the animals being nothing more than 'money machines' long since faded. They were as much a part of the family now as any pets they had ever owned.

With the male at eighteen months and the female a year, the attempt at coupling began in earnest. Bobby took down one side of the fence to allow them to share the yard as a couple while he and the wife sat back and waited for the inevitable.

It was about that same time when Bobby received a rare (and completely unwelcome) visit from his neighbor from the east, Roy Akins, or 'Big Roy' as he was apt to be called by people who either

44

feared or revered his presence. Bobby didn't fit into either category. Roy Akins was six-foot six, two hundred seventy pounds of hot air balloon filler in Bob's less than humble opinion. Akins raised cattle in two large pastures about three hundred yards to the east of Bob's place. Just the constant reek of cow dung filling his nostrils was enough reason for Bobby to consider the man less a 'friend' than an 'acquaintance'.

As he exited his shiny F150 pick-up, cowboy boots the size of manhole covers kicking up dust in thick clouds as he neared, Bobby leaned out from underneath the hood of the rusty Buick Skyhawk (the wife's ride. He would personally never be seen in anything resembling a 'passenger car'), where he had been adjusting the timing.

"Bob-by, what is up?" Roy had blurted in his cocky, 'I'm the MAN and nobody knows it better than me' tone.

"Long time, no see Roy. What brings you to the slums?" Bobby asked while wiping grease from his forehead. His tone was laced with disinterest, and purposely so.

As was his habit, the large man seemed oblivious that Bobby had even responded, continuing a one-sided conversation before it had ever even got started.

"Kept me up the rest of the night, Bobby, and damned if this mornin' I ain't got two heifers missing."

Secretly wishing the man would jump back in the truck and leave without further delay, Bobby had sighed and asked the question the other man seemed

45

to be waiting to hear.

"What kept ya up, Roy? You eat some bad beef?"

Roy had waived him off rudely and leaned down until his right forearm rested on the Buick's hood.

"You didn't hear that racket over here last night around midnight?"

Bobby shrugged indifferently.

"By midnight I was in dreamland, Roy. I usually hit the sack around ten or so. I ain't the night-owl you ar-..."

"It was this hummin' sound, like a hundred hives of bees flyin' by at the same damn moment," he was interrupted as Roy began reliving every detail of the night's activities in his mind's eye.

Nodding negatively, Bobby backed up a step and ducked back under the hood, attempting an obvious hint to his long-winded neighbor. "Sorry, Roy. You got me on that one. Maybe you was dreamin' yourself. You belt back a few at bedtime, do ya?" The other man joined him under the hood, his large round head barely fitting, as his prominent nose hung less than eight inches from the top of the still-warm engine.

"No dream, Bobby. Woke up Marilyn too, and she slept through the tornadoes we had last spring with not so much as a grunt. Then this mornin' I got two of my best gone and no damage to any part of my pasture's perimeter. Somethin' ain't right, I tell you."

They both backed away from the hood and Bobby had slammed it shut with a loud growl. He began to feel the conversation was sounding a bit too much like an interrogation.

"Didn't hear nothin' and don't know nothin' about missing cattle, Roy. Wish I could help ya but I'm afraid my sleep habits are a bit like your misses. I could sleep through a grenade detonation outside my bedroom window."

Roy had departed without saying much more, obviously flustered at Bobby's lack of information or for that matter, interest.

It had been three weeks since the bassets had been penned together by the time Roy came for another visit.

Bobby and the wife had been in the middle of pork chops, black-eyed peas, homemade biscuits and gravy when the knock interrupted their mealtime bliss.

After a ten hour workday at the plant, spot welding trailer parts and hauling metal panels, Bobby was not in the mood for more 'mysterious' night tales from his pompous, self-proclaimed 'richest man in town' neighbor.

Roy had been sweating profusely, his shovel-sized hands shaking like a frightened child, as he practically dragged Bobby outside by the collar of his shirt.

He said the strange noises had awakened him again the previous night, and that this time he awoke and walked over to his bedroom window to investigate. He said the landscape to the west of his ranch looked like someone had built a large bon fire, as the light coming from over the rolling hills was lit up like a football stadium.

47

Roy claimed he had been pulling on his pants and boots to go outside when the light flashed off like someone had hit a switch. Just like that, all was back to normal, or so he assumed at the time. Later that morning he discovered the two heifers that had been missing back in the pasture, albeit with a few very noticeable alterations.

Normally an ultra-calm, docile animal, Roy said the two were gallivanting around the pasture, kicking and biting the other cattle, as if marking specific parts of it as their own. He sent in two men to harness them in order to separate them from the herd, and the men were also attacked. He said the heifers looked different somehow, especially in the eyes. Roy stated that neither owned the bland, blank stare that was commonplace among the species. He swore that they glared at him with an obvious disdain he could almost feel.

Bobby advised Roy to see a vet and check them for Rabies or some similar disease, then strolled angrily back into his house to finish his supper.

The next day around 6 AM, while loading up his tools for work, Bobby found the cat. Or what remained of it, anyway.

It was a brown-colored tabby stray that had been hanging around their house for a few days. It lay just to the right of his right front truck tire, gutted from tail to breastbone. It's mangled, semi-peeled head looked like someone had shoved it through a meat grinder.

"Hope ya saved up some lives, cat, 'cause this one is sure shot to hell an' back."

That afternoon, the wife met him at the front

48

door to pass on the news that the backyard fence had been torn open.

"Butterball" and "Chubby", the bassets, were among the missing, as were most of the chickens.

She said it had been that way since she got home an hour earlier.

Both she and Bobby searched the woods behind the house and barn, neither having any luck finding the dogs, although the mystery of the missing chickens was solved. Bobby would have rather it hadn't, truth be told.

He found the torn carcass of one hanging from a low oak limb, its neck twisted like the ravel of a robe. He discovered another wrapped around a downed tree limb, half of its head above the beak sheered off.

The wife had, unfortunately, also spotted one. Or maybe it had been two or three, since the pile of various parts (stringy pulp for the most part) she almost tripped over were many and confusing as to the origin of the previous owner (or owners).

As they trudged slowly back to the house, Bobby held her trembling body close as she whimpered and cried. She had always been the sensitive type concerning animal welfare and inhumane treatment, and whatever had done that to those poor chickens, Bobby deduced, was definitely being inhumane with a capitol I.

Three of the dead were his best laying hens, and he felt his blood pressure flying off the charts as he loaded his twelve gauge and prepared to hunt down the responsible party.

Nothing or Nobody messed with Bobby Drake

and walked away unscathed.

He gently kissed the wife, who was already fretting about the bassets, and strolled purposely back down the same trail they had just covered.

The sun was already down and the darkness closing in as Bobby re-entered the forest.

It was a half-hour later that he found 'Chubby', the female basset.

She was battered and bloody, lying on her left side in a tall pile of oak leaves, but Bobby could see she was still breathing, albeit harshly.

"Jesus, girl, what did this, a bear?" He whispered as he bent to pat her head.

Just before his hand made contact with her blood soaked skull, her head arose and she growled at him, her lips curled over teeth that seemed far too lengthy and razor sharp for the foam drenched jaws encasing them.

Bobby had quickly backed away from her reaction to his touch, whereupon she again dropped her weary head into the moist leaves.

He had glanced around, suddenly aware of the possibility that the culprit might still be close by. When he glanced back down, relatively sure he wasn't being watched, he realized the basset's breathing had stopped.

He leaned down and patted her side, noticing how bloated and strangely warped it felt. As he stepped away, Bobby glanced back a final time at their fallen pet, and could have sworn he saw something bulge underneath the torn and shredded skin of her abdomen.

"Let's get the hell outta Dodge, Bob old buddy,

'fore you start imagin' little green men carryin' cattle prods," he had mumbled, the rifle clutched tightly in his white-knuckled hands.

It was pitch black by the time he made it back to the house; a virtual choir of crickets ringing in his ears as swarms of mosquitoes fed on his exposed neck and arms.

The house was deafeningly silent as Bobby casually leaned the shotgun by the backdoor and made a b-line for the refrigerator.

He gulped down the entire contents of a frosty Coors Light in four long swallows, the echo of his belch magnified by the surrounding quiet.

"Honey, could ya come in hear for a minute? I got somethin' I gotta tell ya," he had mumbled solemnly beneath his beer-soaked breath.

After waiting a few moments for a response that never materialized, he walked briskly through the living room and into the back bedroom, calling her name a few times (louder with each refrain) along the way.

Standing in the center of the living room, the TV sound set low but the picture blaring images of that day's news headlines, he debated on whether to begin the hunt for his wife right away or guzzle an additional brew.

The faint but still alarmingly distinct sound of his wife's screams a split-second later settled the argument.

Bobby flung open the front door and almost ran through the half-open screen, never thinking about the loaded shotgun he'd left behind.

Her shrill cries were cut off just as his boots hit

the northern edge of their front yard. Changing directions, Bobby whirled around and sprinted to the left, following the dirt trail that led deeper into the woods from the west side of the house and gasping as fresh sweat began to pour into his eyes.

A gully that had been used as a land fill a decade earlier was straight ahead, and it didn't hit Bobby until he saw the blurred movement just a few feet ahead that he was completely unarmed.

The wife's feet, one of them shoeless, protruded from behind a large shrub to the left of the ancient garbage mound. As he peered around the thick bush, his breath frozen in his lungs, Bobby felt his heart skip several beats.

"Hon? Are you oka-.." he managed just as her entire form came clearly into view.

His wife's throat was torn from ear to ear, the front of her dress coated in what looked like literally gallons of blood, which in the dark of night was as black as coal.

Trembling uncontrollably, he reached down with one callused hand and gently closed her wide, terror filled eyes even as his own filled with warm tears. He noticed the half- empty bowl of dog food she had mixed with chicken leftovers laying next to her right arm, and his throat clicked in utter despair.

"She was j-just tryin' to feed the bastard, t-that's all. Tryin' to feed her lost dog," he sobbed, his building rage overcoming the fear he had felt before the discovery.

"Come on out, ya murderin' sombitch! I'm right here if you think you can take me!" he bellowed, his arms wound tight and his fists

52

clinched.

At that moment, the fact he was unarmed was a ridiculously moot one.

The surrounding forest was eerily tranquil, although Bobby knew without a doubt he had witnessed movement while approaching the landfill.

He quickly kneeled back down to his fallen partner and kissed her still warm forehead.

"I'll… come back for ya, hon. I have to…get somebody down here to help first."

He fast-walked/jogged back towards the house, the hair at the back of his neck standing out like quills.

Bobby somehow fought off a series of wracking sobs that threatened to bring him to his knees.

He was only a few hundred feet from the front of the house when he spotted Roy's truck pulling wildly into his driveway, thick clouds of dust engulfing everything but the hood and roof as it skidded to a stop.

The man leaped from the still-running vehicle and was trotting madly towards the front porch as Bobby yelled out in a cracked, croaking tone.

Bobby's grin was hideously warped. Just the man he wanted to see. A theory had been running through his mind on why this insanity had come to pass. He needed a little clarity on the matter from the most reliable, albeit a bit untrustworthy, source available.

Roy halted on the second row of porch steps and turned, his face beat red and coated in thick beads of sweat.

As he neared the larger man, Bobby gestured as

if to ask what could possibly be so urgent as to interrupt the horrific events of the past half- hour.

"Bob, old buddy, we have to get outta here, man. We have to vacate, make tracks, vamoose, and I mean now!" Roy gasped, wiping his soaked face with one thick forearm.

Bob rushed by him with a snarl, his expression a fury-fueled mix of rage and determination.

"Get to you in a minute, Roy. Gotta get Sheriff Van Zant's ass over here pronto."

His slim left arm suddenly gripped roughly, Bobby was spun around like a small child by an angry parent.

"Already done, Son. I called him a few minutes ago. He's on his way. Now listen.." Roy began before being thrown back a few steps as Bobby lurched forward, freeing his arm from the stronger man's grip with one lightning fast jerk.

"My wife's dead, you asshole! I don't give a good rat's ass what your problem is at this particular moment!" Bobby ranted, whirling back towards the front door.

He barreled through the kitchen, making a b-line for the wall phone hanging on the back kitchen wall. He could both hear and feel the vibrations of Roy's footsteps trailing close behind as they bounced off the hardwood floor.

"H-how... did she? Was it an... a-animal attack? Y' see, I just found Josh and Rick, two of my employees, dead as a... hammer in the east pasture. They were...r-ripped apart, Bob. I mean seriously shredded. Hell, I found four of my best bulls in the same condition. I think it has somethin' to do with that funny light I've been seein'.."

Bobby turned on the man just as he pulled the phone from its receiver.

"Lights my ass, Roy! It's that illegal steroid shit you've been shovelin' to your cows to make 'em prize winners, don't you see? You said your cattle had been freakin' out, and now some other animal, probably a black bear or a wolverine, has gotten into it, and they're big, stout, and obviously extremely pissed off."

Roy's expression instantly mutated from simple shock to mock humor.

The smile he displayed was as false as the bridgework revealed there.

"S-steroids? I ain't feedin' my animals that dangerous shit, Bob. Where did ya hear that crap?.."

Bobby tossed the phone aside and strolled purposely towards the back door, reaching for the shotgun he had leaned there earlier.

"Cut the bullshit, man. Your man Rick let me in on that little secret months ago over a few dozen beers at Chuck's bar and grill. If you're responsible for this, Roy, I swear I'll blow your pompous ass away myself. You knew how unstable that stuff was, but greed has a way of pushin' common sense to the side, am I right? It makes 'em bigger alright…bigger and a damn sight meaner."

Bobby lifted the rifle and pointed it calmly at the man's midsection, his own smile nothing short of predatory.

"You might wanna leave now, Roy. I'm a bit unstable myself at this particular moment."

Roy turned quickly and jogged back towards the

55

front door, almost tripping over the corner of the living-room couch as he went. He paused at the open door and spoke without turning around.

"I'm not gonna take the blame for your wife, Bobby. We'll let Van Zant sort that out. I'm waiting for him at the front of my ranch. If I was you, I'd get the hell away from this property. Whatever killed my men and those animals, and probably your wife, is still lurkin' around."

Bobby was reaching down to retrieve the phone from the kitchen floor when he heard a low, somewhat muffled growl. It seemed to be originating from the dense woods just beyond the fenced back yard.

He had only taken a few steps into the yard when the shape came into full view, sprinting clumsily from behind the base of a large oak tree that sat just beyond the yard line.

"Son of...a ..." he managed, taking a step back and tripping over a piece of shattered two by four he had planned to use to shore up the damaged fence.

The creature was only twenty yards away and closing fast when he whirled around, realizing with no small amount of fear that he had left the shotgun lying in the kitchen.

Instead of re-entering the house, he decided to make a b-line towards his truck, which sat parked at a crooked angle in the front drive.

He turned the corner of the house at full speed, his pulse pounding at his temples, and was hit full force by the cruiser's headlights as they swung into view.

Ignoring the man who slowly exited the still

running vehicle just a few feet from his own ride, Bobby leaped into the cab of the truck and desperately dug into his jean pockets for the ignition keys.

"Bob, just what in Sam Hill is goin' on here? Roy Akins met me at the edge of the highway and told me your wife was dead and that you pulled a shotgun on 'im," the man said as he approached the rolled down driver's side window. Sheriff Mac Van Zant was approximately Bobby's age, but years of hard drinking (town scuttlebutt) and suffering through three divorces (cold hard fact) made him resemble a man at least a decade older.

Bobby began rolling up the window madly, his eyes darting spastically from the edge of the house, then back to the Sheriff. "Mac, get your ass inside your cruiser, man, and I mean now!" Van Zant backed away from the truck a few feet, his right hand now resting on his revolver's holster. "Bob, get outta the car. I need to call for an ambulance if your wife is hurt, and we have to talk about the situation here. I've never seen you like.." The Sheriff's mouth remained open but his words ceased once he heard the distinct sound of pounding feet approaching from the side of the house. Bobby opened the door to the truck and reached out wildly, gripping the man's uniform shirt at the collar and pulling him forward. "Get..in here, Mac. Jesus man, it's comin'!" He bellowed, attempting to pull the larger, lankier man inside the cab.

The sheriff threw him back inside and backed away in a shooting crouch.

"You tryin' to grab my thirty-eight, Drake?

57

Your under arrest, son. Now get your scrawny rear outta that truck and get down on your knees…"

Slamming the truck door shut once again, Bobby gestured towards the front of the house with his left hand swinging back and forth like a pendulum's blade. The comical look that covered Van Zant's face only lasted a split-second before transforming within a single blink into one of pure, shell-shocked horror as the shape sailed towards him in a frenzied blur of bared teeth and slashing paws.

Bobby saw the thing pin Van Zant to the dusty driveway, its impossibly wide jaws clamped around his neck like an oversized vise.

Small screams escaped the Sherriff's squirming, purplish-tinted lips as his life force was being slowly, meticulously severed.

Bobby whimpered aloud as Van Zant's jugular vein gave way and a perfectly horizontal gush of crimson three feet high sprayed into the air, an ample portion landing on the hood of the truck like a stream of spray paint from a pressurized can.

Bobby could hear the creature growling as it continued to clamp its lifeless victim's neck, and realized he had a choice to make and possibly only seconds to make it. He could stay in the truck and remain a prisoner of the creature (praying it wasn't strong enough to somehow force its way inside), or make a run for it while it was still occupied by the sheriff's mangled corpse.

Leaping from the driver's side door like a man escaping a burning building, Bobby dashed for the back of the house, hoping to get inside and have time to retain the shotgun before the thing forced its way inside. He had gotten a good look at it (too damn good, he shivered) and realized that the wooden doors and glass windows of the house wouldn't hold it back for more than a minute or so.

As he turned the corner towards the back of the house, he heard the echo of pounding paws and the guttural howls that accompanied them.

Knowing he probably had less than a minute's lead on an animal that was much faster than himself, he decided to bypass taking the chance of stopping and opening both the screen and inside backdoors, and instead headed towards the barn without a hint of hesitation in his stride.

He realized he was cursing under his breath as he ran, the irrational portion of his brain clinging to the offbeat hope that the entire afternoon was nothing more than a very realistic nightmare, and that he was even now lying comfortably within the comfy confines of his own bed.

Jumping a pile of loose wooden planks that fronted the barn's wide double doors, he scrambled inside and forcefully pulled the doors shut, the creaking hinges screaming their disapproval.

He kneeled down, then spotted the pitchfork hanging on the far wall.

**

He waited; the sound of his own heartbeat pounding like thunder claps at both his sternum and temples. He ran forward and plunged the end of the pitchfork in a downward arc with all the force he could muster. The Basset-thing glanced up just as the forks came down and punctured its eye balls, popping them like rotted grapes. Bobby fell back as the Basset-thing continued forward, it's massively mutated shoulders shoving their way inside as more planks cracked and tore away. It halted once it's upper body was all the way inside, shaking its tumor- ravaged head from side to side as if attempting to rid itself of a bothersome flea. Bobby could only sit, his legs splayed out, propped back on the palms of his hands, and stare at what had been only days before, his loving and loyal pet.

The thing had two mouths. It looked as if the upper one had literally grown out of it's snout. It was filled with tiny teeth that reminded him of pictures he had seen of piranha fish, the newly grown tongue flopping lazily back and forth like a worn leather belt. The lower mouth was somehow larger than normal and seemed locked open, as if unable to close on its own. The top mouth had done the deed on the sheriff, he knew, since it was coated in blood and stringy gore that ran in fine lines into the lower one.

The pitchfork still imbedded in its skull and eyes, its thrashing began to become noticeably slower, more sedate.

Bobby stood up and cautiously made his way towards it.

He gripped the fork's suspended handle and pushed downward, practically pinning the thing to the hardwood floor.

It released one final, pathetic whine which sounded like less Alien than pained canine, its body jerking and trembling several times before all movements mercifully ceased.

Bobby gave the fork a few forceful tugs for

testing purposes, then carefully stepped over the foul smelling carcass and out of the barn.

"My...dog...my damned dog did this. That bastard Akins is gonna pay for this...I'll see to that personally, yes sir. I will take care of that bit of business myself right here and now!"

After retrieving his shotgun from the kitchen table, he walked across the vast pasture that led to the ranch of Roy Akins. Bobby's outside demeanor, if observed from afar, would have appeared calm and collected. Inside, he felt as if his guts had been ripped out, scrambled with a blender, then placed back inside. He had lost everything he cared about in a half- hour's time, and somebody had to...would answer for it.

Grinning devilishly, he stepped through the fenced walk and up to the large oak front door. It was a massive three-story brick that, if put on the market, would have sold for upwards of half a million. He had never stepped foot inside, as he had never been invited to do so. Bobby felt no remorse as he repeatedly kicked the locked door until the locks gave way under the force of his size ten and a half Wolverine boots.

"Roy! Where you at, boy? We got us somethin' to jaw about, you and me!" he bellowed, his voice cracking with emotion halfway through the sentence.

The living room was filled with leather loveseats, a lengthy sectional couch, and a matching set of marble-surfaced tables. An entertainment center the size of Bobby's truck centered the next room, and it wasn't until he passed a narrow hallway

61

filled with family portraits that Bobby felt something was terribly amiss.

A long, dark-crimson etched a thick trail towards what looked like the kitchen entrance. A sour, coppery smell filled his nostrils, accompanied by a musty scent he had become quite familiar with inside his own barn.

The shotgun raised to chest level, Bobby made his way gingerly towards the kitchen's wide, open entrance.

"Roy? You in here? N-no use in hidin'....we're gonna talk eventually..."

He heard the faint scraping noises just as he took his first step inside. The kitchen blinds were drawn and the overhead lights were off, so it took his eyes a full thirty seconds to adjust to the scene. At precisely the same moment that the visuals cleared to an identifiable level, other noises became apparent.

Chewing, sucking, slurping noises. The sounds of bones being sucked dry.

"Roy? Good Lord in h-h-heaven...." He mumbled, the rifle frozen in his grip like it had been welded to the flesh of his palms. Bobby discovered that his lower extremities, other than his suddenly emptied bladder, hopelessly unable to adhere to his mental commands.

There was at least a dozen of them. Their sizes were that of newborn puppies. Their tiny tails wiggled back and forth in pure delight. Two of them raised their sloped heads from where they fed and stared at Bobby, growling as if to protect their kill from the newly arrived intruder.

Another raised its lumpy cranium from the ripped, torn chest cavity of Roy Akins and seemed to literally smile at Bobby. Smiled with both of its tiny, teeth filled, slightly drooling mouths.

It seems the wife's breeding plan had come together after all, Bobby mused as the final strands of sanity snapped in his mind like severed banjo strings.

Bobby found he had neither the strength nor the will to attempt to fight them off.

Within moments, they fell on him.

Late that night, oblivious to the townspeople, a bright light lit up the surrounding countryside.

The forms, nothing more than swerving rays of light to the human eye, quickly retrieved the bloated, well-fed creatures, as well as what remained of their victims, and departed the area with a simple flash not unlike a single, random lighting strike.

They would return, as would their present cargo, albeit in a dramatically altered state of being.

Maintenance would have to be performed, especially on the specimens that had been fed upon.

Eventually they would retain the same look, the same outward appearance.

They would act, however, quite differently.

They would then be dropped off at the original pick up site.

Further observation would then commence.

Observation, followed ultimately by increased scenarios of forced acquisition and transformation, multiplied a thousand-fold.

A transformation that would take inordinate amounts of time to complete, but that would eventually, painstakingly, alter the landscape of the planet earth to resemble an entirely new world altogether.

A new World entirely, that upon its inception, had literally gone to the dogs.

***

"What the hell, over? Twilight Zone maybe?" The Sarge asks no one in particular just as the final scene faded to black, quickly replaced by narrow waves of static.

"TZ was never that gory, Sarge. Did you notice the lack of credits? It flashed a title, but nothing else. Anybody recognize any of the actors?" I answered, fast forwarding the disc to insure the remainder was blank.

"Not a one, and I was a TV/movie junkie in our other life. Wasn't a cheap production, either. Good special effects. Those dog-things didn't look computer generated either," Airman Legs said, standing to yawn and stretch.

Private Brain Dog posed in front of the now blank big-screen, shaking his head in disgust. It was an expression and tone we were all nauseatingly familiar with. If Dog wasn't complaining, we all figured he'd been secretly cloned for a more 'cheerful' version of himself.

"Damn, that's all we needed to see…some mystery broadcast 'bout the World bein' overrun by aliens… sound familiar, troops? Why couldn't it have been Top Secret footage of Jennifer Lopez takin' a bubble bath or something similar?"

Lieutenant Lava shoved him playfully aside, then struck a martial arts pose as if to dare him to return the favor.

"Save it, Dog. You'd bitch if J-lo had a pimple on her butt. I think it was cool, like one of those old 'Tales from the Crypt' episodes. The basset monsters were borderline cute, in a ravenous, mutated carnivore kind of way. Check out another disk, Radar. Its not like we have an appointment to meet….at least, not yet anyhow. Right, Chief?"

Shrugging his shoulders, the Chief turned and gestured without speaking; a wry smile that translated to mean affirmative on the Lieutenant's query.

I quickly retrieved the second of the disks from the nearby table top, easily dodging the Sarge's feeble attempt to trip me up as I strolled back towards the player.

"While you're reloading, I'll go check on the Kid to make sure he's not nodding on post. Mighty quiet up there," the Chief announced in a weary, sheepish tone.

"I'll go, Chief. I'm really not in the mood for the Horror Show, anyhow. Never could stomach that shit. Even with the real life crap we've lived through lately, I find that fact ain't changed a single iota," Private Brain Dog blurted, his steel-toed Wolverines thumping loudly upon departure.

"Write if ya get work, Rap Master Dog-Doo," The Sarge barked sarcastically, soon followed by Coporal Chatty's smirking laughter as Brain Dog re-entered the room just long enough to shoot them the bird.

"Power that puppy up, Radar….my gray hair ain't getting no darker," The Sarge grumbled.

"Hopefully the next segment will contain something a bit more...redeemable in nature," Father Pete muttered solemnly.

"I agree wholeheartedly, Father. There was an entertainment factor, and it wasn't boring, but I think we could all better utilize a laugh in lieu of murder and mayhem," the Chief said before a building yawn cut off any further opinion.

"Powering on, team. Let's see what this bad boy has to offer," I practically yelled as high-pitched static waves filled the room. After quickly adjusting the volume, we again observed the scene fade in from murky darkness to a gradual coating of light as the title (and nothing else) briefly appeared before vanishing into the light fog of the presentation's ivory backdrop...

Chapter Three
Sibling Rivalry

October 21st, 2004

9:39 Am Monitored Subject: William White White Male Age: 39 Height: Six feet Weight: One-ninety six. Up nine point three pounds in the last seven calendar days.

Current Physical Description/Mental State:

Weight continues on upward spiral. Losing substantial amounts of hair from top of scalp. Cultivating beard and mustache, both of which remain uncombed and as inadequately groomed as the day they began growth. Eyes are noticeably, consistently bloodshot. Sleeps an average of ten hours a day, up from eight and a half per night from seven calendar days past. Eating habits are deteriorating noticeably. Less vegetables and trimmed meat: increased sugars and starches. Increased moodiness as days pass. Becomes easily irate and is prone to physical threats to staff members.

Diagnosis:

Subject will undergo final physical scan and psychoanalysis following today's taped results. Decision by counsel will then proceed as to subject's further usefulness in future stages of the project.

***

Weakly pushing himself up from the cluttered mattress, overrun by semi-emptied potato chip bags and coke cans, Bill leaned to the left, casually lifted his left leg and farting loudly.

Glancing over at the brightly lit alarm clock on the headboard, he sighed heavily while gently rubbing the back of his stubble-coated neck.

"Getting later every day, my man. I realize it ain't like you have a lot to get up for on most of them, but you need to pull your head from between your butt cheeks this AM. Once you become useless to 'em, you will become quickly expendable. Besides, today's the day you begin a little experiment of your own, remember?"

Dressing in haste, as much as his fatigued body and exasperated mind would allow on such short notice, Bill departed his room (careful to lock the thick metal door and double check the knob) and practically jogged down the antiseptic smelling hallway towards the 'Feed Bag Wing'.

"At least I ain't lost my appetite. My sanity maybe, but not the appetite," he whispered, his nostrils stinging as he walked further into the misty fog of cleaning spray that blazes a hazy trail out of the 'Forty Winks Wing' and into the glass breezeway connecting the buildings.

"Jesus, smells like my butt-bandit namesake has been at it again. I'm gonna stick that can of Lysol up his...waitaminnit...no, on second thought, he'd probably enjoy that," he croaked, madly waving his bare arms in front of his face along the way.

The early morning sun pierces the glass dome breezeway and Bill is forced to squint like a man staring directly into the sun. He's noticed the sensitivity to his eyes of late, as well as the burning sensation his increasingly pale skin suffers at the hands of daylight's rays.

Dark freckles frequent his arms, shoulders and chest. His stool is beginning to acquire a reddish, plum like color to it.

"One more trip through the blender and I'm buttered toast for sure. No doubt about it, my man, one more Zerox and you'll wake up a bubbling, throbbing pile of goo with one eye, one testicle, and with the strange ability to crap through both nostrils. Ain't...gonna let it happen. No Sir, No Way, No How...."

Sniffing like a bloodhound on an escaped convict's trail, Bill inhales the scent of freshly cooked bread and fried bacon as it radiates through the relatively small seating area just outside the main kitchen.

His stomach growls as he forcefully shoves the double door entrance to the kitchen askew and enters wearing a wide, somewhat demented grin.

"Damn, Swish-Me. You are one busy little beaver this morning, ain't ya?" he beamed while reaching for a clean plate from a shoulder high cabinet.

The man he has addressed is bent over a sink full of murky water, scrubbing and rinsing dishes maniacally. The man has the exact same physical build as Bill, less twenty or thirty pounds. His hair is a bit longer, and there is substantially more of it up top and hanging down onto the forehead region.

He turned to Bill with pursed lips, his rubber-gloved covered hands parked femininely on his relatively narrow hips.

"Well, well. If it isn't Rip Van White in the flesh. Why not just wait for lunch? It's only an hour and a half away, you know," he spat, a slight lisp to his high pitched shrieking.

Bill tossed a handful of still-warm bacon onto his plate, adds an ample helping of scrambled eggs, and then poured himself a tall glass of pure Florida orange juice from the first of two consistently well stocked, oversized refrigerators.

He turned to the other man with a section of bacon hanging from one corner of his mouth.

"Gotta have my beauty sleep, Swish. Thanks for keeping it warm for me. You're the best, girlfriend."

The other man bowed dramatically, then arose with a smirk.

"I get it all from you, DNA-Me."

Bill shot him a quick wink then backed out of the kitchen and towards the nearest eating booth.

While scarfing down his third biscuit with a wad of bacon acting as chaser, Bill first heard (as is normally the case) then watched 'B.A.' stomp and tromp his way towards the kitchen area like an enraged bull.

"Morning, B.A-Me. Swishy pee in your Wheaties or what?" Bill asked through a mouthful, little specs of bacon flying from his mouth like fluttering insects.

The man, whose physical characteristics again mirror his own except for the added layers of muscle on his arms, chest and legs, acknowledged the question with a hateful stare.

"Kindly eat shit and die, pin cushion, or I'll find a way to center my anger on your ass instead of Tiny Tim in there." Bill waived him on nonchalantly, filling his mouth with another bite of crusted flour. "Excuse me for recycling," he mumbled in between bites.

He couldn't help but catch every word of the exchange that followed inside the enclosed kitchen a moment later. He also couldn't refrain from giggling at the content of said exchange.

B.A: "Damn it to hell, Hoover lips, when I say I want my eggs over easy, I mean sunny side up! You've been cooking my breakfast for over a month now. Every day for thirty days plus, and you have yet to cease to amaze me at how fucking dense you are!"

Swish: "You always say 'over easy', B.A. Over easy and sunny side up are two separate entities. Every day I am tasked to prepare and cook three meals for eight remarkably finicky individuals. None eat the same thing, ever. This means twenty-four varied meals per day. You expect me to recall the fact that you.."

B.A.: "You fucking-A right I expect you to remember, you fudge packing, suck-the-chrome-off-of-a-trailer hitch, twinkle-toed freak! Get it right tomorrow or I'll stick something up your

Swish: "Do not threaten me, you brutish clod, or you'll find yourself eating bologna sandwiches and stale crackers three times per day. Now, go partake in one of your intellectual pursuits, like lifting weights or.... finding an animal to skin alive or something."

There was a slight pause, then the sound of pots and/or pans being flung forcefully against a nearby wall before bouncing off hard tile flooring.

B.A.: "Pork chops baked, not fried; green beans and white rice for lunch. Get it right, limp wrist, or I'll throw your bony rump in the oven with an apple stuck into both ends."

B.A. departed in a huff, no doubt headed towards the 'Sweat and Strain Wing', Bill deduced.

October 21st, 10:03 AM:

In phase one of his carefully mulled over and meticulously mapped out plan, Bill sought out and found Sloth-Me lying in one of the TV/Rec rooms, watching a taped rerun of "Gilligan's Island." As per usual, Sloth-Me's eyes were half closed and he looked on the verge of a deep slumber. His skin was chalky white, his eyes bloodshot and droopy.

Bill slouched down in the coolness of the leather chair next to Sloth's and smiled cheerily.

"How's it hanging, Sloth old pal? You been sleeping okay, dude? Ya look like hell warmed over..."

It took Sloth a full ten seconds to respond, the slow motion shift of his bleary eyes the sole acknowledgement of Bill's presence.

The tone of the man's voice was weariness personified.

"I dunno, D. I wake up a lot, you know? I'm gonna start taking more power naps.

They say even the presidents of countries take a daily sabbatical every now and then. Is it lunchtime yet? I'm famished." Sloth had a face full of gray stubble and a pot belly gut that hung over his lap like two large-sized pillows packed in a single sized case, but otherwise was the spitting image of the man addressing him.

72

"That's why I'm here, actually, Sloth my man. You seen B.A around?"

Keeping his steadily blinking orbs locked on the boob tube, Sloth responded quicker than normal, just a hint of sarcasm creeping onto the edges of his usually sardonic tone.

"Fortunately no, I haven't seen that hateful bastard since dinner last night, when he bounced a partially chewed pork chop off my dome. He's probably off strangling a cat somewhere."

Bill slapped his left hand tightly over his own mouth to prevent howling, managing to hold it down to a faint snicker before regaining control.

"Well, if you do, tell him Swish-Me said to pass along the following message: he's cooked up some special eggs for lunch just for him. Dunno what that really means, but ol' Swish was sure fired up about it. That is, as fired up as a light-in-the-loafers fairy such as he can manage."

When Sloth-Me didn't respond other than to wink rapidly, Bill patted him on his soft, toneless shoulder and retreated to the second phase of what he had become to think of as 'Operation Elimination'.

He bounded through the bland, colorless hallways that led towards still another glass enclosed walkway, whistling loudly as he entered the 'Drown Your Sorrows Wing', which consisted of two spacious lounges and several separate but similarly constructed wet bars.

Bill found the island's version of Batman and Robin at their usual posts. Perv-Me and Rehab-Me sat across from one another, arguing boisterously

73

over an open bottle of Jim Beam and two long glasses filled with semi-melted ice about who was the sexiest blonde porn star in the annuals of smut-dom.

It was like observing a man yelling incoherently into a mirror at himself. Perv-Me's hair was a bit shaggier in the back, his back seemingly bent into a permanent slump. Rehab-Me was attempting to grow a beard, with mixed results at best, and his teeth displayed a dark tint from not only the five-pack-a-day cigarette habit, but also the lack of contact with anything resembling a toothbrush in the past five months.

"It was Seka, you moron. I've got all her greatest hits on tape back in my room. She had it all; the lips, the hips, that sexy glare that turned men's knees into Jell-O and their jeans into instant pop-up tents. I wanna choke the chicken every time I think about that luscious babe," Perv shouted before slurping down a fresh shot of firewater.

Rehab calmly lit up a smoke and sipped his drink more conservatively. Rehab wore dark sunglasses at all times of the day, no matter what the lighting of a particular room.

"I say it's Amber Lynn by a landslide, man. I could pop a bottle of Valium, wash 'em down with a quart of pure grain alcohol and still play a mean game of 'hide the sausage' with her."

Perv-Me leaned back, visibly disgusted. Perv-Me was constantly rubbing his privates, or 'checking his package' as he put it. He admitted to masturbating at least a dozen times a day, usually while viewing the never-ending collection of porn tapes that had been so conveniently provided for his sole entertainment.

"Lynn? Overrated, doped up bleach-blonde. Funny how we both picked two from the golden age of porn, though."

Bill took a seat between them. The TV in the distance was showing the Playboy channel. Nubile young women were allowing various forms of liquid refreshment to be poured onto their heaving chests for a drunken, raucous audience of mostly teen males.

"How goes it, guys? Seen the Prof anywhere?"

As per normal, Perv-Me didn't bother to acknowledge his presence. Perv-Me had never cottoned to the originator of his existence. It was almost as if he were embarrassed that the embodiment of his perversion was a walking, talking separate entity.

Rehab-Me lit another smoke, sucking the first draw lovingly, like a parched man with a newly poured glass of ice water.

"Baby Prof? I'm sure he's off building an arc or a spaceship in the 'Sandcastle and Shovel Wing."

Professor-Me was referred to as 'baby Prof' due to his being the most recent addition to the 'community', a relatively infantile five weeks.

"Well, word has it he's been instructed to cut off the cable access temporarily for some scheduled maintenance. In fact, he may have to cut off the power for a day or so. Break out the candles and blankets, I guess."

Perv-Me's mouth dropped open like a hinge had snapped free. Rehab poured himself a triple shot of

Jim and emptied the glass in a single swallow.

Bill rose quickly and headed towards the exit leading to the next wing, a sort of do-it-yourself project/construction room equipped with assorted tools and building materials.

"He's supposed to let us know the details at lunch," he added, staring at his wristwatch with a wry expression.

"Heck, that's only forty more minutes. See you guys there."

Perv-Me massaged his genitals and smirked.

"Power outage my ass. Not on my shift."

Rehab lit up his third smoke in six minutes.

"That kind of crap wasn't in the resort brochure I was handed."

Bill shrugged his shoulders and departed.

On to phase III.

Moments later, his breath a bit labored from a frantic pace his cardiovascular system wasn't accustomed to handling, Bill finds Prof-Me diligently tinkering away in the 'Metal-works' department. Bill eyeballed a few of the items spread across the lengthy worktable and grinned mischievously. Prof-Me raised a single eyebrow as he neared, then fell back into his work-is-never-done daze that is his reason for being.

Prof-Me has lean, muscular arms formed from countless hours of lifting, twisting, shoving, and project-related labor-aerobics. "Looks like you're right on schedule, Prof. Forty minutes and counting until D-day. You gonna be all set by then?" His face moist with sweat despite the cool, conditioned air, Prof-Me nodded once and stepped back to survey his progress. "Noon. Possibly five minutes past. I have a few minor adjustments. You wanted twelve-oh-five, correct? Not exactly on the dot."

Bill smiled amiably. It never ceases to amaze him that such a being within himself existed. Hell, he used to hate screwing in light bulbs. He now understood and honestly believed the old scientific tidbit that 'people only use a fraction of their brains'. Proof stands before him that is undeniable.

"Twelve-ten would be even better, actually, Prof old pal. Problem?"

"Not at all. Twelve-ten it is then."

Bill takes a moment to really look at the man, and feels something within himself that, while not quite pity, brings an unwelcome tear to the corner of his right eye.

"See ya, Prof," he babbled while strolling away, the nearest exit leading him towards the gym, long ago ordained the "Sweat and Strain Wing."

Bill unexpectedly runs into Shaky-Me in the connecting walkway.

Shaky was talking to himself again, a trait more necessity than habit being that none of the others would grant him the courtesy.

The ticking of the large overhead fan as it spins on its never ending mission of controlled movement mercifully interrupted the man's insistent babbling, and revealed Bill's presence to him after a short pause.

"D, you ever wonder whether this is hell we're occupying this very minute? I mean, is there a place in the entire universe worse than this? Trapped on this godforsaken island with no hope of escape? I

77

mean, they couldn't allow it obviously, but how do we know there's really anything out there to escape to?"

Bill noticeably shivered. Shaky was in the middle of his daily 'Hell is Here' rant. Shaky never ate and rarely slept. In his four month reign as 'King of Nerves', he had dropped at least forty of the pounds he was provided since inception. His fingernails were jagged nubs, each bitten deeply to the quick.

His hair was perpetually uncombed and literally dripping oil.

"May be, Shakes. You're asking the wrong guy. You seen Bad Ass-Me in the last few minutes?"

Still transfixed on the shifting ocean of sand outside the glass, Shaky half-heartedly thumbed towards the gym building and then grew instantly solemn.

Despite a strenuous effort, Bill never found a useful part for Shaky-Me in the building scenario. Somehow, it bothered him more than it probably should have.

Minutes later he stood before Bad-Ass-Me, who was in the middle of a set of bench presses, his breath spat out in harsh gasps, the veins on his forehead and neck sticking out like cable cords. His bulging biceps and forearms were easily twice the size of the twin model standing over him.

"Working out again, B.A?" Bill asked for want of anything else to say.

After allowing the weight bar to bang nosily onto the supports, B.A sighed in apparent repulsion and spoke through tightly gritted teeth.

"My gawd, you are truly one of the great minds, partner. What gave me away, the fucking weights hanging over my head? What the hell do you want, guinea pig? You know how much disruptions piss me off."

Bill leaned back onto a padded nautilus machine, 'thigh burner' machine he believed it to be called, and vigorously scratched his chin.

"It's Perv-Me, B.A. He cornered me in the lounge and wanted me to speak to you about something that's...bothering him quite a bit. As the group's unofficial spoke's person, I thought it my duty."

B.A arose from the bench and strolled purposely towards a hanging hard bag, sizing it up like a hunter would a fallen buck before providing the killing shot.

"What does that sleazy little shit have to complain about? Didn't get this month's copy of Butts & Boobs?"

Following B.A's lead, Bill walked around the hard bag and held it firmly on both sides, positioning his knees for impact.

"Uh...well, it's kind of...awkward to say."

The first set of hard, short jabs threaten to send Bill flying backwards. As it was, his teeth rattled and his knees came close to buckling under. B.A held up for a moment, stepping back to suck in a deep breath.

"Spit it out, test tube. I'm all ears."

With every fiber in his deteriorating torso crying out to spew forth laughter, Bill managed to keep a straight face by pinching what later became a blood blister onto his left thigh.

"Perv wants you to…lay off of Swish, and not just the constant insults."

After halting his forward motion towards the swiftly swinging bag, a low click was audible from B.A's throat. Bill saw the familiar, visibly throbbing vein begin to swell on the man's moist forehead.

"What exactly does old pud-wacker Perv mean by not just the insults?"

Bill cleared his throat and broke eye contact in fear of losing self-control, instead concentrating on a wall covered in nude posters of various young women.

"Uh…he said he knows that you're…how did he put it? Bopping Swish on a regular basis, and he wants this to cease. He says your brand of rough sex is keeping Swish from 'being in the mood' on certain occasions. Basically, he doesn't want to share."

It was essentially like watching a horror movie special effect come to life. B.A's eyes narrowed to slits, his teeth gritted together like matching ends of a tool clamp. The flesh on his bare, bulging arms, neck and face turned a shade of crimson so dark it was as if he had fallen into a coma while lying in a tanning booth and not awakened until he had reached 'well done' status.

He was a walking, throbbing testimony to how all men would appear if their inner rage was revealed in a physical sense. He was a new breed of super-hero. He was "Captain Pissed Off," or possibly "The Crimson Rage". He was "Irate-Man."

"Perv thinks that I'm.....old pudding pants told him I was....Oh hell...ohhhh hell!" he bellowed, the skin of his biceps on the verge of splitting open from the massive strain.

Bill stood quickly and held up both his arms, hands palm up, as if to halt B.A's apparently impending, quite hasty exit from the gym.

"Whoa, big boy, that's not all, I'm afraid. Rehab has been hanging around Perv quite a bit lately and...he said he is backing Perv on this all the way. You see, he wants a...piece of the action as well. Perv pretty much convinced him that sex with Swish is better than none at all."

B.A froze, the comical look of exasperation on his face at that precise moment easily the most difficult test of Bill's will power yet.

He narrowly passed, although his sides began to shake involuntarily.

"Rehab wants...? You mean old bottleneck himself is turning queer too? Son of a bitch! What hath you wrought, pin cushion? You gotta be living in a world of pure shame no other man could ever claim."

Bill folded his arms defiantly and sneered, feigning anger.

"B.A, how many times have we covered this ground? All human beings are multi-faceted. If my whole persona had been built of just your physical strength and short-fused rage and my calm, cool logic, I would have more than likely been a freaking serial killer with the emotions of a turnip. There has to be more to the make-up, more spoons in the evolutionary soup, don't you understand that? Like it or not, pal, we're siblings one and all"

B.A rushed forward in a blur, his hands pressed against Bill's chest.

Bill was sent airborne, landing on a soft set-up mat a dozen feet away from where his last word had been uttered.

"Bullshit, Guinea boy. Those freaks of nature are your offspring, not mine. I was the first hatched, so that makes me the prototype. I was what was supposed to be...not those mentally defective assholes."

After regaining the power to again inhale fresh oxygen into his battered lungs, Bill pushed himself to his knees and flashed a smile of unrestrained pity towards his bullish twin.

"You could look at it that way, B.A. Or you could consider the Prof's theory, which the others wholeheartedly agree with, I understand." Standing with his buffed, sweat-glistened arms propped across his heaving chest, B.A frowned as if he were a victim of a weeklong bout with constipation. "Yeah? And what might that pearl of wisdom be, lab rat? The pathetic smile faded into a sour grimace. He could only hope the repercussions of his words wouldn't result in permanent paralysis.

"He seems to think the only reason the process was repeated after your birth was due to the sole fact of the obviously inferior product that was created. In other words, they simply thought; if at first you don't succeed...."

To Bill's shock and relieved surprise, B.A did not leap forward with incisors exposed.

The response had simply been a weak shrug and an expression of apparent acceptance.

B.A walked over to a nearby free weight rack and gently toweled his face. He then sauntered past Bill in a somewhat slumped gait, pausing only long enough to utter a series of clear, concisely spoken words; at least the majority of which Bill had not only expected, but sincerely hoped to hear.

"After I finish butchering them, I'm coming back for you, my older sibling."

Bill's reaction was finely tuned, well rehearsed.

It was to simply not react at all, and to avoid eye contact with the side of himself that he despised the most; the one he could not begin to either understand nor manipulate.

He heard B.A whisper before pushing through the exit door, and despite the fact that none of what was happening hadn't already been preordained in his mind days before, the chilling tone utilized nevertheless caused the short hairs on his neck to stand at rigid attention.

"I'll bring you back a memento to remember 'em by, big brother."

Bill glimpsed at his watch and saw it read eleven thirty-two AM. He had a scant twenty- eight minutes to kill, so to speak, before high noon, a time span that he realized would soon seem like an eternity.

He left the gym and entered the pool area, making his way ever-so-casually around the Olympic-sized watering hole, his thoughts frantic and spastically fleeting.

It had been ridiculously easy to first gauge the

involved personalities (they were his own, after all) and then set the grisly, simplistic plot into motion.

Perv had been flirting with self-incest with Swish for weeks, although whether or not the relationship had ever actually became physical was still a mystery to all but them. Rehab was easily persuaded on all matters, depending on his level of inebriation at the time. The Prof was a doer, and didn't possess the natural willpower to turn down any request that called for his assistance in a mechanical and/or construction related means. He was the ultimate 'yes' man, no questions asked.

The catalyst, or nucleus of the atom bomb in this instance, was of course the subject most easily enraged at even the slightest suggestion of wrong doing at his own expense. B.A was unable to harness his anger in a positive way, and the condition of his jagged psyche had been worsening for weeks.

Bill had a point to prove to the ones who had lied to him about their intentions. They had to be shown that even a lost cause such as himself, a man who takes another's life and is condemned by his own kind for the act, was not to be toyed with like a hamster in a maze. He had agreed to the first, but the entire process had gotten cruelly, despicably out of control.

Exiting the 'Sweat & Strain Wing' for the brightly lit, glass entombed walkway that would eventually lead him to view the fate of entities representing distinct portions of his scattered, splintered soul, Bill sat lotus style at the dome's center.

He leaned his head back onto the cool glass and allowed the sun's intrusive rays to warm his face and neck, his ears pricked for even the slightest hint at a distant scream.

The peaceful semi-slumber was only broken at the feel of the wet, warm stickiness that dripped onto his brow.

Shaky was propped atop the finally stilled fan, his head dangling between two of the metallic blades, void a sizeable portion of his nose and with his right eye ball hanging from its socket like a child's hyper-extended slinky toy.

Bill pulled himself up and only then noticed the pool of partially congealed blood he had been so unceremoniously squatting in.

He departed the walkway without grief or sadness, but with the strange vibe of sweet, overwhelming relief. It was as if a portion of his ravaged soul had been returned to him, like an armless man given a new appendage, but without the complete knowledge of its use.

He just wished his rage hadn't been so damn hard on his nervousness.

Shaky hadn't deserved that.

Rehab and Perv were found still occupying the 'Drown Your Sorrows Wing' a half- hour later, although in a vastly different condition than earlier that morning.

Perv was bent over one of the spacious leather couches, his pants pulled to his ankles, a few inches of pool cue (the thin portion) sticking out like a meat thermometer from between his butt cheeks. The thick end had burst through his chest cavity, dragging more than a few sections of his lower intestine along for the ride. Perv's horribly contorted, wincing expression indicated that the procedure had been anything but painless.

Rehab still sat at the card table, his arms splayed out across the top with fingers still gripping the last hand of poker he would ever hold. His eyes were frozen agape, and were focused straight ahead in the opposite direction of his torso, as if the devastatingly accurate carnage to his neck had been measured off at a perfect one-hundred eighty degrees before being twisted and snapped like dried kindling. An empty bottle of rye whiskey had been forced between his lips and shoved inward until his mouth was torn and shredded at the corners in order to allow such an oversized intrusion. Bill had to wonder what had come first..the shoving or the snapping. Just the thought induced a shudder.

As he departed for the TV/Rec room, Bill again felt the sensation of something gained deep within. His heart fluttered in the throngs of a series of fierce palpitations, then fell back into it's normal rhythm.

Sloth was found laying spread eagle in front of the mangled large screen TV, the bashed screen of which still emitting thick tendrils of smoke from it's ruined contents. A cable line was wound tightly around Sloth's bruised and bloated throat. Bill squatted onto one knee and leaned down cautiously, the left side of Sloth's battered face coming gradually into view. Bleached bone protruded from where his lower jaw once set, and the imprinting of the TV's remote buttons covered the flesh underneath his eyes, the tip of his nose, and across his dented forehead like some macabre abstract artwork. Bill snickered uncontrollably as he stood, the surreal image of B.A beating Sloth to death with the remote control very nearly too much for his brittle psyche to compute devoid of taking that first unconscious step down the highway to irretrievable madness.

He felt a tear form for Sloth-me, whom he had formed the closet, securest bond with since the inception of the program.

Once again, something inside him clicked upon the realization of another distinct section transpiring, and the sudden, almost crippling need for a nap came and went like a seaside breeze between two gently swaying palm tress.

His heartbeat now increasing rapidly, the breath from his lungs escaping in brief, asthmatic hitches, Bill felt his knees grow instantly weaker as the plan neared its crescendo.

Only the kitchen remained.

Bill dreaded and rejoiced simultaneously.

From the rec room he practically sprinted, allowing his thoughts to scatter haphazardly without landing on a single specific subject.

Entering the kitchen area like a lost soul released from a decade's indenture, Bill found the scenario disappointingly predictable. It was an epilogue he had long envisioned, but also one he had hoped wouldn't be without a sense of mystery or a Hitchcockian twist or three.

His primal rage still intact but seemingly on a much smaller scale after the earlier sessions along the trail, B.A had performed the fateful deed in an almost mundane, subdued fashion.

Swinging the kitchen doors askew with casual aplomb, Bill couldn't help but feel a bit cheated at how uncreative and alarmingly banal his personal representative of rage and mayhem had apparently become.

Swish had been lain out on the large wooden table that had served as the cutting board stand. His bloated jaws had been stuffed with the partially cooked eggs he had been in the process of scrambling, his chin sprinkled in fragmented shells. The brown wooden handle from what Bill deduced was a meat clever jutted out from his midsection as if at half-staff, the blade completely concealed by the torn flesh that engulfed it.

The crimson smeared blade of a slim, slightly curved boning knife lay beside his tattered right hand, three fingers of which had been systematically sliced away and lain out like chopped carrots for a vegetarian salad.

Bill had despised his feminine entity, although he had gone to great lengths to hide such feelings. He was embarrassed that such a specimen existed, a vibe that was undeniable in the proof of its constantly annoying, always cloying presence.

He had at least found something to admire about the others, despite their glaring faults. In his opinion, Swish-Me had been the true dark side of his other selves. Not Rehab with his addictive needs; nor Perv with his pornographic ones. Sloth and Shaky had been relatively harmless and rarely involved themselves with group dilemmas. B.A was a sadistic pain in the rear, never so evident as in the carnage he had just left in his lunacy filled wake, but he also commanded respect and gave no quarter when it wasn't received.

Bill could at least feel pride in knowing that such fearlessness and mental toughness was a part of his varied persona underneath the cool exterior.

His watch read eleven fifty-five. Fifteen minutes until the Prof pulled the plug on the whole miserable affair.The powers that be had underestimated his talent for creating, for hazardous invention. Bill had been a closet mad scientist since his early teens, and had breezed through chemistry and biology classes without a hitch. The Prof had been handed every single thread of memory and knowledge he had ever forgotten on the subject, thus the creation of an explosive powerful enough to crack through one of the glass dome walls had been a simplistic cake walk.

Bill had known from day one that the desert surroundings were a cheaply produced façade, a special effect hastily thrown together to shelter and sooth the weak minded subjects being kept at bay in the outer recesses of time and space.

It would take nothing more than a pin hole in the glass dome to cause the implosion that would turn the station into a floating rubbish pile of steel, wood, plastic and seared flesh.

Mere minutes and counting, Bill thought morosely. He wanted nothing more than the sweet relief of feeling absolute nothingness in a white landscape void of all shapes and sounds.

He departed the kitchen, not in fear of being the last living target of his own inner fury, but in stoic disbelief that it had actually come down to such a final, desperate act. He hoped this would prevent future projects of such ilk from even being considered.

Man had gone too far in the name of science countless times before. Bill could only hope the destructive plot he had initiated would cause more than one of the upper echelon to reconsider before throwing down a similar gauntlet to the scientific community anytime in the near future.

Bill roamed the bland, deafeningly quiet halls that would have led him to his sleeping quarters in due time. His watch read twelve oh-nine and thirty seconds. As of yet, he hadn't seen nor heard a peep from his ill-tempered, rampaging twin. Bill wondered how the Prof was spending his last few moments, waiting for the crudely constructed time bomb to detonate.

Bill then wondered a similar query about Bad Attitude.

His watch read twelve-ten and fifteen seconds, but he felt no initial panic. It hadn't been a synchronized deal with the explosive, after all.

He entered the hallway leading to his quarters.

His watch now read twelve-eleven on the dot.

The door to his quarters was partially agape, a wide boot print smeared at its center, just left of the knob.

His watch now read twelve-eleven and eleven seconds.

Bill began to panic as he cautiously shoved the door inward and saw the shattered inner latch-lock bent back awkwardly. He had time to sympathize with Shaky just as the interior of the room swam into view, his central nervous system suddenly placed on instant code red alert.

The foil-wrapped, homemade bomb was curled tightly inside the closed fingers, which were ghostly pale and bent to resemble the grisly legs of a predatory spider. The hand had been severed surgically clean just underneath the wrist bone, not a single spatter of blood evident on the pillow case it had been so carefully rested on in the center of his neatly made bed.

"Oh my god. Prof. He got to Prof before he could..."

Realizing Bad Attitude's sleeping quarters were a scant three rooms down, Bill instinctively scooped up a nearby iron-handled putter he had brought along as a whim the day he volunteered for the project, being that he had been an avid golfer once upon a time in a distinctly different life.

He hadn't anticipated such a scenario, thinking the explosive would have already eliminated such a ghastly possibility.

When faced with the choice of either dying by lightning fast implosion of the compound or being stabbed and mutilated by one's own rage come to maniacal life, the choice would have been painfully obvious. Now it was more than likely going to be painful, period.

Bill virtually tip-toed down the eerily quiet hall, the golf club held at the base like a baseball player awaiting the opposing pitcher's best heater.

"Hey, hey, B.A, are you there? It's just me, your spliced DNA twin here. Calm down, man. We

91

really need to settle this without further....uh, incident," Bill moaned, his attempts at masking his anxiety failing miserably.

As with his own moments before, the door to Bad Attitude's abode slid open half a foot as Bill stood ever-so-shakily before it. "Are..ya..here, man?" he asked between lips pursed and slightly purple, using the tip of the putter to ease the door back ever further.

The series of gasps that followed were issued in-between short pauses, as each portion of the horrifying scene came clearly into focus to Bill's bloodshot, rapidly blinking eyes.

The initial gasp was released at the sight of the pulped mass of humanity lying in the center of the now crimson-drenched carpeted flooring.

Bad Attitude had displayed a similar grimace in death as in life, his teeth gritted, jaws wound tight and eyes narrowed. His upper chest and abdomen were literally layered in pointed, sharp-edged kitchen utensils, the handles of each pointing towards the ceiling in balanced perfection. It reminded Bill of a gag birthday cake jokingly riddled with a vast collection of candles, set up as to be impossible for the blunt of the joke to blow out in a single huff.

Some of the utensils had been shoved so deeply and with such force, they had pierced through the flesh of his back, as what looked like literally gallons of blood had encircled his entire frame from head to feet.

Bill barely had time to inhale an ample supply of oxygen when something caught the corner of his left eye and instigated the second, more pronounced cry of shock.

It was his handwriting all right, clearly evident even through the clumsily smeared, still freshly dripping blood that trailed down the dresser mirror in ever-thickening layers.

"T-then again, w-we all have the same h-handwriting, you I-idiot..." Bill whispered harshly, the putter falling uselessly from his sweaty palms.

The message conveyed was simple and brutally to the point:

Pin cushion, my ass.

The third and final gasp resembled the wailing of a thrashing wild animal with its paw caught in the jagged metal jaws of an iron trap.

It forced its way through Bill's desert dry lips the moment his vision was unexpectedly diverted from the ravaged, battered corpse, his own anger finally silenced, to lock onto the empty palms of his own hands.

They were coated up to his elbows, the blood only beginning to solidify, the majority still liquefied and dripping freely onto his shoes below.

A cautiously fearful glance into the nearby mirror revealed his once snow white T-shirt encrusted with spatter marks that ranged in size from that of a penny to the circumference of a regulation softball.

Upon further inspection of his faculties, Bill noticed his jeans were also not without a stain or twelve. It was like someone had gone insanely reckless with a paintball gun and used him as their sole target at ludicrously close range.

Perplexed ever further a split-second later, Bill noticed that the putter he had entered the room with no longer took up space on the copper-scented carpet floor, but had been replaced by a pair of medium sized hedge clippers whose twin blades held tips as maroon-shaded as his clothing.

A thick line of drool now making it's way gradually down his chin, Bill reeled back in a lurch, almost tripping into the hallway head first, then took off in a mad sprint in the direction of his own room. Unable to produce a scream sufficient enough in volume or range to match the horror he had just witnessed, Bill had allowed his pumping legs and flailing arms to initiate the final command on his personal panic checklist.

It hadn't been the body of Bad Attitude-Me nor his own plasma-smeared body that had pressed the button that had permanently shut off what little sanity had remained within his fevered brain. It had been the mirror. The words had changed, although such questions as how or why presently escaped query as he rambled up the hall with hands pressed to the wall, leaving long, thin trails of blood in his wake.

Words not written in bodily fluids, but seemingly written in a type of ink manufactured only within the darkest, dankest depths of hell itself.

Eight simple words that needed no translation or assistance from Webster in their meaning to the man they were written for.

It is you, Billy-Boy…. It always was...

His neck locked in permanent nod mode, side to side in a jerking motion that transformed his face

94

into a wavy blur, Bill babbled and mumbled to the empty corridor walls as he once again neared his humble abode.

"It c-can't be...no. C-can't be. I w-was crashed in my room, that's all. The headphones were blaring....Blue Oyster Cult..or AC/DC...I'm not s-sure w-which. It w-wasn't m-me..."

Bill pulled the bomb from the cold, stony fingers and tossed the Prof's hand away like so much cheap packaging.

"G-gotta detonate this Sombitch....c-can't go on like this anymore. Have to blow the shit out of this filthy, r-rotten place..." he muttered, the tendons in his neck beginning to audibly pop from the constant pressure of the wild thrashing of his head from side to side. Spittle flew from his mouth like a rabid animal in the throngs of a violent death spasm.

"W-wasn't me...don't care what any of t-them say...Was not me. They..w-were my...b-brothers, for god's sake..."

The trembling of his entire body began to match that of his head, only the shockingly normal steadiness of the hands that continued to smother and maul the small, square object in their grasp maintaining a façade of normal movement.

His words became jumbled and incoherent in meaning even as he dropped the object and began to wildly drop-kick it from one side of the room to another.

Bill refused to notice or acknowledge the men who soon surrounded and then gently subdued him. The men wore ivory white shirts buttoned to the collar with generically colored matching pants, and nametags sewn over their right shirt pockets. One particular man held a loaded syringe that was soon plunged into his upper right shoulder; another pushing a gurney complete with thick leather tie-down restraints.

As he was being wheeled away, Bill never heard the intercom click on overhead, nor the voice that reverberated over its speakers a moment later.

"Please transport the patient into treatment room number two and prep him for intravenous feeding, people."

***

The gray haired man rubbed his eyes vigorously and removed the thick, black-framed glasses whose nose pieces were digging a pronounced grove onto his nostrils. He sat down at the console with a heavy, drawn out sigh.

He reached for the small recorder next to the intercom switch and wearily clicked the 'play and record' buttons simultaneously.

"Subject: William Wesley White. The time is now five-eighteen PM. Subject sedated and taken for daily feeding via IV. Videotaped episode will show subject again in the mode of role playing; talking to himself, complete with varied body language and distinct physical characteristics of each personality portrayed. We thought moving him to the abandoned government housing area might possibly alter his pattern of thinking. Again, and for the third time this month, we were sadly mistaken. Updating his medication and raising the level of daily doses has also been ineffective in treatment. To reiterate the core of the dilemma; Subject William White

96

suffered seemingly irreversible psychological damage when, at age sixteen, he was placed in charge of his five younger siblings, four brothers and one sister, by his parents. They were departing the residence for a late dinner in celebration of their twentieth wedding anniversary, leaving William in charge for the first time, feeling his level of maturity had reached a point where such an action was justified.

Police reports stated William was found unconscious in his room, a large but non-fatal wound to his forehead, his mouth, hands and feet duck-taped somewhat haphazardly.

His four brothers and lone sister had been brutally murdered, each of them stabbed numerous times. Two of the brothers had been found with knife handles, later determined to have been taken from the family kitchen cabinets, still protruding from their bodies.

Only William survived the slaughterhouse that became his home that night. He found returning to a normal existence impossible, and has spent the last twenty-two years since inside the walls of various psychiatric hospitals. Authorities had even suspected him for a time, since nary a single suspect was ever unearthed in the killings. No hair fibers other than the families were even found inside the home, nor fingerprints that didn't match a resident. Prints on the weapons found at the scene were wiped meticulously clean. Charges against young William were never forthcoming however, and eventually the case was closed and remains one of the most unnerving unsolved crimes in the history of the state.

My belief is that William Wesley White will continue to relive the murdering of his siblings every day of his existence despite our best efforts to free him from this horrendous guilt.

Each day he awakens and greets them, then eventually plots their death. A murder spree kept from even his own tortured mind until the realization that he is the sole perpetrator is finally revealed at the session's conclusion.

Today it seems he utilized the 'bombing' scenario, in which he would allow his intellectual side to build an explosive that would detonate inside the 'cloning' dome his personalities were trapped inside, this after sending his anger based clone to kill all but himself. This has become a standard plot, the alarm clock again viewed as the weapon William attempts to unsuccessfully 'detonate'.

We will move William back to the hospital grounds tomorrow and continue to study future treatment options, although I have my doubts at this point that the man will ever find true relief until the day passes that his guilt-ridden soul is put to final rest.

This is Doctor Elliot Wesley White, Dean of Experimental Testing, Psychology Unit, Marimont University Hospital, signing off at five-thirty PM."

Watching his lone surviving, long suffering son being wheeled from the corridor, taunt leather straps wrapped tightly around his arms, legs and forehead, Doctor Elliot White reached without hesitation into the top desk drawer and removed the object of his intention.

98

Holding the syringe high as to view it directly through the fluorescent light above, he stared at the blue liquid it held and smiled sadly through obvious agony.

The first of many tears to come fell onto the clipboard resting atop his lap.

"Tonight my son, you will finally find sweet relief.

Tonight it will mercifully end…for us all…"

***

"Geez Louise, that was less than uplifting, wouldn't ya agree, Father?" The Sarge cackled through a tight smile. He was obviously on the verge of howling amid Father Pete's miffed groans of disapproval.

"Disgusting, vile, unsubstantial nonsense….," Father Pete grumbled with a barely submerged grin of his own.

"…..Wonder what's next?" he concluded with great interest, enticing everyone in the room but the Chief into instant hysterics.

"What is this, Tales of Depression and Death? Again, not a single credit or recognizable actor in the whole crowd. Damned strange," The Chief said, although sounding more bored than actually exasperated.

Airman Legs ignored the remark, standing to stretch while providing her own review. I saw the Sarge eyeball her hungrily. He might as well have had 'horny as hell' tattooed on his forehead.

"Again, the special effects were top notch. Trick photography sure made 'em all seem like the same guy, even when the pissed off version

99

slammed the main clone against the wall. Good stuff....computer generated magic at its best."

"Came off like one of those warped reality shows that were so popular before the swarm. Man, whoever produced it didn't skimp on the fake blood. Must have used a tractor-trailer full of the stuff," I add while strolling over to the player to eject the disk.

"Another?" I asked, a new disk already positioned for entry.

"Why not? Our appointment book seems blank at the moment. Troops?" the Chief answers just as Brain Dog re-enters the room with a wide yawn.

"Speak for yourself, Boss. I can think of at least one thing I'd rather be doin' than ogling the tube..." The Sarge smirks, squinting at Airman Legs like a ravenous grizzly at a cornered doe.

Legs ignores the obvious advance and sits back down with a mild huff as Father Pete glares in disapproval. I hear Corporal Chatty snicker at The Sarge just as Lieutenant Lava grips my shoulders from behind and playfully squeezes.

"How about another... counseling session after the movies play out?" she whispers seductively just inches from my right ear.

I turn to respond, already feeling the throngs of arousal warming my groin, just as Private Brain Dog leaps forward in a mock attack on the Lieutenant's exposed flank. She easily avoids his telegraphed right hook, side-stepping to allow just enough room for a leg sweep that sends him flailing backwards into the portion of the sectional occupied by The Sarge and Corporal Chatty.

"Son of a...!!" The Sarge barks as the back of Brain Dog's skull smacks solidly against his upper left shoulder. Brain Dog slides to the floor with a pained grimace, rubbing his head vigorously.

"Damn, girl...you are pumped, primed and professional," he barks while rolling away from The Sarge's playful barrage of punches to his injured appendage. Brain Dog's feelings towards the Lieutenant are similar to mine, I know. It's extremely difficult for either of us to expound on such emotions while standing at such a dark, desolate crossroads. What would it accomplish other than to complicate matters that will soon be sadly moot?

The Sarge leans over the couch's edge, staring at Lava with pure awe while addressing Brain Dog, who stands and flashes a peace sign in her direction.

"Dog, you're about as flexible as a brick. How many times you gonna fall for the same move? Lava's tripped up your carcass with that leg sweep at least half a dozen times. Ya ain't exactly quick on the uptake, are ya?"

"Not to worry, Sarge. The bugs ain't up on such moves anyhow, right? First one of those hairy bastards I see usin' martial arts, I figure my ass is grass regardless," Brain Dog replies without a trace of humor, although he shoots me a quick wink afterwards.

"Good point...I guess,' Sarge concedes, staring up at the stone ceiling as if in deep meditation.

"How's Kid Cadet holding up?" The Chief inquires as I press the 'pause' button on the players remote.

"Little dude loves the duty, Boss-man. Same old visuals though. There's so many of 'em now, looks almost like their welded together into one being, you know? Creeps you out if you watch it long enough…like hypnosis."

"Think I'll go join him for a while. Get a fresher set of eyes on the case," The Chief says, his knees popping like rocket fire upon rising from the couch.

"Damn, boss, you need a splint for those breaks?" Brain Dog says, then backs away quickly upon viewing the Chief's stern, humorless expression.

"Little WD-40'll do the trick, Clarence, but thanks for the sincere concern. Carry on, troops," he replies while practically limping out of the room.

"Now sit your scrawny ass down, Brain Dog, unless of course ya need one of the females to assist you in doin' so," The Sarge grumbles, Corporal Chatty, as always, nodding agreeably in the background.

Tina leans over and gently suckles my right earlobe as I power up the player, then steps forward to take a seat directly in front of me. Suddenly I desire nothing more than for the rest of the discs to be completely blank. Instead, a familiar visual fills the screen….

Chapter Four
Ravaged

Bud Morton is a short stocky man in his mid-forties; has eyelashes as thick and bushy as caterpillars, but little hair remaining on his shiny dome. Bud works at a large city Zoo as a handler. Strong as an ox, despite the only regular exercise he gets is the occasional jog to the john when his bladder is on the verge of implosion, or the infrequent roll in the hay with the better half.

Bud is literally sweating bullets. He can smell a mixture of nervous sweat and stale cotton candy spilling from his open pores. The keys to his brand-spanking new two-thousand three Mercury Cougar are being dangled in front of his exasperated mug like a carrot to a ravenous Jack Rabbit.

Bud says (albeit a bit shakily) "Come on fellas, I really h-have to get going. There's an appointment I can't afford to be late for, you understand."

Clifford J. "Spike" Parker is tall, at least six-four. His age is impossible to gauge (possibly as young as twenty-five or as old as forty-five). He has a pitch-black ZZ Top-like beard that hangs onto his bare chest, which is smothered in tattoos of various naked female forms. His teeth are rotted from years of obvious neglect, his breath reeks of George Dickel whiskey and stale Marlboros. "Spike" is a connoisseur of regular workouts, whether it be isometric (banging the old lady) or cardiovascular (beating the living crap out of the old lady). The bike he rides (stolen from a lot in Reno, Nevada two years earlier) is a '97 Harley FXDWG model.

'Spike' says (spitting profusely) "Soon as you turn over the wallet and it's contents, asshole. You either hand it over willingly or I'll allow the Mangler over there to begin removing body parts, balls first."

Barry "The Mangler" Fuchs is a walking, talking bowling ball with a head. He stands no taller than five-six, but tips the scales at a less-than-svelte two-forty. His arms (both one continuous tattoo from shoulder to knuckles) are as thick as phone poles, but without a semblance of definition. His hair is Marine cropped on tip, but hangs in long beaded ropes from the sides and back. His ears are huge, elephantine. 'The Mangler' rides a black 2000 Harley Buell Blast (illegally 'borrowed' from his brother-in-law over a year earlier).

'The Mangler' says "Can I butt-bang him first, Spike?"

Bud feels his bowels instantly loosen at the thought. Now he wishes he hadn't gulped down that second Whopper with cheese a half-hour ago. He glances back at the Cougar's closed trunk, then back to 'Spike'. Again to the trunk and back to 'Spike'. His expression is like a scolded child on the verge of tears.

Bud says (removing his wallet from the wrinkled Dockers adorning his backside) "You can have my c-credit cards, but I've only got about twenty in cash. I never c-carry cash these days, you understand. N-not safe these days, if…you know what I mean."

'Spike' guffaws as he snatches the wallet out of

Bud's trembling hand and begins digging through the contents.

'Spike' says (his smile fading into an angry scowl) "Yeah, I know what ya mean, pal. You're the second dumb bastard to attempt a free pass through the valley of the Brotherhood. Fucking weasel actually copped an attitude with me when I mentioned the toll fare we charge for such obvious trespassing. Now he's missing fifty bucks and his front two teeth, right Mangler?"

Now picking his nose furiously, 'The Mangler' nods and begins to cackle mischievously.

Mangler replies (flicking a moist, green booger into the cool, misty air) "Lost his virginity to boot. Happens every time a carney comes to town, boss."

Brenda 'Cheeks' Miser claps him on the shoulder playfully. Brenda is 'The Mangler's old lady. She is five-feet six, one-hundred seventy pounds, with short brown hair that is literally dripping oil at the ends. Her ample gut protrudes from the T-top she wears that reads 'Born to Raise Hell' like a thickly rolled slab of dough.

Most of her top plate of teeth have long since fallen away (or been violently dislodged). Brenda rides atop a '95 Harley, pink in color with a skull and crossbones emblem displayed proudly on the gas tank.

Brenda says (in between passionate sucks on the roach clip hanging between her blood-red lipstick smeared, slug-like lips) 'Let me have a shot at the nerdy little shit, Spike. I ain't had a good scrap in days. Can we hurry this up, though? I wanna get over to that carnival and start hockin' wallets."

'Spike' says (his voice growing shriller by the second) "Mangler, put your old lady back in her cage, will ya? This four-eyed sack of horse shit is mine unless he comes up with a better stash. The Carney can wait 'til we bleed Mr. Peepers here."

Bud (cringing while being slapped in the face by his Gucci wallet) glances back at the trunk, ignoring the stinging of his right cheek, which is now Beet red, says "I really h-have to go now, fellas. I'm s-sorry I trespassed on y-your territory. This little two-lane is a short cut to the 'burbs, that's all. I u-use it when the interstate is backed up, you understand."

Bud continues to sweat profusely, thick beads cutting a trail from the top of his bald head to the tip of his weak, quivering chin.

Bud reiterates. He places his chubby hands together as if to beg.

"This is kinda'...it's an emergency, you understand. A me-medical emergency you might say. I'm s-sorry I invaded your space. I just take this road whenever the interstate is packed, you understand. You fellas go ahead and take my credit cards and get wh-whatever you need with them, but I really have to g-go now. Y-you'll love that carnival. G-got lots of rides and g-great food. J-just like w-when I was a kid. Great f-freak show, t-too boot."

'Spike' lunges forward and punches Bud in the solar plexus, then plants his bony knee solidly against the right jaw of the already crouched over man. Bud sails back against the Cougar's driver's side door, then slumps onto the gravel. Bud's mouth is bleeding and he is gasping for air like someone in the throngs of a severe asthma attack.

"The Mangler' steps forward gleefully and beams down at the fallen man.

'The Mangler' says "Let me take out his teeth, Spike. I still have those pliers we used on that dude in Memphis."

'Spike' holds up one thin but tightly muscled arm in a halting gesture. 'Mangler' pouts and backs away.

'Spike' says (casually scratching his crouch through his leather pants) "Too messy, man. That guy almost ripped your eye out, 'member? Let's drag his worthless carcass down into that ravine down there before some other jackass decides to tool on down the highway and spots our little pow-wow. About one weak-kneed S.T.S is all I can handle at the present time."

'S.T.S' stood for 'Slave to Society,' an acronym 'Spike' had attached his unofficial copyright on years earlier. It basically meant anyone who didn't share their 'treat everyday like your last' way of life. If you worked for a living, you were a S.T.S. If you laid your head onto the same pillow in the same home night after night, you were a S.T.S. If you paid bills, you were an S.T.S. In the opinion of the Brotherhood of The Skull, if you didn't spend your time stealing, boozing, ingesting dope or getting laid, you were an S.T.S.

Creating new and clever acronym's was one of 'Spike's favorite past times, right up there on the charts with rape and armed robbery. He was thirty-two and had never held a job, other than the ones

107

provided him by the county or state while he was serving as their unwilling guest in an eight by ten cell.

'Spike', 'The Mangler', 'Cheeks' and Bobby 'Shovel-hands' Klein (the group's youngest member at the tender age of sixteen. He was nicknamed due to his proud ownership of hands roughly the size of dinner plates; with long, thin, spidery fingers to match) each take an appendage and begin to drag Bud roughly across the gravel shoulder towards the grassy ravine.

Bud leaves a trail of urine in his wake, his concern about the contents of his vehicle's trunk now paling as compared to the grim seriousness of what is about to transpire. Still, even as he is tossed onto his back in the center of a small clearing and engulfed on all sides by thick, dense shrubbery and low hanging limbs from nearby pines and oaks (they seemed to be reaching down to either help or assist in his demise), he can't help but wonder.

Bud thinks (just before the large, steel-toed boot lands on his forehead with a muffled thud) "Just how long is that tranquilizer gonna last?"

***

Jimmy Barksdale is a large human being. A large, rather pissed off human being. He stands (looms) six-five and weighs in at a slim and trim two-twenty. His close-set eyes, overly thick lips and jug ears give him the appearance of a man who has endured much ridicule in his time on earth, although truth be told, he has dished out substantially more than he has taken.

Jogging three miles a day, plus an hour a day

(five days a week) in the weight room keeps him from developing 'dun lap disease (i.e. 'his gut dun-lapped over his belt') despite his advancing years (forty-five this coming July). An agent with the Federal Bureau of Investigation for over twenty years (next December), he couldn't help but feel a bit perturbed at the case he was presently assigned to.

A lab animal had been stolen from a government lab six weeks previous, a species his superiors had informed him was 'irreplaceable' and 'vital' to the veterinary field. Rumor had it a traveling carney show had it stowed away in it's 'Gods Freak Zoo' exhibit, displaying it as some kind of 'Mother Nature on Crack' example. His mission was to retrieve it as soon as possible to the scientists that had reported its theft. A Zoo employee who had PETA ties was suspected in the animal's theft from the carnival grounds earlier that evening.

The carnival's head man, a white-haired, skinny as a broomstick old grump who had identified himself to Jimmy as "Mr. Henry Lobo of Lobo's Traveling Wonders of The Universe" had been absolutely livid in reporting the theft. This was despite being duly informed of his own detainment in the original disappearance of the creature. Waving one gnarled, trembling fist in the air as if cursing the Gods above, Lobo had referred to the missing animal as 'the Wonders' main attraction', stating he would post a five-thousand dollar reward for it's timely retrieval. Jimmy's only response to the old man's ramblings was to immediately contact local authorities and order all Carney employees be detained until further notice. Jimmy feels the searing sensation on his bare neck as he leaves the scene, turning to catch a glimpse of the old man just before departing. Leaning heavily on the thick wooden cane by his side, Lobo's expression is equal parts sarcastic smirk and comical bliss, as if he were privy to a secret which held vital information within the scenario, but had decided to keep said tidbit locked stubbornly away for his own deranged amusement.

Lobo shoots Jimmy a playful wink before turning away.

"Good luck, Agent man. Lord, are you gonna need it."

As he stands outside his vehicle, barking orders into a cell phone so petite his hand practically engulfs it, Jimmy fells suddenly nauseous.

The overwhelming aroma of overcooked hotdogs, melted chocolate and undercooked beef fills his flaring nostrils. The paying crowd has long since departed, leaving only the occasional carney worker to straggle by hastily.

He sees the tiny circle of figures glaring at him from the edge of the carnival compound. It wasn't until he pockets his phone and leans into his vehicle that their faces and forms become entirely visible through the dim light provided by nearby ground lamps.

He instantly feels a cold shiver run up his spine like a mild electric shock.

They stand shoulder length apart, a gathering of souls so diverse in size and shape it was as if they were actually stone statues carved out by some hopelessly insane New Age sculptor.

The line-up:

A man so gruesomely thin it reminded one of a cantaloupe shoved atop a narrow stick, his grotesquely long, needle sized arms propped on hips the width of a normal man's single calf.

A woman so large that the massive rolls of her upper body seemed infinite, her own noggin resembled a raisin propped atop a colossal beach ball.

A man with an extra arm (actually only a curled hand and knobby wrist) sprouting from his enormously thick neck..

A woman with a small, pert, and perfectly rounded breast protruding from her overlong forehead.

A set of male-female midgets, both of whom stood approximately as high as the thin man's left knee.

Maintaining his composure as any professional was trained to do, Jimmy drives calmly from the site, then sighs heavily and with no small amount of relief once he reached the nearest bend.

"Jeez, I thought such places vanished along with the dial phone and manual typewriters," he mumbles somewhat nervously.

He had found out through interviews with some of the Zoo handler's co-workers that he sometimes had the habit of taking a rural, back roads shortcut to his home from the Zoo location, thereby bypassing the congested interstate. As fate would have it, the 'Wonders' exhibits and mini-carnival had been stationed just a half-mile from said shortcut, just a stone's throw from said interstate ramps.

Jimmy had met many Bud Morton types in his time. Bud Morton had entered the carney compound with a single mission in mind; to save the nearest creature of God he deemed 'most deserving of sweet freedom from the steel cages of man's inhumane cruelty'. Jimmy huffed in disgust. He would never understand such warped bleeding hearts. So many humans suffering across the globe that were discarded and ignored, mainly helpless children, and these bozos saturate tons of Kleenex over the 'plight' of fur-bags everywhere.

The road is one big pothole, the shoulders almost nonexistent in spots due to the overgrown weeds and grass that had been allowed to flourish.

Jimmy Barksdale glances down at the watch on the dashboard of his year-old Ford Explorer. It reads nine-twenty six PM. Huffing in frustration, Jimmy Barksdale pounds his fist against the steering wheel. A missing lab rat. He was cruising on an abandoned, narrow as a stripper's waistline, two-lane, in the middle of absolute nowhere, looking for some nut with a stolen lab mouse.

He knew he should put aside his anger and lock his thoughts on the mission to be done. He was a professional, after all. He had always been nothing if not that.

As hard as he tried to fight it, he found he didn't give a rat's ass. The only thing he knew for a fact was that if he were white and a twenty year vet with a decade of near-perfect job evaluations, he would more than likely be assigned to an unsolved homicide or the disappearance of someone the agency deemed worthy enough to search for. He definitely would not be on the trail of some flea-ridden rodent first utilized as a pincushion by mad scientists, then by a greedy old man as some sort of freakish display at a roadside carnival.

Speeding through the darkness, the road growing more curved as the landscape becomes increasingly hilly, Jimmy Barksdale realizes another fact; he has to piss like a Russian racehorse.

***

'The Mangler' says (drool dripping from the corners of his mouth like froth from a rabid dog) "Is the sombitch dead, Spike? I want to hit that carnival 'fore it shuts down for the night."

'Spike' leans over the body until his sweat-covered face is just inches from Bud's, which now resembles stomped upon ground beef.

'Spike' says (lips parted wide in a sneer of pure satisfaction) "Nope, he's still breathing. Tough little fat man, ain't he? Hands, ya wanna do the honors? We'll consider it your final test to join the Brotherhood."

'Shovelhands' Klein pulls an object from behind the large metallic belt buckle that covers roughly half of his slim midsection, and a split second later displays the shiny six inch blade, it's smooth edges reflecting the moonlight's rays into the other's wide eyes.

'Shovelhands' says "I'd be delighted, boss. It'll be like carvin' up the turkey at Grandma's on Thanksgiving Day."

Bud thinks (although the thoughts are a tad on the fuzzy, unfocused side due to several broken ribs,

113

a mild concussion, and the fact that most of his teeth have been violently dislodged)

I bet it's waking up about now. I bet it's highly pissed off, as well. It was mighty perturbed when it ripped off that carney worker's arm and swallowed the damn thing whole a few hours back. Just like a KFC drumstick, it was. Spit the bones out like small shards of splintered wood. That cage won't hold it. Neither will the trunk. Maybe it's full for now...I hope. At least it won't ever get at me, at least...not while I'm alive.

Bud hears the sounds of faint laughter; maniacal laughter. There is a moment of complete silence just before the shrieks cut through the air like foghorns on a desolate beachhead; high pitched female shrieks that originated from the highway above them.

Bud thinks (before mercifully passing out)

Uh-Oh. G-Gonna be hell..to pay..now.

***

Jimmy Barksdale decides he's going to pull over and utilize 'nature's mens room' just as soon as he passes through the sharp, winding curve presently in his site.

He rounds the crest of the steep hill that lands him on a flatter, straighter stretch of road and begins to brake, his bladder screaming it's disapproval with even the smallest of moments. His mind drifts back to the macabre collection of freaks that had watched so intensely as he had driven away from their makeshift campsite. He found it downright astonishing that such lives were still being led in the 21st century. He also found it a damned site creepy.

He spots the Mercury and the cycles parked at its rear in the distance, just at the bottom of another rolling stretch of road. Instinctively, he turns off his headlights and slows almost to a complete stop.

Jimmy Barksdale whispers (pulling onto a wide, rocky shoulder) "What do we have here? Looks like a late model Cougar with a Hell's Angels' escort."

'Spike' bellows (scrambling up the ravine with arms and legs pumping) "Get your fat ass up there, Mangler! That sounded like my old lady yelling!"

'Mangler' replies (His Jell-O-like gut flapping free from underneath his multi-stained T-shirt) "Maybe a trooper rode by!"

Bud thinks (after spitting a chunk of what had been a crown on one of his rear molars).

What kind of lunatic...dreams up that kind of ...cruel, inhumane shit anyway? The ultimate security weapon of the future...my fat white ass. They should..have known they..couldn't contain it. Lobo..kept it doped up for display...but...got careless. Hope that team of crackpot eggheads..fry for all the killings that are...imminent...Lobo too.

Cruel old bastard....

Bud passes out again, but not before realizing with surprising aplomb that he cannot feel his lower extremities.

'Spike' tops the hill in the lead and is the first to visualize the massacre revealed in all its hazy orange colored glory by the bright desert moonlight.

'Spike' says (side stepping the carnage towards his overturned Harley) "Son..of..a..bitch. What the fuck, over?"

'The Mangler' huffs towards him like a derailed

115

freight car, twisting his bulky frame to one side just in time to avoid body-slamming his fearless leader. Unable to halt his momentum, he tumbles forward and trips over an object that seems comically out of place on the weed infested, trash strewn shoulder. 'The Mangler' does a belly flop onto the edge of the pavement and instantly feels something warm and gooey spread onto his exposed abdomen and upper chest.

'The Mangler' says (rolling over onto his rear end and then shoving himself up, his face frozen in disgust) "Holy shit! It's a friggin' leg bone, Spike! With the friggin' b-boot still attached!"

'The Mangler' kicks at the object as if attempting to hold an aggressive dog at bay, then cringes back a few steps, wiping furiously at the warm stickiness clinging to his shirt and the pale, hairless skin beneath.

'Spike' wasn't paying the slightest attention to his suddenly passive, less than fearless sidekick. He busied himself retrieving the Glock Nine Millimeter from the storage compartment of his ride, which was presently lying on its side in the center of the two lane.

At almost the exact same moment that he secured the revolver's magazine into place, he spotted the head. It sat upright just a few feet from the front grille of the Cougar, so neatly displayed it resembled an abstract art sculpture. The overwhelming odor of copper filling his nostrils, 'Spike' turned and gagged. The identity of the severed head had become crystal clear upon further study.

116

Kathy 'Legs' Monroe had been his old lady since he picked her up at a local dive roughly three months and two and a half states ago.

She had sported long (down to her dimpled butt cheeks) auburn hair the color of a raging inferno, and legs that seemed to invite even the most prudish observer to undertake a test climb.

'Spike' had really grown fond of her. She allowed him to beat her with a minimum of lip, and whatever type sex he was in the mood for on a given occasion was usually agreeable with her (and if not, a quick jab to the ribs made it so).

Whirling back around, his ears pricked for even the faintest of sounds, 'Spike' couldn't help but think as he stared at Kathy's pulped, torn scalp and partially open, bloodied mouth:

Damn. Guess a last screw is out of the question.

'The Mangler' says (his own eyes on the verge of literally bugging out at the sight of the decapitated skull) "Cliff, let's g-get the living hell…o-utta here pronto, what do ya say?"

The younger man is tugging on the elder's shirt collar like a desperate child leading a parent towards the toy section of a crowded discount store.

'Spike' says (after a quick punch to the chest that bends the younger man over in gasping pain) "Do me a favor and shut your pie-hole, Fuchs. I always knew you were a pussy. Whoever or whatever just made a hood ornament outta my old lady has got some serious payback coming, and DBD-9 and myself are gonna make sure that happens."

'Spike' had a habit of naming his weapons. The

117

serrated combat knife strapped to his left thigh was the 'S & D (Slice and Dice) Special'. The Glock revolver was nicknamed 'DBD-9' (Death Before Dishonor, taken off a slain Marine reserve private he had ran down with a stolen Monte Carlo in the parking lot of a juke-joint in North Carolina a few years back).

'The Mangler' swivels his watermelon shaped head around in all directions, his throat clicking noisily. 'The Mangler' says (a small switchblade held out in front of his chest like an ancient talisman) "Where the hell is Shovel-hands? He was r-right behind us! And where is Chong? He w-was up here with Kat. W-was that his l-leg I tripped over or h-hers?"

As if to provide a hint to the possible answers to such distressing queries, both men simultaneously hear and then yelp out loud from the roaring crash that mercifully interrupts 'The Mangler's' whining jag.

'The Mangler' has time to release a low, squeaky fart before the figure bounds from atop the Cougar's now deeply dented roof and wraps itself around his round dome, the force of the contact sending his massive frame temporarily airborne.

'Spike' begins to giggle madly, his boots seemingly super-glued to the asphalt mere feet away from where his former partner-in-crime is being shredded like a side of beef through a meat grinder.

'Spike' manages to fire off two wild, inaccurate shots at the impossibly quick figure, both sparking off of the pavement like exploding M-80's before sailing uselessly into the surrounding forest.

'Spike' says (his giggling now transformed into something closer to a pleading whimper) "Jesus....you g-gotta be k-kidding me, man. What the hell...i-is it?"

'Spike' drops the revolver and discovers his feet and legs are back under his mental command. His inner mind instantly sounds retreat at the knowledge. He sprints past the rear end of the Cougar and peers down just long enough to catch a glimpse of the ragged, circular hole that has been torn through it at the center. The metal (fiberglass?) is curled and ripped, and faces up towards the star filled sky. 'Spike' deduces while hastily retreating that it looked as if someone had detonated a grenade inside the trunk.

'Spike' also sees the headless corpse of his former lover lying on its side a dozen or so feet up the highway towards the east. The corpse resembles a discarded mannequin. A small, pathetic shriek escapes his throat as he stumbles ahead in a state of total panic he never considered himself capable of.

'Spike' is about to leap from the shoulder of the road into the thick underbrush when a familiar face presents itself for inspection.

'Spike' says (falling back onto the shoulder, his butt cheeks landing somewhat painfully on a pile of broken glass) "Shit! C-Chong?"

Milton "Chong" Demartini was six-feet and two-hundred pounds of certified meanness. He had joined the Brotherhood in Kansas City six months earlier, after the group witnessed him single-handedly clear out a pool hall (and all inhabitants unfortunate enough to cross his drunken path) with a series of reverse round-house kicks and quick-as-lightning jabs, backhands, and open handed chops. He was half-Korean, and was a second-degree black belt in Tai Kwon Do. 'Chong' had also displayed the God given ability to lie and/or con his way out of almost any situation with the authorities. The gift of gab and the gift of jab had been his assets to the gang.

As he waddles incoherently and comically doe-eyed just a few feet from his former boss, it was horrifically apparent that Milton "Chong" Demartini, a young man of many talents, was no longer feeling or looking like his 'old self'.

The pulpy mess that had been his throat was torn open like a soggy grocery bag, his formerly white T-shirt now a crimson-soaked second skin draped over his chest and stomach. Both of 'Chong's' arms were missing below the elbow, white bone protruding from the jagged, bloody stumps like busted conduit pipe. Something trim and slimy hangs free from just above his belt buckle, like the dead weight of a limp snake.

'Chong' says (a thick gout of blood spewing forth like a volcano eruption) "S-Spike? G-get me..a d-doctor...will ya? I can't f-find my a-arms, man. I h-have to...find t-them so...the doc can...s-sew t-them b-back o-on. Help m-me find t-them, will..y-ya?"

'Spike' says (warm urine trickling down his leather chapped jeans) "G-get the h-hell away from m-me, m-man...y-you're d-dead.." and begins a series of rolls, not unlike a man on fire attempting to extinguish the flames, that takes him a safe distance

120

from the walking corpse who is now shambling away in the opposite direction.

'Spike' now visualizes the lengthy, bloated trail of intestine that 'Chong' drags in his wake and begins to gag uncontrollably as he continues to side step away.

'Spike' jogs down the highway's centerline, crying and whimpering like an infant trapped in a dark, confined closet.

He hears the rapid movement gaining on him a moment later, and what had remained of his hopelessly low energy supply dwindles ever further towards absolute collapse mode.

'Spike' says (turning to face his attacker with an expression of unbridled surrender) "D-don't..k-kill...me...p-please.."

'Spike' trips and falls forward, landing directly on top of the figure that had been nipping at his boot heels so quickly and with such maniacal ferociousness it had actually run in front of him.

'Spike' cackled with what little breath he had remaining. Despite knowing his life was about to end, possibly in the throngs of indescribable pain, he couldn't resist.

'Spike' thinks (just before his chest cavity implodes) Feels a warm, fuzzy Teddy Bear.

***

Jimmy Barksdale remains in a crouched, shooters position as he painstakingly makes his way through the increasingly steep, overgrown ravine leading towards the perp's vehicle and the overturned bikes surrounding it.

His snub-nosed thirty-eight held tucked in and

shoulder high, Jimmy is overcome by a sense of foreboding he hadn't felt since seventy-nine, the night he discovered his first dead body: Double homicide inside a heroin-house on the outskirts of Lincoln, Nebraska. A local dealer with a coil-wire necktie; his girlfriend riddled with bullets. He had witnessed quite a few varied, gruesome examples of human cruelty since that specific scenario, but only now was again the feeling of pure dread even comparable to that initial shock.

Literally crawling onto the shoulder as he nears the passenger side of the Cougar, Jimmy spots the first casualty, although whoever it had been, looked to have been pulled apart like a half-completed jig saw puzzle.

His eyes feverishly scanning the surrounding landscape, Jimmy leans over the victim and gives the tattered remains a quick study.

It had been a big kid, white male, no more than twenty or twenty- three.

The kid had huge ears, like mini-boat sails. Hair was short on top, military cut, but hung like reggae style rolls in the back. Arms (actually only the left remained entirely intact) were heavily tattooed, the majority of which were crudely designed and more than likely homemade.

His face was frayed, like someone had broken out the yard tools and metaphorically wiped away his identity. His eye sockets were empty pits filled with seeping fluids, like coffee cups left out in a rainstorm. His right arm looked mashed somehow, like it had been trapped underneath an object of enormous weight and simply crushed, then the flesh,

Jimmy turned his head in the direction of the howl just as 'Spike's' back split apart like a ripe melon struck by an axe blade.

The figure leaps from the detonation of shattered vertebrae, perforated bowel and projectile spattering bodily fluids and bounces off of the asphalt, halting its forward movement three feet to Jimmy's right.

The body it had so violently emerged from was left looking like something that had swallowed a bazooka blast from an insanely short range.

'Spike' has a circular hole punched through his chest cavity and back that would have measured a foot horizontally and at least eight inches diagonally.

Jimmy decides against taking the time to measure.

He is far too busy soiling his size thirty-eight (a bit loose these days due to a daily set-up regimen) Fruit-of-the Looms at the mere sight of the specimen before him. The specimen that seemed to hardly be acknowledging his presence as it nonchalantly shakes the fresh gore off of its furry coat.

Despite its small stature (no more than fifteen inches high from paws to backbone; thirty-six to forty in length at the extreme), it owns two very specific physical characteristics that takes center stage. Characteristics which quickly dismiss its less than imposing size as insignificant in terms of imposing stark fear in its prey.

Its front and back claws are slightly hooked, thick at the base and slim at the tips. Even drenched in layers of dried blood, Jimmy has no doubts at their razor-sharp effectiveness when utilized on an opponent's tender flesh.

Its snout sports teeth that seem far too large for the mouth that contains them.

Its fiery red eyes meet his own for the first time, a low pitched, drawn out growl reveals both the upper and lower sets it all their hideous, terrifying glory.

Jimmy thinks (trying desperately but failing at keeping completely still, even as the odor of his released bowels fill the air around him).

The ugly little bastard looks like a hybrid mix of some kind. Those egg-heads must have been doing some seriously dangerous experimentation at that lab. Kinda resembles a Wolverine, but with a touch of Grizzly or black bear thrown in for good measure. Jesus, I cannot believe I've actually crapped my pants. Shit! How many rounds did I load? It's been so damn long since I unloaded I can't remember.

The creature lifts its head and Jimmy can see its tiny nostrils flare. He knows it is sniffing the crap that has now soiled through to his pants. He also knows that it realizes his fear, engulfs it; relishes it.

Jimmy gets off one round before his shooting arm is slashed on the inside of his elbow. The bullet ricochets off the pavement and into 'Spike's' left thigh, although the former biker, drug dealer, woman beater, and all around upstanding citizen seems well beyond the point of caring.

Just as he feels an overwhelming burning sensation on his left calf, Jimmy quickly surveys the damage to his gun arm, which feels strangely weak and a bit numb around the crock of his elbow.

Jimmy lifts his damaged arm to eye level, and is

instantly spewed in the left orb by a stream of hot, sticky liquid. With no other reaction available at that precise moment, Jimmy begins to giggle at the deformity hanging before him. His forearm and hand still point directly towards the roadway at his feet, even though his bicep and shoulder are positioned in an upward arc. He sees the jagged white bone sticking through, cut clean as though by a bone saw. He sees the slim thread of muscle and tendon that grasp onto the severed appendage stubbornly, preventing his upper arm from separating from their host.

Jimmy kicks his stinging leg forward with the majority of his waning strength, and watches the creature sail forward in a lurch, landing in the center of the quagmire that is 'Spike's' upper torso. The impact causes 'Spike's' head and a portion of his backbone to roll forward face up. 'Spike's' expression is one of excruciating pain one might associate with victims of the Spanish Inquisition. His eyes are open but only the whites show; his mouth is agape and stretched impossibly wide; he has chewed off the top portion of his own tongue.

Jimmy Barksdale has little time to sympathize.

As he turns to run towards the Cougar for temporary safety, he falls forward and scrapes his forehead and nose onto the pavement. Glancing down to his injured calf, Jimmy begins to whimper helplessly. His pants ripped entirely away from knee to ankle, he has a clear view of the missing area where his fairly muscled calf once occupied.

The bone is frighteningly skinny between the knee and ankle, he deduces.

Jimmy thinks back to a Warner Brothers cartoon he once saw. The Tasmanian Devil had just whittled away a large tree trunk to the size of a number ten pencil with his razor-like choppers at literally the speed of light.

Jimmy's lower leg was a bit pulpier, but had a similar look to it. The fact that his foot remained planted in his shoe and was completely untouched only added to the surreal feel of the situation.

Dragging himself forward on his remaining arm, Jimmy hardly noticed that the other had become detached and been shoved to the side with his thirty-eight still locked in its grasp.

Jimmy whined (his blood filled eye beginning to settle into a rhythmic tick) "G-gotta..get inside…the car…maybe..a c-car phone…g-get some h-help…"

The driver's door is slightly ajar, but it still takes Jimmy a full minute to drag himself in. Blood is leaking from his body from three separate but equally ravaged points. From the area in the roadway that the initial attack had occurred, a glutinous, snail-like trail of blood led to the Cougar's driver's door.

Jimmy shuts the door with a grunt and groggily looks around for a cell or car phone.

Jimmy thinks (his eye lids only half open, bloody spittle leaking from the corners of his mouth)

What a way to go out. Taken apart like a Christmas Goose by an overgrown Gerbil. That asshole Lobo knew…knew I'd get my head handed to me…w-where the hell is my gun, anyway?

Jimmy wearily looks down to the space his arm

should be. Jimmy smiles sheepishly.

Jimmy thinks (closing his eyes and sucking in one last supply of oxygen)

That is......one ....mean fucking.... rodent, man.

The windshield shatters, and Jimmy Barksdale thinks no more.

The creature departs the blood soaked interior of the vehicle and makes its way up the roadway a few dozen feet, where it stops to begin the arduous task of self-cleaning.

Its plans are simple; to find a place to den. A safe haven minus the probing, studied presence of human eyes. It feels the sneaky chill settling into the night air, and part of its mind screams for a long, peaceful slumber, especially now that its insatiable appetite has been temporarily satisfied.

The rage that it had awakened with has only subsided a touch, and that part of its mind screams to kill and savage whatever moves into its sights.

It rises onto its hind legs and sniffs, the fresh scent of pulsating flesh filling it's heightened senses.

The first round blows its left paw into a dozen meaty chunks.

The second hits the pavement a foot to its left.

The third catches it directly between its wide-set, searing eyes and sheers its head away in a misty spray of fur and bone.

The creature spasms once before lying still.

Bud Morton crawls from the edge of the road's hilly shoulder, spitting a small chunk of tooth from his battered mouth along the way. He tosses the Glock pistol into the ravine and waddles painstakingly towards his vehicle, stopping only momentarily to glare down at the specimen whose test-tube initiated life he has so abruptly ended.

Bud says (in between hacking coughs that threaten to make him faint) "S-sorry about that, little fella. W-wasn't your fault the crazy bastards screwed with your...both of your DNA's. Maybe...the surgery they proposed would have created a gentle side to you, a side that would have made you controllable. A side that w-would have made you marketable as the p-perfect security pet. At least you w-won't kill again or s-suffer at the hands of those b-butchers at the lab. No more time in a cage being stared at by groves of ignorant thrill seekers either."

Bud pulls the ripped apart form of an unidentified black male from the front and back seats of the Cougar, wincing in both pain and disgust as he does so.

Bud drives away, leaving what the media would later dub 'Slaughterhouse on Walnut Road' in his bloodstained rearview mirror.

In his dazed, injured state, Bud had neglected to check the vehicle's trunk.

Three small creatures lay curled inside the wheel-well of his regulation size spare tire.

They would waken hours later and begin to suckle on the severed, tattoo-infested arm that their now deceased mother had so lovingly provided only hours before.

Bud discovered them three days later while residing in a rat-trap hotel just outside Reno, Nevada.

They had grown considerably since inception.

Their first taste of live, pulsating flesh had definitely agreed with them.

***

The old man scans the grounds from just inside the propped open door of the RV. He watches one of his foremen waving frantically for the third of the four semis to cut a sharp left as it backs over the rocky terrain onto the edge of a grassy knoll.

He is about to retreat into the coolness of the air-conditioned vehicle when he first hears and then sees the form sprinting frantically towards him, the sound of untied shoelaces whipping back and forth filling his ears. "Mr. Lobo! Mr. Lobo?" the man shrieks as he nears, his long black hair matted in thick waves, as if previously dipped in used motor oil.

Lobo turns, using the stout oak cane at his side to pivot upon.

His voice is weary, worn. Forty-two years of eating back road dust on the outskirts of towns with names like Blue Rock, River's Edge, and Mud Flat Hills have chiseled both his physical and mental beings down to the dullest nub. His level of tolerance for stupidity is set permanently at the lowest human ebb imaginable, especially following the incident two states back. The only thing that had saved him from a lengthy confinement had been the lack of an identifiable animal at the scene. Authorities had found the mangled remains of something not human amongst the carnage, but giving the scattered or altogether missing parts of the corpse, obtaining a positive ID had simply been an impossible task.

131

"What is it, Becker? I'm very, very tired, and need my rest before we re-open our doors tomorrow night," Lobo grunted, wiping his bleary eyes furiously.

White spittle flew wildly from the man's mouth as he spoke, causing Lobo to grimace in disgust.

"Jennings and Markum found 'im, Sir! That guy that stole the 'Devil-rine'.

He was hidin' out in some fleabag hotel a few hundred miles to the south.

Actually, they only found...part of him, but.."

For the first time in a week, Lobo felt a twinge in his gut not affiliated with negative news.

"I don't care about the thief, Becker! What about the creature? Was he..?"

The man smiled so widely Lobo thought the skin on his jaw would soon split open like carved fruit.

"Three of 'em, Mr. Lobo. Seems that animal they found on the road that night was our girl, for sure. She birthed her litter 'fore they blew her away, though. We got three of 'em. Each of 'em no bigger than a beagle pup."

Lobo practically beamed.

"Any problems in the capture?"

Pete "Pig Pen" Becker's smile quickly transformed into a shaky, slightly gruesome contortion. He looked as though he were suddenly wracked with stomach cramps.

"Uh, Markum lost a finger or two. They cornered the vicious little bastards in an abandoned lot outside the hotel and shot 'em full of sleep-juice. Marky got...a little careless and picked one of 'em up 'fore it was completely conked. Otherwise, smooth as snot...uh, Sir."

"Where are they now?" Lobo asked, already descending the RV's rusty metal steps.

"Double caged in Jennings' van, sir. The doc shot 'em up again a few hours ago. They were beginning to chew on the bars. He said we have to get a new glass cage since that asswipe broke the other one when he stole the mama."

A half hour later, Henry Lobo stood over his newest prize display, a trio of thick-bodied, short legged creatures coated in fine layers of slick, pitch black hair. Even in sleep their razor sharp claws were bared, the stubs of their lower set of prickly teeth revealed in all their grisly glory.

Smiling like a man holding the winning Powerball lottery ticket in his taught, closed fist, Lobo's head fell back and he began to howl in joyful glee.

"Won't lose you this time, my pets. You will be guarded twenty-four seven. You will be given the royal treatment, yes sir. Such glorious benefits you will enjoy. I know what you crave, young ones, and I can guarantee complete satisfaction in that particular department."

Leaning down until his ancient knees popped in disapproval, Lobo placed his chin atop the cool glass top and gazed unblinkingly at the unmoving entities below. His weathered face bore the pride of a newly ordained father.

"Besides, mama wouldn't have had it any other way."

The next day, one Pete "Pig Pen" Becker came

up missing, his meager belongings no longer stashed in the supply van with the other workers' items, his cot stripped bare in the one-man tent he had previously called home.

No one questioned Becker's absence for very long. The carney lifestyle was one long associated with 'gypsy' type personalities, and the revolving door of faces who maintained its rare appearance came and went like busboys in a big city restaurant.

Stored behind a thick metal door adorned with various sized padlocks, three forms began to slowly awaken from the foggy haze of an afternoon nap. A semi-dry, crimson liquid hung to the corners of their tiny mouths, falling away in moist chunks as they yawned.

For now at least , their bellies were comfortably full.

It was almost Showtime, and they were, undoubtedly, destined for stardom.

***

"Cripes, could we possibly view something a bit gorier, please? If I see another detached lung or severed appendage, I think I'll forever lose my appetite for boiled liver and onions," Father Pete growls, practically leaping from the couch.

Private Brain Dog joins him at the entrance, griping his midsection with both hands. The dog always seems to relish the role of drama-queen.

"I'm with you, Padre. That crap is for splatter-hounds only. Sure as hell is realistic, though. Filmed like one of those episodes of 'COPS', the camera shaking and bobbin' up and down. Made me belch up that corned beef hash we had for lunch...and let me testify, regurgitated CBH is as nasty as it sounds."

"Best episode yet, I say. That furry little beastie was one lean, mean, pint-sized mother. Ya think it was animatronics? Didn't look computer generated either," The Sarge chimes in, clearly focusing his attention on Airman Legs as she again rose to stretch.

"Definitely wasn't hand puppets,' she says, fighting off a yawn while continuing to ignore The Sarge's personal Quality Control inspection of her slim, toned form, 'this girl has sat through her share of Hollywood horror and sci-fi, boys, and I'm telling you....that was as close to the real thing as you're gonna get other than boogieing down with the Cy-sects."

"Suds break, anyone?" Corporal Chatty injects blandly, invoking a comical glare from The Sarge, whose eyes bulge even as his squared jaw drops open.

"That's three more, Chat. That flappin' tongue of yours is runnin' up a tab I'm afraid you ain't capable of paying. Great idea, though. I was beginning to develop butt-sores."

"Now there's an erotic visual," Airman Legs smirks, sash shaying by with her shoulders pulled back and her ample chest pumped out. The Sarge looks on the verge of drooling as he follows her departure and soon follows suit, basically trampling Corporal Chatty in the process.

"Back in ten...hopefully fifteen," The Sarge announces without actually looking my way. Following the Corporal's somewhat labored exit, I whirl about and grip Tia's taunt, muscled rear end with my left hand while gently cradling the back of her head with the right. As usual, her mouth is warm and sweet; an inviting, magnetic safe haven for the unbridled lust I feel in her presence.

"Not sure we have the time now, projector man," she whispers as I tongue and nibble her slim, luscious neck.

"I've got your projec-tile right here, Sweet Thang," I mutter between kisses, and the woman known within our ranks as Lieutenant Lava begins to literally melt beneath my touch, as I do her own.

With or without the Man in Black's vocal assistance, the act is fast, furious, and shockingly intense.

We hardly have time to re-tuck our shirts and zip up our camouflage pants before the others begin to shuffle back in.

The Sarge enters first, his nostrils flaring wildly. He flashes me a brief, knowing smile but says nothing. He is sipping a bottled water between filling his mouth with canned peanuts.

Within the next few minutes, all but Private Brain Dog and The Chief take up their previous positions for the next disk's premiere. Father Pete eyes Lieutenant Lava curiously as she takes a seat between himself and Corporal Chatty.

"You okay, Tia? You look a tad winded," he says, then quickly glances my way. I busy myself at the DVD controls, inserting disk number four.

"Yeah, Lieutenant...you do look a bit pale, as much as one of your race can, anyhow. Didn't see ya in the feedbag room. You been joggin' circles around the Hive again?" The Sarge quips as Corporal Chatty openly smirks in the background in between sips of canned Root Beer.

"There are better ways to work the cardiovascular system than pounding Iron, Sergeant Rock-head. What's say we all just pipe down and watch the show? Bar...uh, Radar, you locked and loaded up there?" she asks, and I hear Airman Legs giggle softly.

"Uh, yeah. All systems go," I reply, backing away from the screen while simultaneously pressing the play button. I can feel Father Pete's glare searing into the nape of my neck.

"Then by all means, raise the curtain on act four," he says flatly.

Clearing my throat nervously, I notice the Chief's dour demeanor and far-away glare.

"No significant changes at the monitor, Chief?"

Although the Chief looks directly at me, I feel his inner-eye is visualizing something on a significantly large scale.

"Nothing dramatic, although like Brain Dog said, the wave seems...thicker now. Something's brewing for sure, troops. Something on a massive scale."

We all grow uneasily silent, and I press the play button for want of anything else to do. At the moment, any distraction, however grim, is a blessing.

The dark screen slowly fades into a misty, ivory fog...

Chapter Five
The Dead Sea, Indeed...

It was our 24th day on the Atlantic that we spotted 'er.

At midday, the sun beat down on us without mercy, as if to punish us for invading its space. I heard Winston, our second in command, bellow out 'ship ahoy' in his nasal, whiny tone. Myself, my oldest friend and shipmate, Carl, and Willie Cohn, were down below in our bunks, taking a quick respite before our shift up top began that afternoon.

We all gave each other a curious glance, then trudged topside.

Our ship, the Bullmask, held a crew of around forty men, practically all of which shuffled to her starboard side to view our mysterious visitor.

Captain Walt, all six feet ten inches high and three hundred pounds of 'im, stood erect and motionless at the wheel, his rugged, heavily bearded face not unlike carved granite, as was usually the case regardless of the situation.

Winston was babbling to him a mile-a-minute, his arms gesturing wildly.

You would have thought our little supply vessel to be under attack by Blackbeard's Ghost. Winston was a fool, everyone agreed, but if he had been warning Captain Walt of possible danger, he surely would have been the only sensible man among us that day, I concede.

The Devil himself called upon us that faithful afternoon, you see. That's the only explanation I can logically conclude.

My name is Barnes, Dale Barnes, although even that fact is in some doubt at this particular moment in time. I had worked on supply docks and sailed most of the Atlantic in my twenty years on the job ever since my stint in U.S. Grant's Army as a peach-fuzz faced young lad. The Bullmask was a ship I had become quite familiar with in the last five falls or so. The pay was reasonable, the work hard. I only wish I had decided to say on the docks for this trip. If I had, perhaps sleep wouldn't escape me so, maybe I wouldn't wake up in a cold sweat each time exhaustion did win the battle (rarely) with fear. Perhaps I could dream of other things; riches, former lovers, money I haven't yet made.

Instead, I dream of what I saw that day. The day we met up with the vessel that Satan steered.

We came about two-hundred feet or so closer to the ship and threw out our anchor. It was a fairly large boat, maybe a hundred footer in length and with a wider girth than the Bullmask. It was also obviously a floater. Her sails blew steadily, but no one manned her, at least, no one we could see.

Captain Walt ordered a few of the hands to take one of the side rows and go aboard to investigate and see if anyone was there to lend aid to.

Slowly, a few of the crew went back to their duties, but even they kept an eyebrow raised in interest to what might be found in the other vessel.

Myself, Willie and Carl leaned on the edge and watched. We were still a good two hours from our work shifts, and this was a mystery worth staying up top for.

In my time at sea, I had encountered floaters before, usually smaller vessels whose inhabitants had either escaped or hadn't the vengeance of a nasty storm or sudden squall. This was different, only because of the size of the vessel. It was a fifty or sixty crew tub, and I had never heard of such being totally abandoned and still afloat.

Carl joked they would probably find the entire crew down below passed out from a night's drink. We laughed, but all knew better. I remember the hair standing up on my neck as we awaited word from our mates, who had boarded the ship a few minutes earlier from the starboard side.

It was over a half-hour later that a second group was sent over to check on the whereabouts of the first. More than a little uneasiness spread throughout the ship, I can tell you. Captain Walt sent Winston with the second wave. I can still vividly recall the look of stark fear on Winston's pale, gaunt face as he led his charges into the dead quiet surrounding that mysterious craft that loomed in our wake.

The sea itself was eerily calm during this time. I couldn't quite recall if it had been that way before we came upon our unknown visitor.

Captain Walt paced slowly, his head pointed downward, while the rest of the crew went about their duties almost as if dazed. Our attention was directed completely to the situation developing on our eastern starboard side.

Ten minutes passed like ten days, and Captain Walt pointed his spyglass in the direction of the other ship. His gaze wavered a moment later, the glass dropped to his side. He instructed myself, Carl,

140

Willie and another man named Billy to arm ourselves and go aboard. His eyes were full of terror as he instructed us, a look I never had seen before in our stoic leader, and one I wished I hadn't seen at that time as well. As we loaded the last of our ship's side crafts, the Captain leaned over us and said six words that chilled my bones: "I saw nothing move over there," he whispered, his eyes darting from side to side, never meeting our own. It was the look of a man who was about to send more of his mates to die. I was hoping I was mistaken in that regard.

Billy, a mountain of a man who stood as tall as Captain Walt and whose body rippled with thick muscle, rowed us away from our ship. My hands ached from the tight grip with which I held my revolver.

Not a word was spoken from any of us on the way, my own teeth gnashing together as if I was suffering through great physical pain.

From an outside view, the mystery vessel seemed to be almost glistening in it's appearance, not at all resembling a boat that had possibly been drifting at sea for months or even years.

As we threw our line over and climbed topside, the stillness of not only the ship but also the sea itself was as foreboding as any tropical storm I had ever faced in all my years at sea.

We moved very slowly, almost shuffling as we made our way towards the center of the craft.

Topside was clean, practically glowing. Nothing seemed out of place, as if we ourselves were readying her for a mission of our own.

The hair on my arms raised towards the clear

141

sky, and I felt a sudden chill.

The wheel of the craft soon stood before us, defiant in its isolation, seemingly beckoning us to take her in hand.

We gave one another a worried glance, then headed down below. Billy went to check the engine room, Carl and Willie the mates bunk area, and I the galley and kitchen.

What I found in the galley chilled my bones to the marrow. I felt my legs grown numb almost instantly.

Cups filled with still steaming black coffee sat on a long wooden table that centered the room. The pungent scent of the freshly brewed Java filled my nostrils a moment after I entered the otherwise dark and dank space. The chairs that surrounded the table were all pushed underneath the table top, as if no one had ever been there to consume what lay before me and that had obviously only been brewed within the last few minutes. Empty food plates were lined up in a row on the table as well, as was the cutlery that accompanied them. I left the galley and felt a sudden dizziness as I walked slowly down the narrow hallway that led to the sleeping quarters. I wanted nothing more at that moment than to find Carl and Willie and let them confirm what I had discovered. The absolute silence on the vessel as I made my way through its core was almost unbearable. I was a man who valued peace and quiet during times of rest, but this was a different species of quiet. This was the kind that had been known to drive men insane.

I met Carl and Willie halfway. Their faces clued

142

me into what they had found before they spoke a word. His breath labored, Carl said the bunks had been unmade but totally vacant. I passed on what I had seen in the galley, and led them back in its direction. By the time we got there a few moments later, the coffee wasn't steaming quite as actively as before, but the cups we felt with our hands were still very warm indeed. We all stood quietly for a moment, lost in our own dreary thoughts, when Willie suggested we seek out Billy. Carl and I wholeheartedly agreed. Anything to spare us another moment in that particular room.

The engine room was beyond the sleeping quarters, just past the Captain's private bunkroom. We all descended a small set of creaky, rotting steps and saw the heavy wooden door that served as the engine room's entrance; it was standing wide open. Carl gestured to me playfully to enter first, whispering 'age before beauty' with a nervous grin. Willie slid behind him with his sights set on the hall we had just walked down. My stomach grumbled from a mixture of hunger and nerves, causing Carl to laugh hysterically. I smiled back and waived him off as I stepped into the dark, musky smelling room.

Once inside, I called out Billy's name several times without shouting, which wasn't at all necessary due to the thick silence. The room was so dark I paused to light a small candle that I had been carrying in my shirt pocket.

The light that shone was sparse but adequate enough to give us a view of what stood directly in our way. The metal parts of the engine looked to be in fairly good shape, and in some places looked to have been recently oiled and wiped free of built-up soot.

Billy didn't respond, and the room was much smaller than what I had anticipated before we entered. I shrugged towards Carl and he gestured for Willie to turn around and go back out towards the hallway. Willie took a few steps forward just as Carl turned to speak to me, accidentally touching the elbow of his jacket against the candle flame, dousing it. I cursed, backing up a step and reaching for a fresh match stick from my trouser pocket. I re-lit the candle and jokingly told Carl to make a day of it soon to go see an eye doctor about purchasing some spectacles. We turned back towards the door and noticed Willie had already left us behind.

We slowly made our way back towards the stairway that led to the deck, all the while I quietly wondered why Willie was nowhere to be seen in the hallway ahead of us. Carl called out for him several times as we went, but no response was returned. For some reason, as I felt a chill run up my spine, I knew there would be no reply from Willie, nor would we find him up top.

I do not know how I knew this, but the premonition that Carl and I were alone on the craft was overwhelming. We checked the galley and kitchen for both our mates, and could do nothing but glance at each other and shrug helplessly when we found nothing. We turned to walk back up to the deck and Carl sidestepped quickly into an open room that was across from the galley.

I heard him whisper Willie's name as he entered the room, and I myself whirled around to glance

144

behind me, as I thought I had heard a bumping, shuffling noise coming from the kitchen area.

Stepping forward after being satisfied there was no further activity to my rear, I peered into the small supply room that my friend had been checking on.

I felt my chest turn to ice and my head begin to tingle madly. I fell back against the far hallway wall, sitting down hard enough to cause my teeth to grind roughly together upon contact. The supply room was only the length of a man, and barely as high. It held canned goods and unopened bags of rice and wheat, but what it did not hold was Carl.

As I sat with my eyes staring straight ahead into the small dark space that only a moment before I had watched my best friend duck into, I could feel my heart beating through my clothing as if it might burst free. I do not know how long I sat in the deafening silence of that dank hallway before I arose.

It might have been only minutes, but could have been hours. I screamed the names of Billy, Carl, and Willie Boy at the top of my lungs. I bellowed for them until my throat burned like I had just downed a quart of cheap scotch. I wanted to cry, but the stark fear that was confining my being would not allow it. I got to my feet and half jogged towards the light that led to the deck above. I had to get back to Captain Walt and the others and give them fair warning of the haunting events that were taking place. As I topped the steps and pulled my body onto the deck, I suddenly realized that the outside air was no different than the wet, dank smell that swirled as thick as fog below. I was greeted with no breeze, no familiar scent of the sea. I was also thrown back by another fact. It was pitch black. I paused, my feet frozen to the slippery deck. Hadn't I seen the light coming in from up top just a moment before? Hadn't it only been midday when my mates and I paddled over to this Godforsaken ship? I looked up into the dark sky and saw no stars illuminating above. I ran towards the edge and peered down into the water to check on the side row we had come over on. The still, unmoving sea held nothing. My head pounding madly at my temples, I jogged over to the other side, almost slipping halfway, and was greeted by the same blank stillness.

The sea that held the ship afloat resembled water sitting in a tub. It did not even gently slap the edges of the vessel.

I whirled around in a circle, glaring into the dark nothingness that surrounded me and was not shocked in the least to find the Bullmask as invisible as my missing mates. No moon shone in the sky, so it was difficult to visualize anything beyond a few hundred feet from the deck I occupied, so again I yelled and hollered out for my crew. Not even an echo of my own cries were returned.

I laid on the middle of the deck and found myself drifting into an uneasy but merciful slumber.

***

I awoke with a start and tried to push away the sunlight that was baring down on my sight. I practically leaped to my feet and found the temporary blindness slowly fading. I gasped when I realized that I now stood on the deck of the Bullmask. It had taken me a moment to recognize

146

the surface I had spent many hours swabbing, or the Captain's bridge on which I had on many occasions had the pleasure of steering while the First Mate supervised.

I took a deep breath, the sea air filling my nostrils and immediately lifting my spirits. The hand that softly touched my left shoulder was gentle, almost caressing. I turned and Captain Walt stood before me, his large hands gripping my shoulders weakly. I smiled and sighed in relief, and was about to ask him about the missing crew when his grip on me became as tight as a vise. His face began to transform then. He grinned widely, his teeth as black as slugs. He was screaming I believe, but no noise escaped his lips.

His grip was like steel, and try as I might, there was no escaping it.

His mouth stretched so wide the skin at the corners ripped and flayed loose like torn sails. The top of his head fell back like it had been severed by a blade, and I could smell the stink of rotted meat as the mouth neared my own in what I knew to be not a kiss of adoration, but of slow, painful death…

***

I awoke with a start and jerked myself up, my hands covering my face defensively. I was alone aboard a side craft, and the unrelenting darkness that surrounded me gave the illusion of total blindness until my eyes had blinked madly for a few moments and made the adjustment. The water lapped softly against the sides of the small vessel, which I quickly noticed held nothing but me in its narrow hold. I dismissed the depressing notion of attempting to

147

hand paddle myself to land without an oar. It was too hysterically sad for my mind to contemplate at that moment. My vision was limited to a few feet in each direction due to the blanketing blackness. After a moment I stood shakily and attempted to peer through the ink black night for the shape of a larger ship, or at least be able to hear the sounds of an approaching one.

I kneeled back down and placed my hands on the edge of the boat and closed my eyes, which felt as if they were filled with sand. I reopened them just as the hands came out of the water and grabbed my forearms.

I recall a sound escaping my throat, but it was more a long, drawn out whine than a piercing scream. I was unable to muster anything stronger. I was able to focus on the figure's face as he scrambled to hang onto my arms with his wet, slick fingers. The face of Winston, the first mate, glared back at me. His hair was matted down to the left side of his face, a long strand of sea weed hanging off one ear onto his shoulder. I recall feeling total euphoria at just seeing a familiar face, even one I had never actually been very fond of. Just as I braced myself to pull him into the boat, a splash from the craft's opposite side pulled my attention toward its origin.

I laughed aloud as I recognized Willie and Carl slinging their arms over the side, their faces strangely slack and expressionless. I felt warm tears run down my cheeks as I pulled them in one by one. It wasn't until we were all aboard that my laughter became more of a groan that stuck in my irritated throat like a hook in a fish's maw.

Winston reached out to me with his right arm, a look of dazed confusion on his bone white face. His arm only raised half way before it separated itself from his shoulder and fell like a piece of driftwood at my feet. The bony fingers still wiggled and clinched, one of which tapped the tip of my boot softly. I glanced back up and watched unmoving as Carl tugged at his right knee until with a loud crunching sound, he pulled it free and tossed the knee, ankle and foot into the water. Willie clawed at his own chest, ripping the shirt and skin until a sickening, bone-splintering noise filled the air. He grinned at me with teeth suddenly razor sharp at the tips as he opened up his own rib cage like a ripe melon. My eyes darted from his grimacing expression and those piranha teeth back to his open torso. He whispered six words to me as I finally saw the darkness he so gleefully displayed to me through the gaping wound. The dark of the night shone like a falling star compared to what was inside that ruined chest. I found myself hypnotized by the absolute desolation I found there. His words rang in my ears as I continued to stare and somehow felt I was being carried towards the wound itself.

'...it's so warm in here.....'come..."

'...come...it's so warm in here...'

'....it's so very, very warm..'

I was only inches from his exposed chest when I looked up expecting to see Willie grinning down at me. I looked into my own eyes instead, my teeth rotted, the sockets of my eyes as red as a fire pit..

***

149

I awoke with a start and rolled flat onto my stomach.

My woman grunts on her side of the bed and turns over nosily. I found myself drawn to her house, one she insists I built, less than a week past. Trying not to be to obvious in my inquiries to her, as not to upset her with my personal madness, I have learned a few surprising facts about who I am.

I run a farm here on this small hilly countryside, and have, according to her, for over twenty years. She and I have been keeping company for twenty-five.

We were both born and raised here, and have never been closer than four states to an ocean of water. We have three children, two sons and a daughter. They all live east of here and have their own families. I also raise livestock and am an expert tracker and hunter. I desperately want to ask her how I received the anchor mark tattoo on the underside of my forearm. I do not want to ruin what is more than likely a fine life I have with these bouts of madness brought about by night scares and bad dreams. I think I love her, although there are times I feel I do not belong in this existence at all. There are times I smell sea air, even out in the middle of a dusty field. I hear sea gulls calling just to look skyward and see blackbirds instead.

At night she comes to me and we share each other's bodies.On this night I am on top of her and I pause our kiss to lean up and stare into her deep blue eyes, slightly wrinkled by years of sun exposure and hard field work. As I lean back down, her eyes begin to glow red. She smiles and her teeth are sharp and moist, the red liquid seeping from the side of her mouth onto her shoulder blades. Her hands grip the back of my head forcefully and pull me towards the mouth, which is now opening wide enough to devour me whole. I smell salt in the air. I hear the waves hit the side of the bed....

I awake with a start...

***

"So what's the deal, Lucille? Is Popeye the Sailor man certifiable or what?" The Sarge barks just as the screen fades into thin static waves.

"Should be obvious, even to the mentally challenged such as yourself, muscle boy, that the poor guy's living a humdinger of a bad dream," Airman Legs answers with a frown.

"Twilight Zone, I tell ya. These must be from that updated version they did a few years back. Got axed after a season or two," Brain Dog announces matter-of-factly.

"Least this one spared us the drippin' spleens and steamin' intestines... for the most part anyhow."

"Campfire story. Bermuda Tri-angle bull crap. Then again, a few years ago, who would'a believed a Planetary takeover by an army of overgrown gnats?" The Sarge grumbles.

Kid Cadet sprints into the room at full gallop, flying into the Sarge's lap while giggling madly.

"I take it Queen-Bug is still conspicuously absent from the swirling masses?" The Sarge asks, jabbing the Kid's midsection playfully.

"Not hide nor hair, Sergeant beer-gut, Sir!," the Kid replies with obvious glee.

"Uh, shouldn't we rethink the Kid's presence at

this little shin-dig? This ain't exactly Saturday Morning Disney, y'know," Brain Dog snaps, walking over to muss the Kid's lengthy blonde locks.

"He's seen a hell of a lot worse in the past year, Dog," I answer, cutting off

Airman Legs, who then shrugs as if to agree with my assessment. "Yeah, Kid Space-Cadet here is practically a man now. Let him enjoy the show with us," Corporal Chatty injects blandly.

"Father Pete?" Lieutenant Lava asks with a cocked eyebrow. Father Pete rises from his slouch like a man waking from the recesses of a decade-long coma, not responding until he has practically departed the room. "Why not? Sadly, the innocence of his youth was stolen away long ago." "You heard Pope John the Last, Radar. Roll that film," The Sarge quips, gently tossing Kid Cadet onto the couch between himself and Corporal Chatty.

"What are they, dirty movies?" the Kid says with a sly grin, sending the Sarge, Corporal Chatty, and Airmen Legs sailing into a fit of barely restrained giggles. Brain dog just shakes his head from side to side, fighting to maintain the frown he's manufactured. Lieutenant Lava pats me on the back and nods.

"Well, like Father Pete said, innocence lost is a sad thing indeed." It never ceases to amaze me how adaptable the human species can be. We are probably less than 24 hours from the final battle of our lives, but an outside observer might mistake us for a comically aged frat house. I insert the next disk and engage the remote as the lights so soothingly fade.

Chapter Six
Donner (Dancer, Prancer & Blitzen?) Party Revisited

"Damned if that old man can't run like a spooked rabbit, Pete, even in those clunky looking boots," Willie spouts between huffs and puffs as I barely avoid the pointy end of his spear as he whizzes by in a frantic blur. Passes me like I was standing still, he does. Then again, 'Will the Chill' is twelve years my junior and a former College b-ball player.

"He'll poop out soon enough, my man…no where to go except to retrace his own tracks. Besides, he's libel to drop dead from heat exhaustion any minute, what with that red parka he's wearing," I reply just as Cynthia catches up, playfully bumping my elbow with her own.

"Can you believe the luck, Pete? You think…we're dreaming? Some kinda, group mind meld or somethin', like on those old Star Trek episodes?" she asks, her rail-thin arms pumping madly. The once drop-dead gorgeous specimen of the female species now resembles a skeletal model from my tenth grade biology class, her long black hair matted onto her bony skull in coiled clumps.

"No dream, Cyn…more like a bonafide miracle straight from a Hollywood screenplay," I answer between gasps, switching the small pocket knife from my left hand to my right to refrain from accidentally poking its rusty tip into her already bleeding rib cage. I can clearly visualize the red, seeping gash just beneath her exposed and quite horribly shrunken right breast. It had taken the four of us a full ten minutes of ducks, weaves and wild thrusts to bring the first animal down. The others, including the herd's point man (the one with the 'shiny nose' of fame), had been severely injured in the crash, instantly marking them as easy prey. I felt a twinge of pity as we all waded in to deliver the fatal blows, even though it was painfully obvious that the majority were mercy kills, after all. Hunger overrides any and all other emotions…to this I can testify without a shred of doubt.

"But…it can't really be…him..right? I mean…it just can't be, right?" she queries while ducking a low hanging palm branch that seemed set directly in our path solely for the purpose of clothes-lining us both.

"You're asking the wrong man, Cyn. I haven't believed since age five," I reply solemnly, although the remark was meant to be humorous. Seems we're all past such trivialities. Over the hill and around the bend, so to speak.

Cyn picked up the pace, leaving my weary bones in the dust while whistling (I swear) the opening notes to 'Santa Clause is Coming to Town'. I would laugh aloud if my winded torso would allow it. At this point, crying is much easier to accomplish. Drinking water is the one shortage we haven't yet faced…thus bodily fluids are plentiful.

***

Clay had given the herd's master a choice even as the lone remaining animal struck up a defensive pose a few dozen feet from its fallen, deceased

155

peers. The man had shaken his head defiantly as he slowly removed a bulky, stuffed duffel from the overturned sleigh, the side of which was spattered in liquid crimson a tad shade darker than the metal's original color.

"You're either with us or ya ain't, old man. Join us or don't, it's altogether your own choice. Sorry to say, but it's a deer eat, deer world in our warped little corner of the gods' green earth.....," Clay had quipped, frothy drool sailing airborne from his over-moistened lips. A stout, thick-boned two-hundred twenty pounder at the time of our...predicament, good ol' boy Clay had always been the biggest eater of the group, hands down. Despite the dramatic weight loss of recent months, his appetite had remained shockingly healthy despite the circumstances. The man truly has a cast-iron gut. I had always felt a bit frazzled within the man's boisterous, 'southern-born and southern bred' company, especially after that little fiasco with the Chinaman. Figured I'd wake up one fine tropical night just in time to witness him take a Whopper-sized bite from the meaty portion (not sure it actually qualifies as such these days, actually) of my thigh.

Even as he had given the man a choice, I realized without question the answer old Clay wanted to hear. Clay had plotted, designed, and dug out the majority of the food pit after Cyn had accidentally run across the small cave on the Island's southern-most tip. Staring at the herd's master with an expression of maniacal glee covering his reddened, sweat-moistened mug, it was apparent that old Clay wanted to fill that sucker to the brim, and he wasn't the least bit picky on what type meat to stockpile to do so.

The chubby, middle-aged man had backed away from the wreck's carnage as if entranced, his eyes as wide with terror as his once white beard was with the bodily fluids of his former steeds. The calf-high black boots he wore dug deeply into the powdery sand as he prepared to turn and sprint, the duffel thrown over his shoulder like an overtaxed laundry bag.

"The storm…. that horrible storm brought us here…that godforsaken storm…" we all heard him mumble in a low, husky whisper as he stared into the star-filled blackness above our heads as if praying to a god we were all convinced had long since abandoned the human race as a whole.

He then vanished past a thick patch of foliage, a red blur with black boots, moving as if his very life depended on it, which in this rather pathetic case, it most certainly did indeed.

***

I finally catch up to my fellow cannibals ('The Charlotte Clan' Willie had so cheerily donned us all those months ago, when such banter still provided a semblance of comic relief…long since extinct, I'm afraid) near the smoothed edges of a rather steep cliff on the isle's northern-most tip.

No sign of our quarry, whose speed and guile has shocked even Clay into a state of frustrated resignation. "Let's get on back and start guttin' the rest 'fore they turn in this damn heat," he spouts angrily as we all kneel in unison to catch our collection breath.

"Right. Chubby cheeks ain't got far to run and nowhere to hide," Willie echoed, his sunken cheeks and ashen complexion making him resemble the walking dead in those old horror films.

Cyn and I simply follow their lead back to the crash site, my legs numb from fatigue.

***

Clay and Willie do the gist of the cleaning, to which I am immeasurably grateful. As horrible as it sounds, my gut growls uncontrollably as we haul the raw, bloody carcasses to the cave, the meat wrapped tightly in palm and scrub leaves. The coppery stench actually feeds my hunger as the drool begins to build at the corners of my mouth. I see Cyn battling her saliva glands as well, her nostrils flaring wildly. Simply put: what we've become ain't the least bit pretty.

Willie accompanies us while Clay hauls a select slab of venison back to camp in preparation for the night's unprecedented feast, the likes of which none of us have experienced since the days before the stranding.

The time that has passed since that day is a constant source of argument, not that it matters a single iota in the grand scheme of things.

Cyn says eighteen months. Clay is adamant that it's more like twenty-one. Willie is just certain that a full two years have passed. Personally, I had quit caring about such mundane details long ago. Around day three, I had begun systematically marking a palm tree with my pocket knife; a simple horizontal slash originating at the trunk to better count the days as they passed. I had stopped once the markings reached a lower limb a foot or so over my head. Since then, hours, days and months had passed like wind blown pages in a discarded paperback, no longer registering as even remotely vital to our plight. None of us had any idea that another holiday season was upon us. The year-round tropical climate does little to remind one that such seasons even exist.

As the meat cooks, dripping deliciously into the fire's yellow/blue flame, we stand hand in hand like some primitive cult, entranced in a ritualistic daze as we prepare to bow to the gods of good fortune. My patience threshold is utterly pegged out, and I fight the urge to dive into the burning meat even as it just begins to turn pink at the edges. You can only live on coconuts and berries for so long before you start seeing roasted drumsticks in your sleep. This is the first taste of meat since…since… well, more about Michael later. Don't want to lose my appetite for the treat to come. As a diversion from my animalistic urges, my thoughts turn to the past, specifically to that faithful day when five distinctively different individuals were dealt the cruelest of fate's many and varied hands. A fate that, over time, transformed said five individuals from modern, contemporary citizens of 21st Century society into prehistoric, primal beasts with only a single mission to accomplish: survival.

***

April 15th, 2001. The boat was called 'The Pegasus'. Held seven comfortably for a 'deep sea fishing excursion unmatched on the entire East

Coast', read the brochure.

I had met Willie first, a used car salesman from Daytona Beach. Cynthia came aboard next (to everyone's delight, I must say), a legal secretary from D.C. Clay (chomping a cigar that smelled like a wet dog turd) made his less than tranquil intro next, having just departed Atlanta, where he worked as a warehouse foreman. Michael Kim, a twenty-something fry cook/wanna-be stand up comedian from Denver was the last to board for the three day event (three days? Can you believe that? Trite but true. Just like the infamous sitcom that I catch myself whistling the theme song to even today....THE SKIPPER TOO, THE MILLONAIRE AND HIS WIFE, THE MOVIE STAR, THE PROFESSOR AND.... Lord, my kingdom for just a moment's bout with amnesia!).

Having been born and raised in the rolling hills of West Virginia, it had been three decades since my eyes had rested on the Atlantic's cool, swaying waters, when my father had taken the family to Myrtle Beach for a weekend vacation. My company had sent me on a three-day sales junket to 'blanket the east coast', while simultaneously footing the bill for the trip once my week long sales pitch was completed. How could I possibly refuse such an offer? I always was one who dived into the unknown without a parachute and/or safety net to break my fall. Months (years?) later, I've lost considerably more than just the eighty pounds that have melted from my formerly chunky frame, courtesy the mile long, half mile wide uncharted island we all call hell...uh, home. My sanity slipped its gears right around the same time that Clay decided to murder Michael Kim.

We had been run through the mill, no doubt. An emotional roller coaster ride that held few positive highlights. The storm that tossed us about for six hours like a wooden cork in a whirlpool; the subsequent lifeboat fiasco as the Pegasus took a permanent powder to the bottom of the swirling sea. You know the old saying, 'the Captain must go down with his ship?' Well, ol' Captain Thomas of the deep sea fishing tub Pegasus took it literally, pulled into the swirling abyss with only his 'SEA DOG' baseball cap floating atop the surface like a watery grave marker.

We washed ashore like beached fish, the lifeboat ripped into a dozen separate strips when we sailed atop the edge of that coral reef. Took three days of frantic, bleary-eyed searching to find a fresh water supply, all the while being ravaged by mosquitoes roughly the size of Montana. As the days and weeks passed, desperation and disbelief slowly turned to acceptance. We went on daily berry hunts, spent hours attempting to spear shallow-water fish and built individual lien-tos, eventually constructing separate huts as boredom and tedium set in and time seemed to freeze in place.

No one liked Michael from the word go, no argument. It's a documented fact that all have claimed. The man never shut up, his stale jokes and biting sarcasm, a never-ending irritation that severed my last nerve, and I was easily the most easy going of the group. He was also making a habit of raping Cyn at every opportunity, at times violently. She

161

never accused him, but it was damned obvious to the other men. We all...had our turn with Cyn. She came to us individually, however, and willingly so. I think she felt it her...responsibility somehow. Plus, I'm sure it gave her a sense of security; of being needed. I never forced myself on her. A life-long bachelor, I hadn't exactly been a ladies man, but I did consider myself a throw-back to the days of true gentlemen. Still, I must admit I welcomed the contact. We had little else in the form of pleasure on this godforsaken sand dune. Needless to say, the sexual escapades ceased about the same time that the berry and nut supply became dangerously scarce, fish harder to spear and food rationing began. Pretty simple equation; no food, no energy, loss of urges all save one, that being to fill one's gut with anything edible.

Clay had simply gotten his fill of the man's constant prattle and shut off the volume knob once and for all. Clay said Michael attacked him in a jealous rage over Cyn's affections and simply defended himself. There is no justice system on Christmas Island, as Cyn now calls it. No DNA evidence, no court rooms, no judges nor juries. Secretly, we all applauded Clay's actions, as Cyn's bruises began to clear up even as we all slowly melted into skeletal versions of our former selves.

The decision to utilize Michael's body for our own survival and nutritional needs was a unanimous one. I felt no guilt during or after the deed, although a twinge did briefly appear as I pinned for my favorite brand of Barbecue sauce. In truth, it revitalized us all for a week or so, a surging within our veins that hadn't been felt in months.

Unfortunately, it's been slim pickings since, in the protein department. Hence, temperaments have grown a bit testy as stomachs bloat and skin pulls tightly over bones previously covered by hearty meals of old. I'm sure that if by some miracle we were rescued in our present conditions, it's a distinct possibility that society as a whole would certainly reject us as one of their own, possibly putting us on display as a recently discovered race of mutants.

***

Hours later we lay about the fire, our stomachs happily swollen as we pick small shards of gristle from between our blackish, rotted teeth. Willie suggests, while wiping his greased lips with a pencil-thin forearm, that we cook another animal at first light, as the meat would more than likely begin to spoil in a matter of two days hence, despite the pit's relatively cool temperature. We all nod in ravenous agreement, our expressions ghoul-like.

"Better us than the maggots, right?" Clay chimes in with a level of excitement that borders on psychotic. I think we all realize that ol' Clay has slipped a gear or two with our unexpected guest's arrival. He'd been balanced on the edge for quite a while, just looking for a banana peel to slip on as an excuse to blow his final mental fuse. The man is a walking, talking loony tune with a single agenda, one that has nothing at all to do with his fellow islanders' survival. The recent acquisition of fresh kill provides nothing more than a temporary delay to the inevitable. Clay will have to be eliminated least the rest of us end up butchered and packed away in the pit like chopped sirloin. We all heard the words, all of us stopped chewing as one, as though we had all bit into the same sourness. Clay seemed oblivious to his own insanity, but Willie, Cyn and I were acutely aware, glancing at each other while wearing the same shocked, battle-weary expressions.

"It's damn good, no doubt..,' Clay had announced between bites from the animal's hind quarters, '..but the Chink tasted better."

You see, Clay had not only enjoyed the taste of his own kind, he had developed a specific hankering for it. There aren't many taboos strictly adhered to on deserted islands, morals and ideals wash away with the morning tides as the days drone on. However, admitting to savoring the meat of one's own species is a definite no-no.

I drift into a rather uneasy slumber as the fire's warmth heats my bare flesh, keeping an eye trained in Clay's direction.

***

The man in red has apparently killed Wille and Cyn is missing. Clay shook me awake just as the beach began to take light, a chilly breeze instantly raising chill bumps on my leathery forearms.

I was inclined to accuse Clay until he showed me Willie's body a few dozen yards from the campfire. The spindly arrow that protruded from his stiffened neck was constructed from pliable plastic, a child's toy. Its tip, presently coated with crimson-shaded gore from its forced puncturing through the back of Willie's neck, had been filed to a sharp point from its original blunt condition. The man in red had used a toy pulled from his duffel of similar

164

items to eliminate the most agile and undoubtedly quickest of our group. I reach down with shaky fingers and pull Willie's eyelids closed as Clay curses at my back. We grab spears and begin our hunt for Cynthia, who I already fear has met the same fate. After all, the man knows it's us or him. He's simply defending himself from a band of crazed cannibals. We got careless and took his appearance, his reputation, for granted. As Clay and I scour the surrounding foliage, we realize the roles being played out hours earlier have been shockingly reversed. We are now, undoubtedly, the hunted.

***

I check Cyn's hut as Clay investigates the others, hoping she had simply awakened during the night and returned here to escape the beach's relentless gusts.

The fishing line is deeply embedded into the soft flesh of her horribly narrow neck just below the Adams apple, giving it the look of a recently tied-off balloon. Her tongue lolls from her open mouth like a large brown slug, a grouping of flies having already congregated on its moistened tip. The accompanying fishing pole lays atop her lap, its cheap plastic reel and flimsy construction instantly labeling it as nothing more than a pre-teen plaything. Again, the man has used a child's toy to eliminate the enemy.

I sprint from the hut, my eyes darting wildly in anticipation of impending attack only to find that I am utterly alone within the campsite. In checking the other huts, I find Clay's pocketknife lying next to the entrance to my own, the small blade exposed but without moisture of any kind.

Without considering my reasons for doing so, I trudge slowly to the crash site from the night before, strangely feeling the need to walk the length of the island's perimeter to do so. Instinct tells me that the man in red is there, and that he no longer feels the need to remain hidden from my view. I find no logical reason to rush in order to greet my own mortality.

***

The man in red is indeed present, standing beside his overturned sleigh with his right boot propped casually atop its metallic rail. He grins sheepishly upon acknowledging my presence in a nearby thicket, his cheeks rosy and glowing, his eyes sparkling like twin diamonds from the morning sun's reflection. The butcher knife he grips in one white-gloved hand is massive in both length and width, its serrated edge turned outward in my direction, as if to beckon me forward. The tune he so cheerily whistles is hauntingly familiar to me from past holidays, and floods my overtaxed senses with memories of winters past.

"..You better watch out..."

I see, even smell the stout odor of freshly cut spruce, of smoldering kernels of popcorn roasting within a covered iron skillet. My mind's eye is full with bulbs both brightly lit and silver in tint, with just a light coating of angel hair to accent their presence amid the fullness of the limbs themselves. I smell pecan pie and baked chicken and feel my stomach groan as my mind yearns.

"....you better not cry..."

166

Freshly baked bread and just a hint of cinnamon assault my nostrils as I scan a grouping of neatly wrapped presents parked in the shadow of the glistening tree's lower half, just out of my tremor-racked fingers longing reach.

"…You better not pout, I'm telling you why…."

The sweet, intoxicating smell begins to change as a new, infinitely more powerful scent pushes it aside. I feel my gorge rise into my throat; warm bile rising in thick, mucus-filled waves.

"…Satan Clause is coming to town…"

Cinnamon and smoked ham are replaced by perforated bowel and punctured intestine.

"…he knows if you've been bad or good…"

Sweetened Yams and sliced turkey are replaced by gashed chest cavities and carved, hacked torsos stuffed with throbbing parasites that twist and gorge within it's torn, seeping flesh as swarms of fist-sized flies skim the surface for their share of the swiftly-decomposing prize.

"…so be bad for goodness sake!…"

I wake from the trance as the gloved fingers snap a few inches from my bleary eyes.

The man in red backs away like a Shakespearean actor accepting a standing ovation, sweeping his arm dramatically in a circular wave as if to point my attention to his handiwork.

The bodies are stacked like cordwood, arms and legs protruding from the pasty-skinned pile like imbedded quills. Clay lies atop Cyn, what resembles the blade edge of a child's ice-skate sticking from his concave chest like an oversized shoehorn.

Cyn lies beneath him facing upward, her boa-sized tongue lodged in the stringy black hair of Clay's left armpit.

Willie forms the pile's base, the tip of the toy arrow puncturing Cyn's left side like a probing syringe.

The man in red laughs heartily, his ample midsection shaking like semi-formed pudding beneath the thick red coat, his hands propped at his sides while his short, stubby legs bend just slightly.

"...oh, you've been a naughty one, Peter Walton...a naughty boy indeed.....," he yelps while shooting me a playful wink.

"...the others trusted you, my boy...you were the voice of reason; the backbone of the team, a stabilizing force...."

I feel a burning sensation at the heels of my feet, as if I'm standing on searing coals still afire.

"....my goodness, Peter, killing my precious reindeer for nourishment would have been a gesture of loving kindness in comparison to this....this...abomination..."

The man in red begins to transform then, his squat body stretching, elongating as if being pulled from both ends. His full, chubby cheeks grow instantly gaunt as his red overcoat and matching hat peel away like reptilian skin, his black boots splitting at the sides before sailing away like ash in a wind tunnel.

"......then again......I can sympathize your plight, my boy....I am an understanding soul, after all, to the likes of you...."

A new holiday song fills my ears, though the

168

words and music are comically sped up, like an old 33 record played in 45 mode. The tune's familiar lyrics have also been dramatically altered, even as the record's pace begins to slow somewhat…

"….fresh spleens roasting on an open fire….

….Old Pete nibbling at your nose…"

Whether I simply blinked or fell into an hour-long slumber, I can or will never be sure. My eyes fling open and are bombarded with distorted imagery that my tattered mind is unable to immediately download.

The man in red stands before what at first resembles a formation of midgets positioned five rows high and at least fifty across per row. The echoes of their high-pitched wailing threatens to shatter my eardrums as I reach to cover my ears with the palms of my hands and instantly feel the warm, sticky liquid coat my fingers.

"…… Petey the meat-man, was a bloated, nasty soul,

…… with a sharp-edged knife and bloodied teeth..

….....and two eyes he gouged from Clay…'

"Petey the mea-…isn't that supposed to be ..F-Frosty the Sn-Sno…," I manage to babble through lips that seem literally glued together by the moist, sticky substance coating them. The spaces between my teeth feel weirdly packed, as if I had just left the dentists chair.

The man in red approaches me from his conductor position in two impossibly quick, uniquely graceful leaps, now posed just a scant two feet to my front. I swallow hard within his grotesquely mutated presence, feeling a chunk of something distinctly mushy break loose from my molars and slide down my throat.

"......Petey the meat-man, is a nightmare-tale they say,

......he was born in HELL....

......but the islander's bray...

......how he ATE their lungs one day!..."

The man in red no longer dons red clothing, nor any clothing at all for that matter. His skinless body is a pulped mass of muscle and tendon that seeps blood as dark as the deepest cave. The inch-long horns protrude from his temples like insect feelers; probing me, sniffing me. His eyes are albino white and pupil-less as he leans closer, displaying a broad, wide smile filled with squared teeth that are sickeningly short; the teeth of a preschooler.

Behind him the choir of little people (the red man's elves, perhaps?) hums and moans in unison, their heads much too large for the squat bodies keeping them airborne.

Just as the red man's searing hot breath (not unlike blowing steam from a punctured boiler pipe) fills my blood-soaked left ear, the faces of the elfin choir swim horrifically into focus.

The front row is Cyn, all hollow eyed and gaunt.

The second is Willie, jug ears and all.

The third is Clay, good ol' boy sneer intact, albeit less a few teeth.

"They say you are what you eat, Peter....', the red devil mutters, the stench of rotted pork filling my quickly clogging nostrils, '...if that's truly the

170

case, you are indeed my Elves....and my Elves are about.. to become…you…"

I turn to run, but my movements are cumbersome, leaden, my feet seemingly submerged in ankle-deep quicksand. I turn to see the elfin horde take flight as one, their mouths agape and slinging droll as they sweep down like a tidal wave of gnashing teeth….

***

Waking with a scream, I roll away from the burning embers lying just inches from my naked flesh.

Clearing my eyes with a quick, frantic rub from my left forearm (my hands are hopelessly sand drenched), my vision clears just enough to scan the surrounding beachhead.

The fire has long since died out, the last few morsels from the previous night's feast charred and smoking as it droops over what had been the center of a roaring blaze.

Sighing heavily, sweet relief floods my senses as the dreamscape slowly begins to float from my subconscious and dissipate into the salty air. Never before have I experienced such realism, such vivid detail in my slumbering jaunts.

I peer downward to the dried splatter on my chest, abdomen and groin and feel the slightest twinge of guilt knot my gut. "Ah, soon this to will pass. What's done is done, Peter old buddy old salt."

Strolling past the cleanly picked chest cavity and the neck bone that has been meticulously sucked dry, I fight off the wave of regret that seems to automatically surge forth on the morning after.

Cyn was dying anyway, I tell myself. The day we floated onto the island as a group was the day we all began to slowly pass away. Decisions regarding survival had to be made. One by one, they were. The sickly die to feed the less sickly. As I entered her tent last night, Cyn knew. I saw it in her drooping, pathetic hound dog eyes. Yes, there was fear held there as I approached her with the pocket knife, but there was also something else...relief. Her misery was about to end, and for the noblest of causes, to sustain another human life.

Her charred skull lies just to the right of the rocks that make up the perimeter of my cooking pit, a select few hairs still clinging to the scalp like passengers hanging from the sides of a sinking ship. Such Irony in that thought, I muse while turning away.

I plan to allow the ocean's mellow morning waves to wash the remnants of my feast into its infinite belly of treasures, when the tiny configurations within the sand catch my still sleep-blurred eyes.

Hundreds of them. Possibly thousands. Littering the water line and back towards the jungle's edge in a massive circle that blankets the entire beach. Footsteps no larger than a preschooler... I feel my scalp begin to tingle, then itch as though infested with feeding parasites.

I whirl around just as the colossal shadow sweeps over me like a floating body bag.

The final booming chorus from yet another Christmas carol enters my soon to be permanently parted ears.....

"......Petey the meat-man...

......no time to waive goodbye or blush...

......as he tried his best to outrun fate....

......but it chewed his innards to mush..."

As the tiny teeth bore into and begin to rend and tear, my final thought is not of mercy from a higher power...but a startling, rather grisly realization...

...that Santa Claus was indeed real...albeit a Santa from an infinitely lower realm than the North Pole...a forked-tongued, pointy-eared Santa who delivers eternal suffering and indescribable pain ...

***

"Merry Christmas to all, and to all a good freakin' nightmare!" The Sarge bellows sharply, causing all in the room to flinch as if a bee stung. "Damn, White Christmas it ain't. Fresh spleens roastin' on an open fire? What kind of demented shit is that?" Brain Dog whines.

"Did you see the actors? They all looked....malnourished and...their bellies were swollen just like those kids they used to show in Africa...like the starvation was...real," Lieutenant Lava says, nervously biting her left thumbnail.

"Best special effects make-up I've ever seen, bar none," Private Legs adds as Corporal Chatty flips the lights. I walk to the DVD with legs made of the softest, most pliable rubber.

"Special effects my eye. That was real, I say. No computer graphic on the planet could create such a look in a man's eye. That dude was stark raving loony with a capital L," I mumble mostly to myself, unaware of my voice's volume as the cold chills streak up my spine like a runaway freight car.

The Sarge howls while grasping Kid Cadet in a playful headlock.

"What do ya mean real, Radar? You sayin' Santa, Dancer, Rudolph and the whole gang truly met their fate on 'Cannibal's Island'? Actually, even if you're only testifyin' that Santa himself is real, I need to seek out a straight jacket and the nearest rubber room right away."

"No, I...um...but the film... it was shot like a documentary...like one of those National Geographic Specials," I babble, my quickly-reddening face strategically turns away from the group.

Trying to refrain from sarcasm with pathetic results, Private Legs chimes in just as I insert a new disk with slightly shaky hands.

"You mean like the Crocodile Hunter meets Dracula? Come on, Radar. I have to admit it scared the bejeebers outta me too, but it wasn't real. Very professionally produced yes, but about as real as the Tooth Fairy. Besides, if it is real footage, ala Faces of Death, who was holding the camera? Satan's cinematographer?"

"Gotta admit, it was spooky as hell. What did you think, Kid Skid-marks?" The Sarge interrupts, thankfully switching subjects.

"It was okay, but they talked too much. Needed more of the devil Santa. He was cool, 'specially his eyes. Those elves were nasty looking little goobers, though."

Father Pete re-enters the room sipping a bottled water, his shoulders noticeably slumped.

"How's the chief doing? He need some relief?"

174

Airman Legs asks, stifling still another yawn.

"Told him I'd take over after the next show."

Lieutenant Lava walks over and begins re-ruffling Kid Cadet's locks while the Sarge stares a hole through her shapely backside. I feel a pang of jealousy that I instantly realize is as foolish as it is pointless.

"I might join you, Preacher man. My creep-show meter is just about pegged out at this point."

"Ya gotta admit, darlin', despite the subject matter involved, its hard to pry your eyes away," The Sarge replies, blocking the barrage of short jabs Kid Cadet tosses his way.

Brain Dog nods in reluctant agreement.

"Kinda like a train wreck, maybe, or the Jerry Springer Show back in the old World."

"Hit those lights, Chatty my good man, if you don't mind," I blurt in my best British accent, inducing a group groan that had been my precise objective.

"Back into the abyss of terror we go..." I continue as the screen crackles to life.

Chapter Seven
The Lone Reaper

The figure was sitting on the crest of a steep, grass-covered hill the first time any of the caravan set eyes on him. The black steed he rode was a portrait of stillness, giving it the illusion of being a statue instead of a living, breathing animal. He glared down at the trail of wagons being pulled through the valley by the trudging oxen and grinned, spitting a thick trail of tobacco juice to one side. A large Stetson covered his head and shadowed his face, and the long black coat he wore seemed extreme for the spring temperatures of the season.

Gil Morgan was the first to notice him, and pulled on the reins to halt his oxen. Gil shot his wife Martha a concerned look and then hopped off his wagon, pulling his rifle from behind the seat, and gestured to Samuel Levins, who drove the second wagon in line.

Morgan, his long graying beard blowing wild in the strong prairie winds, grimaced as he leaned in to whisper to Samuel, who had struggled to halt his wagon before his oxen rammed the back of Morgan's.

"Do ya see him there, Samuel?" he asked sourly, his eyes darting nervously from Samuel and his wife Patricia to the stoic figure perched above them.

"Yep, I see the man, Gil. You sense trouble of some kind?"

Morgan gripped the twelve-gauge in both hands

and shrugged his bony shoulders. Gil Morgan was in his late fifties, but resembled a man ten years older.He had no front teeth, and had a habit of whistling through the open space as he began or ended a sentence. Samuel found the habit, and the man himself, more than a tad bit annoying.

"I think he may be a raider of some sort. Bothers me I can't make out his face.Remember what Captain Rower told us back in Lawton? He said there were bands of them roamin' the valleys and mountains just waitin' for a wagon trail to attack. Do ya think we should face 'im down or just keep goin'?"

Samuel glanced over at his wife of six months and smiled, his eyes rolling comically.

"Well, he doesn't seem to be bothering us at the moment. I say we just go on about our wa-"

"What's the trouble, fellas?"

Samuel turned in his seat to face John McGraw, the man who drove the third Wagon. A moment later, Lawrence O'Malley joined them at the front of Samuel's wagon.

Wincing, Samuel removed his hat and scratched through his wavy black hair.

He had actually grown fond of McGraw, a chubby, soft spoken southerner from Alabama, but considered O'Malley's company the equivalent of a rabid dog. O'Malley had joined the caravan around Columbus, Ohio, and had managed to insult and belittle everyone involved along the way. He was what Samuel called a 'European stare-downer', meaning a man who had just recently stepped foot in the U.S. from England and immediately began degrading everyone and everything around him. More than once in the week since O'Malley and his clan had joined them had Samuel wanted to tell him to get his behind back to jolly old England if he thought it to be so much more 'refined' and it's people more 'dignified'.

Samuel couldn't help but frown when O'Malley spoke up.

"I think we should arm ourselves immediately and keep a watch, but there seems to be no basis to panic here. He is the first person we've seen since Lawton, not counting those two young Navaho warriors who rode past us a few days back, whom I barely consider humans as it is. I say let us continue with caution, but we do not need to remain stationary."

Gil Morgan nodded agreeably and wheeled back around towards his wagon.

Samuel could feel his face reddening. Why had Morgan bothered to ask him if O'Malley seemed to be the man in charge? O'Malley patted McGraw on the shoulder as if to indicate the meeting was adjourned, then strolled casually back to the fourth wagon, which was the last in the train. John McGraw glanced back up at Samuel and smiled through tobacco stained teeth.

"Looks like the Lord of All He Surveys has spoken, Samuel."

Attempting to refrain from laughing out loud but failing, Samuel howled. In the six weeks they had traveled together, he had never heard McGraw string together so many words in one sentence.

"True enough, John. Let us not disobey our

King."

McGraw shook his head comically and walked away.

As Samuel waited for Morgan to pull away, he turned to face his wife, a tall, beautiful red head he had met in Cleveland almost a year ago to the day.

"Patricia my darling, what we have here is truly a case of the blind leading the blind."

She returned his grin and placed her hands gently on his thick, muscular forearms.

"Just place this firmly in your mind, Samuel, if all goes as planned, we only have his boorish company in our midst for another three weeks at the most."

Samuel whistled loudly as he urged on the oxen.

"I'm not certain a thank-you is in order for reminding me of that, my sweet."

As he allowed Morgan's wagon to build a decent lead on the slight trail that led into the large valley, Samuel glanced upward and noticed the man was no longer surveying them from the top of the hill. He was nowhere in sight, vanishing like a tendril of fog in bright sunlight. Samuel's gut tightened a bit as he ensured his rifle was within reach.

The caravan stopped to camp a few hours later, just a half hour before darkness fell on the wide open space they were approximately halfway across. A line of low hills and mountains was only a few hours to their north, and all present realized they were going to have a long, challenging trek ahead.

Patricia handed Samuel a hot cup of coffee as he kneeled beside the small campfire at the side of

179

their wagon.

"Where exactly are we, Sam?" she asked as she leaned against him softly.

He sipped and placed his thick arms around her narrow waist, taking in the perfumy scent of her.

"Only a few days from the New Mexico border. We're almost out of the panhandle. We picked the perfect month to travel through this region. I hear the winters are hell and the summers are worse."

Patricia sighed deeply, and Samuel responded by hugging her closer.

"What is it, dear? Still having second thoughts?" he asked almost in a whisper as his eyes followed Martha Morgan walk towards a high mound of shrubs a few hundred feet west of the wagons. She was walking with the determination and desperation of a prairie animal who had just found the ideal place to mark their territory.

"Well, we both did have good jobs in Cleveland, and this is such a chance to take. I know your brother is a good man, but just because he has found a rich claim doesn't mean…"

Samuel and Patricia both cringed involuntarily as a shrill scream filled the previously still and silent darkness. A moment later, they watched as Martha Morgan rambled back towards the camp from the area she had chosen to do her business in. Her arms were waiving madly and Samuel noticed with some humor that the outside of her dress hung crookedly, the white bloomers underneath clearly visible.

Gil met her just as she entered the center of the lit campsite and practically had to tackle her to prevent her from overrunning the clearing. Samuel

180

and Patricia quickly joined the others at Martha and Gil's side.

Martha's eyes were wild and her face was covered in fresh sweat, despite a late evening temperature that was more fall than summer like.

"Martha! What is it, woman? Did ya straddle a rattler?" Gil asked as he shook her by her thin upper arms.

"Th-the man was out there...w-watching me. The man..."

Her words came out half-garbled, and Lawrence O'Malley stepped up stiffly, basically pushing Gil to the side. Samuel looked over at

John McGraw, who was standing bow legged in his long johns with a revolver in each hand, and couldn't help but giggle at the sight. John glanced down at himself and scowled.

"What man are you speaking of, Mrs. Morgan? Another Indian, perhaps? I was told Shawnee roam these plains," O'Malley blurted as he placed a hand firmly on the back of Martha's neck. She stepped back and slapped his hand away with a quickness that belied her frailness. O'Malley backed away with the look of a child who had just received a good spanking. Again, Samuel fought back the urge to laugh out loud.

"It was no Indian, fancy pants! It was the same man we saw up on the hill today. I bent to....to water the flowers and looked up from my squat. There he stood, not twenty feet away. Him and that horse 'a his. I couldn't see his face, but it was him...I know it was!"

Gil placed his arms around Martha and led her

away as O'Malley ran over to his wagon and returned a few moments later with his rifle. He glared at Samuel but did not speak. John McGraw joined O'Malley as they walked slowly towards the line of shrubbery Martha had just exited. John turned to Samuel and nodded.

"Watch the camp, Samuel. The snaky som'bitch might try to sneak in camp while we're out lookin' for 'im."

Samuel returned the nod, took his wife by the hand and walked towards his wagon. He retrieved his own rifle a moment later and stood in the center of the camp.

"Ladies, please return to your wagons and arm yourselves. It may not be trouble, but there's certainly nothing wrong with being prepared."

Patricia was hesitant, but finally departed with Samuel's insistence.

She reluctantly armed herself with the revolver Samuel had taught her to fire mere months ago.

A few tense minutes later, Gil and O'Malley jogged back into camp with puzzled looks covering their rugged, unshaven faces.

"Nothin' out there now," Gil managed in between huffs.

O'Malley's eyes darted from side to side nervously.

"Doesn't mean he still isn't watching us. I believe we should post a sentry, just as we did outside Oklahoma City. Two hour shifts for the men."

Samuel wanted to step forward and disagree with the pompous, arrogant snob just for the sake of doing it, but had to agree having someone awake at all times was the logical thing. O'Malley volunteered for the first shift, and Gil would follow. Samuel and John would split the last two hours before dawn. O'Malley was the only member of the wagon train with children accompanying him. His wife, a quiet, refined woman in her mid-forties and son, Bradley, age five, had obviously grown accustomed to their husband and father, respectively, being the absolute tyrant he was so naturally talented at portraying. Samuel hadn't heard his wife, her name being Marion, say more than three words since Lawton, and the son practiced the 'children should be seen, not heard' creed to the letter.Samuel's heart went out to them. Gil and Martha had no children, Gil explaining this by announcing to anybody within earshot that 'Martha was as barren as an Arizona desert', to Martha's shocked dismay by the look in her eyes. John and Loraine McGraw were also childless and, to Samuel and Patricia's delight, did not share their reasons.

Samuel and Patricia Levins planned on starting a family as soon as they settled in California. The house and claim came first, and then Samuel Junior could join the ranks and grow up helping his father run the cattle ranch they planned to build as soon as a rich vein gushed forth. He had not only sold his home and food market back in Ohio, but also four young, healthy horses that he was told would never survive the trip. He bought his six oxen fairly cheap and packed what belongings would fit on the wagon, joining the thousands of apprehensive hordes headed west for a new start.

Samuel had heard that it never snowed in Southern California, and never really got cold enough to worry about the welfare of the livestock he planned on buying and selling. His brother had sent word that there was gold to pan, land to claim, and plenty of open spaces to build homes on and raise families in. Patricia hadn't put up much of an argument, although he felt her nervousness on certain occasions. He didn't mind playing the role of confident breadwinner in the least. It actually helped ease his own secret fears.

Samuel was gently shaken awake by John and took his place by the fire just as the sky began to lighten over the vast horizon. The sweeping plains were deafeningly silent at night, not even a coyote's howl piercing the peacefulness. They had only seen a few nights of rain since leaving Ohio, and even those had barely registered as nothing more than cloud bursts. Samuel realized that luck ran out eventually on such travels, and he wanted Patricia and himself safely tucked away at his brother's home as soon as physically possible.

The sun rose to the west and revealed a sky void of clouds, although Samuel noted the winds were picking up considerably from what they had been the previous days.He was in the act of making a large pot of coffee when he suddenly felt a cold chill ran up his back. Glancing up slowly from where he had been kneeling, he could not shake the feeling that eyes were trained on him from a nearby distance.

Just as the slowly rising sun cleared a nearby mountain and came clearly into view, Samuel spotted the figure. He sat aboard the stiff, dark horse much in the same pose as the day before. Again, the horse seemed unnaturally still while the rider's face was concealed by the brightness of the morning sunlight.

Samuel raised up slowly, both his knees popping in disapproval. He unconsciously had reached down and was now gripping the rifle loosely in both hands. The figure was at least a hundred yards away and sat near the crest of a tall, weed infested dune.

Samuel was preparing to back away from the fire and wake up John McGraw when he saw the rider move for the first time.

At first he thought the man was waiving at him, then he saw the glint of metal in the morning light. The man held a Bowie knife with a blade that had to have been ten inches long and at least three thick.

The man brought the knife up high over his head in what resembled a greeting, then pointed it straight out in front of his chest, directly at Samuel.

Samuel found his legs to be frozen, and the rifle in his hands began to shake uncontrollably.

The man bought the knife back down and performed a slow, calculated 'slashing' gesture across his own throat, then brought the blade back down to his side.

Samuel, feeling as if the blood in his veins was no longer cursing, backed cautiously towards the nearest wagon, and paused.

The rider was gone.

Rubbing his eyes vigorously, Samuel looked down to the ground and then back to the spot where the rider had sat. Had he taken his eyes off the man for a moment? He couldn't remember looking away at all, and as he stared at the bare prairie he was facing, he began to ponder if an overactive imagination hadn't been the true culprit.

He took a few steps forward, just past the freshly lit fire, and kneeled down with a sigh, placing his rifle loosely across his knees. Samuel was not a stranger to fear. He had seen his share of death while serving in the War Between the States. The stark fear of dying on the battlefield was visceral, almost a solid object that could be physically worn and just as easily peeled off depending on the situation. The apprehension and nervousness he was experiencing as he shakily bent to pour himself a cup of coffee was not as easily defined.

A moment later, the steaming tin cup he had been holding fell to the ground as the screams of Marion O'Malley shattered the silence of the surrounding landscape.

Samuel leapt to his feet and ran towards the O'Malley wagon. He got to it just as Lawrence O'Malley was leaping from its rear.

"O'Malley..what the devil is.." he began, his eyes locking on O'Malley's.Samuel recognized madness and pure, primal rage in the other man's gaze.

"Where is he, Levins? Where the hell is my son!?" O'Malley bellowed, his revolver held at his waist, and pointing directly at Samuel's midsection.

Backing off a step, Samuel raised his rifle to his chest defensively.

"Bradley isn't…with you? I didn't see him lea-"

O'Malley raised the revolver until Samuel was staring down its shiny barrel.

"Damn you, man, WHERE IS MY SON?"

Samuel took a deep breath and lowered his rifle, his free hand held out in a posture of surrender.

"O'Malley, I haven't seen Bradley since last night. Since I've been on post, I saw no one but….but the rider…"

His expression transformed from rage to puzzlement, O'Malley lowered the revolver slowly back to the ground. He stepped back and his entire body slumped as he leaned his head back and sighed in exasperation.

"You..you saw the rider? When? The bastard probably has my son!"

Samuel stepped forward and placed his free hand on the other man's slumped shoulder.

"No..he was alone. It was only a few moments ago. Actually, I'm...I'm not really sure if I actually saw him or not. Regardless, Lawrence, no one physically entered this camp while I was on post. Of that I am certain."

O'Malley leaned against the side of his rig and closed his eyes in defeat as both men stood quietly and heard the soft sobs of Marion O'Malley reverberate from inside the wagon.

***

Fifteen minutes later, the men armed themselves and performed a sweeping search of the surrounding area. Gil walked the eastside of the campsite, while Lawrence took the west. John covered the north area

187

and Samuel the south. They all walked out approximately two hundred yars and then returned, fearing for the women's safety, although they were careful to keep the campsite in view as they searched.

Within the hour, all returned with no news to report. They found no tracks that would have indicated that the boy had roamed away on foot. Samuel had searched the area where he had visualized the rider that morning. He felt the short hairs on his neck rise when not a single hoof track appeared.

Lawrence and Marion O'Malley announced a few hours later, just as the caravan was preparing to move on, that they were turning back. As Lawrence was readying his oxen, Samuel and John tried to convince him to continue on with the train until they reached Albuquerque, where he could contact authorities about the missing boy. John tried to explain that they were closer to a city going west than turning back the way they had come, but O'Malley turned a deaf ear. With moist eyes, O'Malley thanked them for their concern and wished them luck in California. Marion was riding in the back of the wagon and her soft whimpering could still be heard whenever the men were momentarily silent.

Gil strolled over and they all shook Lawrence O'Malley's hand and wished him god's speed. Samuel had not particularly liked the man, but nonetheless felt a deep sadness for his plight.

As the wagons pulled back onto the pastureland and headed towards the mountains to their west,

188

Samuel and Patricia Levins secretly felt an eerie foreboding that neither shared with the other. Samuel looked into the darkening sky and noticed the thick, black clouds building on the horizon. He deduced that an unknown evil had hopped aboard this wagon train somewhere along the way, and the ride was far from concluding.

***

That night they camped alongside a narrow passageway between two high, jagged mountain ranges. Although they had started late that day, John told Samuel he figured they had covered at least thirteen or fourteen miles. It had threatened rain since the morning, but did nothing but lightly shower until around dusk. The heavy downpour began right after the group had consumed their dinner of beans, crackers and coffee, and all barely had time to jump into their respective wagons before getting completely soaked.

Samuel and Patricia found a release in being trapped in the back of the wagon as the full force of the storm hit. The mountains mostly blocked off the winds associated with the deluge, but the massive sheets of rain were pelting the top and sides of the wagon with such force they were almost forced to scream to be able to communicate over the noise.

By the time the storm had dwindled to a light shower, Samuel and Patricia were in the throngs of a deep sleep following a passionate session of lovemaking.

At dawn, Gil Morgan awoke to discover Martha was not at his side. It wasn't until he dressed and exited the wagon to search for kindling that the

189

worry began to build. Being that the campsite was in a narrow space surrounded by rocky hills and small shrubs, there wasn't a vast landscape for a person to hide in. It took Gil another few moments before he began to truly panic.

Samuel sat kneeling at Gil's side an hour or so later, both of their faces a mask of despair. They had covered what limited area there was to search without roaming completely out of the seemingly endless passageway, and just as with the boy before, had discovered no evidence of Martha's departure. The ground had been wet and muddy where rocks were not present, but the only footsteps had come from their own boots as they searched.

Gil held his head on both sides with callous covered hands.

"I thought she might have got up to pee is all. I was real groggy and 'member her leanin' her head out the back of the wagon and whisperin' something about the rain stoppin'. I drifted right back off then..."

He sobbed as his bearded chin came to rest on his upper chest.

Samuel patted the older man on the back gently, embarrassed at not knowing what to say or do.

"We'll tell the sheriff in Albuquerque. Maybe they'll send out a unit of troops to search. Maybe...maybe she walked up the trail and got lost up in the ridge somewhere. It'll be alright, Gil."

Patricia was sitting in the back of their wagon, looking up into the cloudless morning sky. Samuel crawled inside and hugged her close and she playfully scratched his stubby growth of beard, which he hadn't bothered to shave off in a week or more.

"What's happening here, Samuel? First the boy and now Martha?" she asked wearily.

"It's more than just strange, honey. The boy I could see roaming off and getting lost on that vast prairie, but we're basically camping in a tin can here. Where could she have went? And why?"

She patted his hand softly.

"Let's leave this canyon, Samuel. Things are...not right here, somehow."

Samuel nodded.

"I feel the same. I can't help but think that unknown rider we saw two days ago, and who I think I saw yesterday, has something to do with all this. I just can't shake his vision out of my head, and I wish by all that's holy that I could."

Patricia laid her head on his shoulder and they both sat silent in thought and watched an eagle soar high overhead, the birds massive wing span temporarily blanketing their faces in a long narrow shade.

"Got to feed and water the oxen," Samuel managed before leaning over and giving his wife a quick kiss on her right cheek.

***

The three wagons pulled away from the campsite a half-hour later, with John McGraw's rig leading the way. Samuel had seen Loraine McGraw's face as they prepared to depart. The flesh was pale and pasty, with eyes that expressed the horror lurking within her fevered mind.

They entered a grassy valley eight hours later,

and decided that the treeless, mostly flat area would serve as a perfect camp. There had been no signs of Martha Morgan along the rocky trail that led from the mountains, and Samuel figured that Gil was more than likely both depressed and relieved. Depressed that his wife was not found alive and well, and relieved she was not found in the condition they all suspected but did not dare speak of.

John and Samuel decided to pull a two man watch around the wagons overnight. They would not just sit in one strategic area, but actually walk around the wagons themselves. Both had pulled roving guard duty in the Army, so dealing with a lack of sleep was nothing new. John had wanted Gil to participate, until he got a good look into the man's eyes, and realized it would be counterproductive. Samuel could sympathize. He couldn't imagine what his state of mind would be if it had been Patricia that had vanished into thin air.

After a quickly prepared dinner of beef jerky and cabbage soup, Patricia and Loriane retired to John's wagon. They had decided it was best to keep everyone together, sans Gil, who was almost comatose and hadn't even left his wagon to eat dinner.

John and Samuel alternated two hours on and two hours off, thus giving each ample time for a couple of quick naps.

Samuel lay next to the dwindling fire and dreamed. His eye lids moved like waves on a stormy sea, and his hands wriggled and spasmed.

He was in the middle of a beat down wheat field and was running madly. He turned to face the entity that pursued him, and recognized Bradley, the young son of Lawrence O'Malley, was right on his heels. Bradley was swinging a large bowie knife out in front of him as if he were cutting corn stalks. It was the same knife the unknown rider had shown him the day before, only now it was blood soaked. Samuel felt his breathing grow increasingly labored, and his legs seemed to be moving in slow motion. As he sprinted further and further into the middle of the vast field, he noticed a lone, still figure appear directly ahead. He slowed to almost a complete stop, and recognized it was Martha Morgan, but with a distinct difference. Samuel glanced at her face and couldn't help but stare. A scream built in his chest, but he found he didn't have the oxygen to allow its escape. Martha had no eyes, only bloodied, empty sockets that reminded Samuel of the small caves he used to frequent as a child. Martha's body was as frozen as a stone statue, but her lips worded a whispered sentence Samuel couldn't quite comprehend. He heard someone speak behind him, and whirled around expecting to see the young child coming at him with the huge blade. Instead, he was face to face with the unknown rider, who had dismounted his black steed and was poised only a few feet away. Samuel couldn't make out the man's face, which was hidden beneath the shadows of the large Stetson he wore, but he did hear the man's words, which were spoken in a deep southern drawl.

"She said, I'll get you too. I'll get ya all eventually…"

Samuel was about to turn and head to the other end of the field when the rider raised his head, removing his hat in one fluid, shockingly fast sweep of his right hand. His face and head were a skinless skull. He had long, impossibly wide teeth that were as white as a freshly painted fence, and had eyes that protruded from the sockets as if they had been stuck there but not pushed all the way into position. There were thick brown lashes stuck to the bony forehead above the eye sockets. Samuel turned and glanced back at the stoic figure of Martha, and noticed that not only were her eyes missing, but the lashes as well. He swung his vision back to the rider, who was mounting his beast and laughing. The rider took his long bowie knife and dug out his left eye. It popped like a rotted grape and hung on the blade like a chunk of sliced melon.

The rider grinned. This time, Samuel found he had ample oxygen to scream.

He practically jumped to his feet as he woke, and heard the far away cries that he realized now had awakened him. The fire had completely extinguished, only a few glowing embers remaining. After pausing a few moments to allow his night vision to adjust to the darkness, he concentrated on the origin and whereabouts of the noise. He heard someone speaking, but couldn't tell how far away. It did sound like John, but he couldn't be sure. He scooped up his rifle and ran to the east of the wagons, where he soon saw the shape jogging towards him.

He took a few steps forward, and was almost run over by John McGraw, who was panting madly and cursing at the same time.

"What the hell is it, John? What's out there?"

McGraw bent and placed his hands on his knees for support, then blew out a short series of long-winded breaths before speaking.

"I..I saw 'im, S-Samuel. I saw…the sombitch…he..he.."

Samuel scanned the surrounding fields as best he could by the dim moonlight, then glared back at McGraw.

"Saw who? I didn't hear…"

McGraw waived him off.

"That same sombitch we saw on the hill a few days ago. Big hat, black horse. Big un. I…I was walkin' around the wagons and I turn the corner to your rig and there he stood, pretty as you please. I don't…know how he got there without me hearin' or seein' him, but he did. I held my pistol not three feet from his nose and told him not to move. He had a bowie knife, biggest one I've ever seen, in his right hand, and I could have sworn he was cuttin' his other hand with it. He was runnin' the blade back and forth on his palm, but I didn't see no blood, Samuel. I thought I heard 'im laugh, or it could have been a cry, hell, I don't know."

Samuel cringed as a coyote howled in the far distance. He realized he had his finger on the trigger of the rifle, which was pointed directly at John McGraw's chest. He removed it cautiously.

"Then…how did he get away from you, John?"

McGraw finally stood straight, blew out another load of air, and shrugged.

"Samuel, I do not know. I do know my eyes never left the bastard. He…was there one second and gone the next. I think…I'm going…c-crazy or

195

somethin'."

Thinking back to the previous morning, Samuel couldn't help but grin.

"No, you're not, my friend. And neither am I."

McGraw suddenly blew by Samuel in a mad trot, almost sending the smaller man sprawling into the grass.

"John, what the...?"

"The women!" he bellowed. A moment later, Samuel had almost caught up with him.

They found Patricia and Loriane sleeping peacefully, wrapped inside their blankets and sheets like cocooned larva.

Gil Morgan, however, was not found.

Without speaking, they divided the useable contents of Gil and Martha Morgan's wagon and split up the oxen before hitching them to their own rigs.

Samuel was in the process of watering the animals when Patricia came up behind him and broke down in heaving sobs. She trembled and wailed until he practically had to carry her to the back of his wagon and lie her down.

"Samuel, I'm scared. Why is this happening? How is this happening?" she sobbed.

Pulling the wool blanket over her, Samuel leaned over and softly kissed her on the forehead.

"Shhhh, try not to think about it. We're only two days travel from Albuquerque. Three at the most. We'll let the powers that be try to figure it all out."

As he walked to the front of his rig, he realized it wasn't the three days travel that worried him, but the two nights that had to pass along the way.

John McGraw strolled up to him as he was checking the oxen one last time before departing.

"Okay, Samuel, what's the plan?" he sighed heavily, his eyes blood red and sagging. John McGraw looked as if he had aged ten years in the previous forty-eight hours.

"I would think to get as much space behind us as we can. We really need to get to the city as soon as we can, John."

McGraw threw his arms up in frustration.

"You know what I mean, Samuel. What about when the sun falls and the moon rises? The nights? What in hell can we do when it turns dark? Playin' guard hasn't prevented a damn thing so far."

Shaking his head as he turned from the oxen, Samuel found no logical reply forthcoming.

"Jesus, John. I have to tell you, I'm lost. I have seriously considered in the past few days whether we are all losing our minds out here. I don't have an explanation. I know I'll hold my wife close to me whenever we do stop to sleep, and by god, I won't allow anyone or anything to take her from my arms."

John McGraw nodded amiably, then strolled away to prepare his own rig.

He stopped just before reaching his wagon and turned back.

"Samuel, is gold worth this? Is fighting over claims and land worth the price we're payin'? I dunno. I kinda wish me and the misses had stayed in Alabama. At least there we weren't bein' chased by the devil. Least ways, not that you could tell it, anyhow."

Unable to find words to sooth his friend, Samuel turned back to the job at hand.

***

The two wagons pulled away from the open pasture a half-hour later, just as the skyline behind them began to grow dark.

In the next ten hours, they passed through two small, bare mountain ranges as well as a half dozen open fields. They spotted a lone Indian rider crossing one of the fields around mid-day, but the rider never gave any indication if he had seen them at all. Samuel found he had little fear of what roamed the prairies and mountain ranges of the land they crossed, for there were other dangers present that made all others pale in comparison, one that seemed less than human and more fierce than any wild animal or rampaging savage.

The wagons pulled to a stop outside the entryway to yet another rocky mountain range. John had spotted a small enclave and pointed it out to Samuel, who agreed it seemed like as good a spot as any.

After a sparse meal of beans and crackers, John stayed with the women as Samuel scoured the area for an alternate shelter. He and John had decided it might be safer if they all slept in a nearby cave or an enclosed area of some kind, given that they all agreed four people in one wagon would feel too confined and uncomfortable.

Samuel returned to the camp within the hour, and reported he had found a tiny cave just over the first ridge. Carrying only their blankets, firearms, and a small oil lamp, they trudged up the hill just as the sun became hidden over the nearby mountaintops.

The cave was at least a quarter mile from the wagons, and was partially hidden by a line of small trees and high shrubs. The entrance was neck-high on Samuel, and was just deep enough to fit all four of them inside without inducing claustrophobia.

They spread out two blankets, one for each couple. The lamp illuminated the small space adequately without giving away their location from the outside.

Samuel had one arm around Patricia, who was snoozing softly while leaning on his shoulder, and the other wrapped around his loaded rifle. He glanced over at John, who was leaning against the back cave wall with his eyes closed and revolvers sitting loosely in both hands. Loraine slept soundly on her stomach, a light snore escaping her lips.

His whisper echoing in the small enclosure, John's voice broke the tension-filled silence.

"You think he went back for O'Malley and his misses, Samuel?"

Rolling Patricia off of his arm and onto the blanket, Samuel slowly crawled over to where John sat.

"I...I don't know, John. Maybe he just wanted the child. I've been thinking that possibly the man has a certain quota to fill. Hopefully we're not needed. We can only pray that's the case."

"Uh, Sam, what in Sam Hill is a quoter?" John asked, his face the definition of puzzlement.

Despite the situation, Samuel had to laugh. He giggled uncontrollably for a moment, sending John into a fit of muffled howls.

A full three minutes later, the men leaned shoulder to shoulder against one another, their breath coming in short gasps. Samuel wiped the tears from the corners of his eyes. It took another full minute for both of them to regain full control.

"A...a quota just means he has a certain number of people to...take. Maybe he's done."

John sniffed and wiped his own moist eyes, then nodded.

"What do you think he wants, Samuel? Why us?"

Samuel frowned deeply.

"He's a vulture of some kind. I had heard some horrible stories about wagon trains coming west and never making their destinations. Some just disappeared altogether. No traces of them were ever found, not even a stamped out camp fire or wagon wheel. Who knows how many of those stories were fact or fiction, but I know I've become a believer."

John leaned forward and for at least the tenth time since entering the cave, checked his rifle to ensure it was loaded.

"I hear ya, Sam. I find myself believin' things now that I'd have laughed at just days ago."

"Try to get some shuteye, John. We'll have an early start in the morning."

Crawling silently over to where his wife lay, John grinned sarcastically.

"That's what I like 'bout you, Samuel. You're one positive SOB."

Returning the other man's smile, Samuel crawled towards Patricia and gently took her into his arms, his rifle now resting within easy reach beside the blanket.

The dream was fragmented, flashing images into his mind in short, frantic spurts. Samuel was leading a wagon across a vast flatland, which held no vegetation of any kind, not a single weed or rock in sight. He seemed to be traveling at an incredible speed, but no oxen or horses pulled the wagon. He held empty reins which splayed out in front of the wagon like thin, black snakes in search of some unseen prey. As he traveled on, feeling the dust fill his mouth and eyes, he visualized shapes sticking up from the dry, cracked desert just ahead.

At first he thought they were small, round boulders. As they grew closer however, he saw that they were human heads, lined up in a neat row like they had been planted there.

As he passed them, the wagon seemed to be gradually slowing. The first head belonged to Bradley O'Malley's, followed by his father and mother.

The fourth was that of Gil Morgan, then Martha. John McGraw and Loraine came next, and the wagon was almost at a complete stop as it pulled up next to Patricia's. All of the heads had one thing in common, he noticed. None had eyes. There had been no blood around the sockets to indicate any force had been used to take them, just empty dark sockets that seemed endlessly wide and deep. Samuel saw a darkness where his beloved Patricia's beautiful brown eyes had been that called to him, attempting to seduce him somehow into being hypnotized by the unknown evil that lay within.

An empty hole was dug behind his wife, just large enough for one more addition to the macabre collection. He jumped from the now completely stopped wagon and kneeled down next to the hole. Looking down into it, he cringed back as the fleshless skull popped up from the tunnel. It was the face of the rider, the bright noontime sun reflecting off its white teeth blinding him momentarily. The large, wide eyes began to spin wildly from tip to bottom, then from side to side. Samuel commanded his legs to take him away from the abomination that lay at his feet, but they were no longer his to order. The rider's white teeth opened impossibly wide, and Samuel cringed as the moist, circular objects rolled around and onto his booted feet. The skull spat out the last one, and it landed with a wet plop onto Samuel's chest and stuck there. He began to scream as the severed eyeball stared back up at him and winked, although it had been lidless. He heard the rider speak, and although the words came out like they had been spoken from a deep dark cavern, he somehow understood their meaning.

"Told you I'd have 'em all, didn't I Sam old man? My work is done here. ...but yours has just begun..."

He jerked awake with a scream, mouthing the words from his dream in a husky whisper.

The light from the oil lamp was down to a miniscule glow, but it was light enough for Samuel to see two things very clearly. The first was that he was totally alone in the dank cave. The second was the shadowy form standing at the cave's entrance. Rolling over quickly, he scooped up the rifle and raised up to his knees in one fluid movement. He pointed the rifle at the shape that stood only five or six feet away from where he squatted, the barrel of the weapon shaking uncontrollably.

"Where are they, you son of a bitch?" he croaked, his finger tight on the rifle's trigger.

The figure never moved, its face once again just a shadow above the neck. It held the bowie knife stiffly at its side, the blade almost chrome-like in its glimmering shininess.

"Deep within you, in the innermost reaches of your mind, you know the answer," the rider replied, its voice seeming to come from outside the cave. It was a deep, gravely tone that chilled Samuel to the very marrow of his bones.

The rifle now pointed at the shape's head, Samuel crawled forward a step.

His teeth were gritted to the point of shattering, and he felt the blood throb at his temples.

"Listen, Mister, I want to know where my wife is....and I want to know right now, or believe me when I say that I will not hesitate to put a very large hole directly in the middle of your forehead."

The rider replied as if Samuel had never spoken. Only his head moved at all, bobbing slightly under his wide hat when he spoke. The remainder of his body seemed frozen in suspended animation. Somewhere in the background, Samuel heard the rider's steed whinny.

"Some are not meant to make it. It is fate, and humans do not have the capacity to understand. You have been chosen for the next cycle. I long to join my wife, my children in the world beyond. You see, we never made it either. You and I are one in the same. All I can tell you is, it will end eventually. I never thought my cycle would, but now the end is finally, blissfully near."

Samuel stood, now only a few feet from the rider, his rifle's handle slick from the coating of perspiration emitted from the slickness of his palms. He stepped forward and poked out the barrel of the rifle until it struck the rider's chest. The rider did not respond except for a low grunt upon contact.

"Jesus, you crazy bastard. If you don't think I'll pull this trigger you keep up this...this...bullshit talk. I don't give a good damn about your wife or kids, I want to know where my wife is, and why you've trailed us since we left Oklahoma!"

"Why? Because, my friend, you are my successor..." the rider replied as it slowly reached up with its right hand and began to remove the large Stetson, revealing it's face from the shadows.

Samuel's eyes bulged as he backed away, half tripping on the blanket that had wrapped itself around his boots. The rifle fire lit up the cave like the brightest of suns devoid of cloud cover. Samuel fell to his knees, dropping his still smoking weapon at his feet uselessly. He glanced back up, but felt no surprise or shock when the form of the rider was no longer blocking the cave's entrance.

His head feeling suddenly light, his vision growing dark and spotted, Samuel had time for one quick flashback just before passing out. He had seen the rider's face. The rider's face had no eyes, just coal black, hollow pits that looked infinite in the depth of their despair.

The rider's face wasn't just a fleshless skull with white teeth, as in his dreams.

The rider's face was his own.

***

The rider watches as the long wagon train begins its climb up the rocky terrain, headed directly into the desert canyon to the south.

They go west for different reasons, of course. Some for riches, some for land, some just for a new beginning and a fresh start. The rider reaches into his saddlebag and pulls out the small satchel bag that is tied tightly at the top. He glances down into it and smiles at the moist sets of pleading eyes staring back up at him. He glares back down at the caravan and grunts in a mixture of satisfaction and eternal frustration. Some aren't supposed to make it, he had been told that day that seemed now like a lifetime ago. He had decisions to make about the wagon train below. It was finally his time, he knew. If he were able to cry in the demon's body he had been supplied with, he would have.

Almost over.

He couldn't wait to see his beloved Patricia again.

He pulled the large Bowie knife free and waited.

Waited for the night to set in.

***

Just as the lights flickered back to life, Brain Dog begins whistling the western theme from the old Clint Eastwood movie, 'Good, Bad and the Ugly'.

"So that's what happened to all the missin'

settlers back in the eighteen-hundreds. I had always chalked up those mysterious disappearances to bad trail grub and hungry coyotes. Lotta second-rate cooks roamin' the plains in those days, I understand. Wipe out a full wagon trail of cowhands with a single pot of horse-meat chili," The Sarge says, reaching over to pinch Airman Legs on the knee. Legs slaps his hand away with a fierce growl, then swings her legs out of range. Corporal Chatty slaps The Sarge on the back in sarcastic consolation, then winces back from the elbow thumping his ribcage. Chat man never misses an opportunity to rag The Sarge, although invariably he receives the worst of any comedic duel between the two. Those two are like an apocalyptic version of Jerry Sienfield and George Castanza. The Laural and Hardy of the hopelessly-doomed set. Personally, I never tire of playing observer to their little two-man play. Humor is a commodity when you spend twenty-four seven locked inside a cement and steel tomb, as vital to survival as H20 or crap paper.

"The reaper-man looked a little like a biology teacher I had back in high school. Same complexion anyway...like a dead fish belly up on a hot patch of sand," Legs announces, shooting The Sarge a seductive wink.

"Wasn't that Bill Shatner in heavy SF makeup? I could have sworn he...spoke..in..a..Captain...Kirk...overly..dramatic... monotone..." Lieutenant Lava cackles in the worst celebrity imitation I've ever witnessed, far worse than The Sarge's frequent 'Duke' Wayne take-offs.

I reach over and punch her upper arm lightly,

covering my grin with the other hand. She jerks back as if I'd nailed her with a fifty-pound sledge.

"Sounds more like Spock after a dose of female hormones," I'm barely able to quip, as Tia's moon-faced expression has me on the verge of guffawing aloud.

"You...had better...watch it...or I'll have...you beamed   aboard...the   Star-Ship 'Cylor'...you....traitorous....a-hole...you.."   she continues with a menacing glare, cocking a single eyebrow while staring me down.

My ribs ache as I bend to howl, her 'a-hole' utterance literally forcing me to one knee. As my vision grows bleary from the warm tears spewing forth, I can barely make out Brain Dog as he rolls to the floor in a similar state of weakness. Corporal Chatty's bland expression and The Sarge's look of stark confusion just adds fuel to my inner giggle-meters engine as I roll to the floor and begin to seriously ponder if a man's lungs can implode from lack of sufficient oxygen.

I hear The Sarge mutter 'easily amused, ain't they?' and it seems an eternity before I'm able to stand and breath normally again.   Brain Dog continues to lie on his stomach like a frozen slug, while Tia hugs me tightly from the rear, reaching up to lightly kiss my neck. True, it is usually the quiet, simple moments that make this hellish existence bearable, but bouts of unrestrained lunacy are just as necessary to keep things locked on an even keel.

"Put in another episode, Private Radar. These are getting good," Kid Cadet pleads.

"Yeah...now that you three are done hackin'

your lungs out. I didn't get the joke, though. Personally, I thought Lava does a damn fine Mr. Sulu impersonation," The Sarge says with a grin, and Tia bounds over and punches the thick muscle of his right bicep, dead center at the crossed-sword tattoo that adorns it.

"A new chapter it is, then," I reply happily, still giddy from the yuck-feast that has my sides throbbing like full-body toothaches.

Moments later, all grows silent just as the shadow of darkness cloaks the room...

Chapter Eight
White Man's Burden / White
Man's Pain

August eleven
Year of Our Lord 1858

Dear Aunt Charlotte,
Don't think I'm going to get the chance to mail this off, but I'm hopin you or somebody else will be abel to find it when you get here so you can know what hapened to us. My writin and spellin might not be so good, cause Im scriblin this in a mitey big hurry. Don't really know how long fore whatever is out there desides to come inside for a visit. I just know there ain't a blessed thing I can do to stop it. I peek out the front window ever now and then, but its as dark as Foley's Swamp out there. All I can see is the edge of the forrist and the growin fog. Finally stopped rainin' at least.

I ain't never been this scart in all my thirteen years, Auntie C. I thought about runnin, but somethin ain't lettin me. Like my feet are stuck in kwik sand or somethin. Papa would have forced me to go, I think, but Papa ain't around no more to do so.

***

The whole blamed mess started a week ago today, when Uncle Cyrus came by to help Papa find a new wellspring. The old one had dried up a few days earlier, so Papa was havin to make trips into town and load up the wagon with water pulled from

Uncle Cy's well.

I was with them when they found the natural spring on the east edge of Kane's woods. I heard Uncle Cy telling Papa to pass it up and keep headin back west for a closer source. Uncle Cyrus is a big man, and probly the strongist I've ever knowd. Stronger than Papa even. But that partickular day, Uncle Cy was shakin like a pup dipped in freezin creek water. He was tellin Papa that the land was damn land, or doomed land. Something like that. He said that the well was to close to an old Cherokee buriel bureal burial ground, and that any water pulled from such a well would be poison to a man's soul. Papa laughed at Uncle Cy and called him yellow, saying that those old injun stories were nothin more than cow chip tales made up by old women with nothing better to do than flap there gums after Sunday prayer meetin.

They dug out the well that very day, and I recall Uncle Cy's face turnin a scary shade of white. Kinda like a dreid up dog turd in the summer sun. Five days passed before Mama got real sick, doublin over at the kitchen table like somebody socked her in the guts. Papa said her head was sizzilin hot with a terrible fever, and rode into town to get Doc Campbell. While Papa was gone, I heard Mama screamin and carryin on like a bobcat with its paw caught in a bear trap. Auntie C, I ain't never heard a human bein make noises like that before. It had the hair on my head standin on end like a lightnin strike had peeled my hide.

By the time Papa and Doc Campbell got here, Mama had stopped makin any noise at all. For some reason, Auntie C, I just could not make my self peek inside that room to check on her. I think I was too scart at what I might see. I recall Papa and the Docter openin the door and both of em fallin back like somebody had just slapped em square on the jawbone.

I also recall the smell comin from that room. Reminded me of that dead squreal I found on the creek bank last summer, all swoll up and rollin in magots.

I heard old Doc Campbell tell Papa that Mama had some kinda food poyson, more n likley. Papa talked about the new well and the Doc's eyes lit up. He asked if me and Papa had drunk from the same, and Papa said we all had. Doc handed over a bottle of some kinda dark medisine that looked like lubercatin oil and told Papa to give Mama a teaspoon full every hour, then call on him late the next day if the fever stayed at a pitch.

When I woke up the next mornin just after sun-up, I was alone in the cabin. I checked on the bedroom after hollerin there names. It stunk like high heaven in there, Auntie C. Like a mashed skunk left to rot on a hot rock. Front door was standin wide open with the mornin chill blowin in pine straw and dust by the handful.

I wondered around outside in my nightshirt and bare feet, but the only livin thing I ran into was my old hound Willie, who looked about as worried as me, with his ears all purked up and his eyes wide as Mama's best servin dish. Willie trailed me as I made a kwik circle around the barn and tool shed. I checked the garden and pasture, but even the cows were stayin out of sight. Wazn't til later that I thought bout checkin the barn stalls. Thinkin back on it, I'm fairly certain they would have been empty too.

I stumbled back into the house and found Papa and Uncle Cy sittin at the kitchen table, both there faces red as beeks and sweatin like somebody had stuck em in the cheeks with a red hot poker.

I tried to ask Papa were Mama was, but never found a place to break in as he and Uncle Cy talked about what they had seen.

From what I gather, cause they was talkin real fast and some of it I wazn't able to understand, Papa had woke up to find Mama gone from the bed. He ran up the road and woke Uncle Cy, and both of em took off into Kane's woods lookin for her. Papa figured she had just wondered off, bein led around by her sickness more n common cents.

Uncle Cy said something about seein her on the creek bank near the old creakin bridge, telling Papa he still wazn't sure it was really Mama at all. He said the shape he saw, Uncle Cy said shape, not person, Aunt C. That kinda sent a chill up my back, if I recall. Anyhow, Uncle Cy said the shape he saw on that bank wore Mama's clothes, but looked all together diffirent. Said its hair was glowin gray, not dark brown like Mamas. He also said he saw its hands, and that they were big, like a man's hands, with fingers as long as a Granddaddy Longlegs, and sportin claws to boot. Claws, I swear he said.

By the time Papa caught up to him, Uncle Cy said the shape had run off, even though he said he never really saw it move. He said it was just there and then it was gone, like a mornin fog pushed away by the sun's early light.

They found Hershel Bettis on the bank where Uncle Cy said the Mama-shape had been standin. I saw Papa look sternly at Uncle Cy, then nod towards me, and Cy droped the subject. Needless to say, Auntie C, Mr. Bettis was more than likely expired, and probly not lookin to spry niether.

A little while later, I was in my room, bitin my nails and listenin to my own stomach growl when I heard Papa holler that he was ridin into town to fetch Sheriff Barton. Uncle Cy stayed at the cabin with me, and he cooked us up some eggs and ham while we waited, not sayin a word as he did so. As I recall, Uncle Cy never did look me in the eyes niether.

The rain started in bout middle of the day, pourin down so hard that it made even peekin out the window a waste of time.

I went into my room after lettin Willie in from the storm, and ended up fallin a sleep soon there after. I was dreamin of my Mama, standin inside the kitchen makin biscuits and gravy and smilin at me like she does sometimes. I could almost smell those biscuits cookin as I woke, cryin a little too, I recall. Willie was sittin in front of my bedrooms door, growlin like he had just treed a thirty-pound coon. The room was pretty dark, so I figured I had been sleepin at least three or four hours. Rain hadn't let up a bit, explanin my sleepin spell. Willie almost tripped me up soon as I opened the door, runnin into the kitchen and out the open back door like somebody shot him out of a kanon. For the second

213

time that day, I found myself alone in the house. Auntie C, I ain't too proud to say how shook I was. I almost peed my briches right then and there. I prayed that Willie come back, even more than for Uncle Cy. Not sure why, but I reckon deep down inside my chest, I knew both of em were gone for good. Just like Mama.

The wood floor was wet from the rain that'd blew in, and Uncle Cy's boot prints were the only ones I saw trailin out towards the pasture. I put on my slicker and followed em a little ways, wishin the good Lord had given me better cents.

Look like he'd been draged through the mud right fore the prints left dirt for grass, then I lost the trail all together.

I shut the back door and pulled the board lock down on the front, then went to the kitchen and got my Mama's biggest carvin knife out of the spoon n fork drawer.

Don't ask me how I knew bad trouble was circlin the cabin, Auntie C. I just knew. Maybe the man upstars was warnin me, I don't know.

Papa beat on the front door for a while fore I got nuff coruage to let him in. I had heard his voice good nuff, but for some reason wazn't real sure it was him. Know that sounds crazy, but it will make more cents in a minnet, Auntie C.

Papa was soakin wet, his hair all stuck to his head and his beerd drippin like a fontain. He ran past me like I was a ghost, payin no mind to me askin him were the Sheriff was. He came chargin out of the bedroom with his shotgun in one hand and his horse pistol in the other, breathin like a train runnin

214

low on cole tryin to climb Stone Ridge Hill.

Right fore he walked back out into that ragin, howlin storm, Papa pulled me aside and placed the pistol in my left palm. He told me that he was goin out to find Uncle Cy and the Sheriff. Said he and Sheriff had taken the Potter cutoff back to the cabin to save some time, and saw something haulin Uncle Cy into Kane's woods by the hair of his head near the old burned out church. Papa never said who or what was doin the draggin. I think he started to tell me, but his lips just kept on shakin and squrmin around without nothin leavin his mouth. He said Sheriff Barton jumped off the buckboard and sailed into the woods fore he even had a chance to tie the team to a nearby oak. By the time he got around the other side of the church's one remainin wall, he said the rain had turned to hale, and he was pretty much blinded. The cabin is only a short run to the old church, so he came back to get some fire power fore startin a new search.

Papa ain't one to look for a fight, Auntie C, but you know like me that he ain't no coward niether. I've heard tell he was a scraper in his younger days, and I saw him shoot a black bear not a dozen feet away on a huntin trip last year.

That said, Auntie C, I could pretty much smell the scartness in him fore he left the house. My father was sweatin fear. I ain' never felt so much like a no count child in my life as right then. I wish I could have helped my family in some way. But what could I do? The pistol Papa gave me might as well be made up of rotten wood, glued together by tree sap and shootin rabbit pelets.

215

If only Papa would have listened to Uncle Cy an dug that gall blamed well somewheres else.

If only Papa hadnt been so blessed stubborn, as Mama always said he was want to be.

Course, I once heard Granpa Wills tell my Mama that frettin over its and butts is like nailin the barn door shut after the cows get out.

That well water was cursed, Auntie Charlotte. Couple of months back I heard Uncle Cy talkin to Papa bout Kanes woods. They was sharin a jug of Mr. Palmers best lightnin, both of em snozzeled to the gils and not payin much attention to me. Uncle Cy was sayin how the Cherokee Chief had put a curse on the whole blamed forest after a US Army solider had killed his sqaw daughter while runnin the tribe further into the woods, up towards Hacker's Mountain. Said the Chief had said that anything that growed out of the ground would be soiled rotten and not fit for the white mans touch. I quit listenin after a while cause my skin started to crawl neath my shirt like a chigger itch.

I never was one to believe ghost stories though. My friend Chester says they al

I had to stop writin for a minnit, Auntie C. M Mama wuz at the door. I was ascart to answer at first cause she sounded diffirent, not like Mama at all. Her skin is fish belley white, almost like the chalk they use on the school bullitin bored. She smells funny to, Auntie C, kind of like pig meat startin to turn. Just like Uncle Cy had said, her hairs a shade of gray now, and moves around like lake water even if the wind ain't blowin it.

The wool gunny sack she carried into the cabin

216

is layin on the kitchen table, leakin something feirce. Leakin somethin redder than a bloomin rose. Something that smells a little like the time Papa took me to that slawterhouse in Macon.

Its Mamas eyes that scare me the most, Auntie C. They ain't blue no more like before. Kind of look like plum pits instead. Her lips are all smered in something, like shes been eatin cherry pie. I got the feelin she was gnawin on somethin else entire, Auntie Charlotte. I'm tryin not to think about that though.

I want to quit writin and go to her as she moves about the room, floatin like a sheet caught in a summer days breeze, but somethin won't let me. My hand wont stop scriblin, Auntie C, even though all I really wannt to do is run away. I cant even breath good no more, like somethins chokin me real slow like. I droped Papas pistol by the door as soon as I let her in. Don't matter none anyhow. It was useles as the day is long, I recken.

Mama is movin towards me, like she just now saw me.

She is openin the gunny sack and empytin it out on the table.

Mamas smile is a terrible thing to see, Aunt C. Worsen than any nightmere I ever had.

Least ways I know what became of Papa, Uncle Cy and Sheriff Barton.

Crazy. At first I thought they wuz big ol' gords layin there. Big red gords drippin soot colored raindrops. Wish she would close Uncle Cy's right eye, all hangin open like a broke window shuter.

Mamas got an injun tommy hawk in her left

217

hand. almost big as Papas ax blade, it is. Funny, she werent holdin it before. saw a drawin of one just like it in my school book. Cherokee or apaches caried em like that, I recall.

Mama wants me to tell you somethin, Auntie Charlotte. Wants me to write down the mesagge real clear like, so there won't be no confucion later on.

Afterward, she promises to tell me a secret. A secret shes goin to whisper to her only son to prove her internul love. My hands aer shakin like craazy…but it won't turn loose

Message is this, Auntie C..

There is InDEED something infinitely WORSE than the White Man's HELL

I aint sure who wrote them words, Auntie Charlotte, but I swear to the lord above that it wern't me

Mama ain't mama no more, auntie C, she aint
Don't rightly think she ever wuz, now.
Don't come here whatever else don't come
p-pray for me auntie c, pray hard…..

***

"Ho-kay, game over. I'm officially throwin' in the yellow towel," Brain Dog announces just as the lights go up and the group grimaces in harmonic unison. He exits the room in three lengthy strides, easily dodging Corporal Chatty's half-hearted attempt to trip him up.

For the second time in half an hour, I feel the hair on my arms and neck stand on end as goose pimples envelop my upper body in waves of

218

cowardice.

"Is it just me or are these stories getting darker and more... apocalyptic with each episode?" Airman Legs asks, leaning forward with her elbows balanced on her knees. The sarcastic edge has, at least temporarily, departed her tone, and the expression she displays is uncharacteristically dour.

"Think that's the whole idea, Legs. I mean, the genre itself is geared towards unnerving those who are foolhardy enough to choose such entertainment, correct?" Father Pete answers, cutting off The Sarge, whose mouth hangs agape in mute response.

"Bingo, Father. My sentimental exactly," he finally croaks, reaching over to pinch Kid Cadet's left earlobe.

"No, I mean...it's almost like Radar said...they're too...damn real somehow. This last one, filmed in black and white and in what looked like sixteen millimeter, it was....I dunno....too lifelike."

"Gerbil pellets, Legs. Folks said the same thing 'bout that witch flick back in the late nineties. Y'know, the one that gave everybody motion sickness cause of the camera movement," The Sarge counters, his eyes turned to the stone ceiling in thought.

"Blair Witch Project," I answer proudly, shrugging my shoulders modestly as the Sarge shoots me an appreciative nod.

"That's the one, Radar my boy. 'Sides, didn't think anybody had access to a camcorder back in the late 1800's, Legs. Not unless the director was named H.G. Wells and his time machine was parked on a nearby mountainside. Am I right or am I right?"

Legs blushes and glares down at her own boots.

"Yeah, whatever, Sergeant Smart ass. I'm just saying...that one sincerely creeped me out, and I don't wig out easily."

Father Pete rises with a low groan, wincing as he uses the palms of his hands to massage his lower back. There are times that his body language and mannerisms add a decade to his actual age. Then again, we've all aged beyond our years these past few months. Even Kid Cadet can seem worn and grizzled when standing beneath the fluorescent glare of the Hive.

"Carry on, gore-hounds. I'm going to go see if Chief Big Cheese needs some orbital relief. Please retrieve me if an old episode of 'Highway to Heaven' pops up on the next disk."

"I'm with you, Reverend. Chief wanted me to check the generator hours ago. We don't wanna be fightin' flies in the dark, right?" The Sarge announces, ruffling Kid Cadet's locks a final time as he trails Father Pete from the room.

"Hurry back, muscle head," Kid Cadet spouts between giggles, then jogs over and leaps onto Private Leg's waiting lap. Between herself and Lieutenant Lava, Legs has assumed more of a motherly role with our young charge while Lava seems more along the lines of 'older sister'.

"Settle down, Spanky, or I'll sentence you to ten minutes of extreme capital punishment," she blurts loudly, tickling the Kid's rib cage until he struggles to breath between hysterics. Legs calls him Spanky from the Little Rascals character of old.

"You know what that means, don'cha? Locked in the small storage room with Corporal Chatty for five full minutes of....con-ver-sa-tion. Arrgggghhh!" she concludes, shooting Chatty a playful wink. His only reaction is the deliberately gradual cocking of his left eyebrow.

"Oh....nooooooooooo!" the Kid croons, only beginning to regain the use of his undersized lungs.

"Roll disk, Radar. Let's see what devilish fate awaits us next in the chamber of horrors!" Lava whispers dramatically, reaching over to goose my left cheek in the process.

"Jeez, I thought I was warped,' I mumble, signaling to Chatty to douse the lights, '..you people are borderline demented." Without further ado, showtime commences...

Chapter Nine
Revelations Within Hell's Breakroom

Placing the fine points of its bony elbows on the tabletop (a wide sort, constructed wholly of melted human bone and covered in a sheet of meticulously sewn flesh of the same), it casually sipped the thick, steaming bile from the blackened mug and sighed in obvious frustration.

Across the table, the other forked a mouthful of raw intestine and chased it with a quick spoonful of kidney nectar.

"DIR-46, you still on Suicide Detail, I take it?" it muttered between noisy slurps.

"You got it, DIR-57. You know the drill. About as exciting as Pit Detail, which I'd actually prefer between the two," replied the other, belching a ball of fire that sailed into a nearby wall and quickly dissipated.

"Pit detail? Ugh. Don't even go there. Spent almost three decades unclogging those damned, if you'll pardon the well-worn pun, flesh canals. Didn't mind watching the surface-vile burn and decompose within the liquid flames, but the aftermath isn't worth the brief thrill. Ton after ton of seared bone and charred hearts. Why is it that the heart of those vile vermin won't melt away like the rest? Sticks to the breast bones like parasites still feeding -...."

"Strongest muscle in the human body. Didn't you read the Detail Manual?"

Forking another huge portion, equal parts liver, pancreas, and tongue, the other nodded stubbornly, a shard of tendon hanging from its pointy chin.

"Just thumbed through 'em. How much is there really to learn about shoveling burnt husks into a waste compactor? Got my fill of rules and regs in Basic D training. Such banal trivialities are for surface dwellers, I say."

"True enough, I guess. I always was a stickler for details myself."

The other groaned, sipping slowly as a fine trail of the mucus colored brew ran down its squared jaw and onto it's scaly shoulder.

"Yeah? Look where it got you. Suicide watch for what, four decades and counting? Brother, you definitely pissed off somebody in lower management; am I right?"

"Not that I know of,' it replied with a wide, sharp-toothed grin, 'fact is my natural talent for the task has trapped me there."

Tossing the emptied plate into a nearby wastebasket made from finely sculpted human skulls, DIR-57's expression was one of dour sarcasm.

"You think? Pray tell, pardon the expression, what exactly makes you King of the self-destructive?"

"Check the numbers, four-six. Since I took over the detail in the late '60's, suicides worldwide have increased fifty-one percent from the previous four decades. Not only that, I've added some much needed creativity to the genre that was sorely lacking in past regimes."

DIR-46 arose and faced the nearest vending machine, digging into the thick, scaly folds of its lower abdomen for correct change.

"Such as?"

Taking a final sip of the fast-cooling bile, DIR-57 then leaned back as if to nap, cautiously wrapping its spiked tail beneath the table.

"Methods were so…crude, so banal before my promotion from Pit Detail. Hangings, drowning, wrist-slashing and such. I was the first to institute 'mass subtractions', whereas an entire group punched the same one-way ticket at precisely the same time. Whether by having one within the clan kill the majority and then himself, or by enticing a higher authority to attack with excessive force. Police assisted suicides, I believe they labeled them. Same general scheme, same result. Group elimination's have become my specialty; my personal forte and calling card. Teens are the easiest. Always have been. Angst is at a premium. It takes little or no effort within their age grouping. Similarly, the aged need only the slightest of shoves for a satisfactory result.

Lately I've concentrated on the forty to fifty year old demographic. I love a challenge, and the 21st Century provides so many varied tools with which to perfect my craft.

New batches of immensely strong and perfectly legal narcotics are added to the mix almost daily. Doesn't take a handful of sleeping pills to turn the trick anymore. Two or three of these babies gulped down with the right bottle of firewater, pardon the pun, and presto, instant freight elevator ride headed south."

DIR-46 slowly inserted a pair of 'soul vouchers' and punched in its choice of refreshment. Sipping from a moistened, blood-red straw made from pulped tissue, it frowned slightly as the rather thick, salty taste coated its forked tongue.

"Typical. Out of date H-8 Juice. Nothing worse than soured plasma. Anyhow, I hate to take the wind out of your sails there, Fifty-Seven, but don't take all the credit for yourself. Lot more misery up top these days, not to mention the increased state of overall depravity within the population. Your stats are padded thanks to innovations such as Cyberspace, instant gratification fads, and increased levels of selfishness within what the dwellers categorize as 'entertainment'. Agreed?"

Raising his clawed hands palms up, Fifty-Seven smiled wryly, the tip of its incisors dripping yellowish gore.

"No argument. Then again, the dark god's crusades are growing stronger as well. More are attracted to his false prophecies each day, a fact that doesn't exactly make our jobs easier."

"A pathetically gullible bunch, aren't they? Massive hordes of mindless sheep, basically," Forty-six spat sourly before gulping down the remainder of the glutinous beverage in two long swallows, followed by a loud, echoing belch that spewed scattered flames airborne.

"How about yourself, Four-Six? Haven't seen you that often since basic. Still working Homicide Detail?"

Gently stroking its pointed right ear with one

razor-clawed hand, Forty-Six grinned happily even as its massive chest ballooned out with obvious pride.

"Nope. Left that humdrum detail behind two decades back. You're talking to the assistant director, second in command mind you, of Region Eight Soul Collecting." Fifty-Seven's mouth fell open in comical shock, a small swarm of slick, bloated flies exiting its split tongue like fighter jets from the deck of a Destroyer. "The HELL you say! Congratulations, you old flint-sniffer! I never would have thought an old bunk mate of mine could climb so low in such a short span."

"Gotta tell ya, Five-Seven, it's a daily rush that never wanes...,' came the enthusiastic reply, Forty-Six's red hued pupils practically glowing from the pitch-black pits encasing them, '..presently, I'm dangling the hook in front of several high-profile wannabees who are edging our way with pen in hand. Several desire nothing more than a successful career in entertainment, you know, SOS; money, fame, drugs, sexual depravity. Consequently, I have another who is reaching for the ultimate brass ring. This one wants nothing less than to bed down in the White House for two full terms. Wants to go down in history as the people's all-time favorite, a nation's savior. I love it when they aim high. Warms my rotted soul to actually discover kindred spirits roaming the surface world, trapped in a mortal coil that can only be liberated through the likes of us."

Patiently tapping its spear-like nails atop the fluid-slick tabletop, Fifty-Seven is never allowed the chance to verbally concur as a loud speaker within

226

the tiny room's confines booms overhead.

"...DEMON IN RESIDENCE FORTY-SIX..REPORT TO CONFERENCE ROOM SIX-SIX-EIGHT....DIR FORTY-SIX TO CONFERENCE ROOM SIX-SIX-EIGHT FOR QUARTER-CENTURY IN-BRIEF..."

Rising with a loud yawn, Forty-Six reached over and playfully clapped its cohort on the right shoulder.

"It seems break time is officially over, my malevolent ally. Been a real pleasure conversing with a peer I truly respect as an equal within our hallowed ranks."

Fifty-Seven stood stiffly, its spiked tail unfurling like an uncoiling Anaconda.

"Ditto, Six. I'll be back on shift myself in a few. Keep collecting those souls. Soon the gist of their pitiful race will be ground beneath our hooves, far from their so-called Savior's grasp."

As their claws clasped in a departing gesture, Forty-Six cocked its oval-shaped dome and carefully studied the others' rather bland expression with awestruck wonder.

"Something amiss, Six?"

Forty-six sighed, bathing the others face and upper chest in waves of thermal heat.

"You're utterly oblivious, aren't you? There are no signs of purposeful deceit that I can detect. Shameful how one can accept such abominable deeds as being personally acceptable over time, isn't it?"

Its own visage now frozen in a confused scowl, Seven attempted in vain to pull its claw free from the others sudden vise-like grip.

"What's this about, Six? Some kind of lower echelon gag? Let me in on…"

"Twin teenaged girls, Seven. Richmond, Virginia two surface years back. Ring a bell, or have you seen fit to invoke self-induced selective memory?"

"I…twin girls? Richmond? I don't have…"

Fifty-seven reached over and gripped the other's shoulder and began trying to wrench free via leverage. The hold seemed forged of the strongest alloy, as did the captors horrifyingly intense stare.

"Fine. Let's try another then. The Hospital Administrator in Tokyo who was on the verge of convincing an entire wing of cancer patients to cash in, to be followed by his own overdose once the others had led the way. That was…three earth years back, according to the files I was given access to by….a very, very concerned lower management head. There have been more recent scenarios, such as that crippled retard in Tacoma, Washington last month. The boy was soaking in a tub of boiling water with a straight razor poised at his wrist when you so inconveniently stepped in and inexplicably….how can I say this without the accompanied nausea, 'spared' his seemingly damned soul?"

Its short, shrill whimpering barely audible as it struggled to free itself, Fifty-Seven collapsed to its armor plated knees just as its captor began to tremor and convulse in a slow, deliberate transformation.

"I d-didn't…t-they weren't r-ready…p-prepared t-to…they w-were so y-young…."

228

"Not your decision to make, Seven! You possess no such authority to alter a soul's ultimate destination! Internal Affairs has been investigating you for the past decade. Rogue demons are rare, indeed, but it is widely know that the dark god has the capability to turn even the most devoted of our ranks given the time. His legions have worked on you hard and long, my friend. He won the small battles until the war for your soul was eventually lost. So subtle was his takeover of your inner core that you never even noticed the alteration. Sad. I was told you were one of the best Suicide Detail ever had."

The demon's chest cavity split open horizontally with a muffled ripping sound, a deep, black crater opening like parted lips stretched apart in a hideous parody of a smile.

Bowing its head in woeful shame, Seven's entire frame slumped in apparent defeat.

"...I deeply r-regret my d-disservice to the one and on-only m-m-master. M-my failure is no r-reflection of the master's g-greatness", it mumbled as its flesh ignited from head to hoof.

"Rest assured, old friend, I will only utilize the best your detached soul has to offer and vehemently discard the spoils that the dark god injected without your permission,' Forty-Six bellowed as the mass of tentacles emerged from the chest crater, caressing the putrid air cautiously, like a nocturnal beast crawling from a pitch black abyss.

The tips of the tubular appendages burst apart, revealing tiny pincers that were slightly hooked at the slime-slicked ends.

"You see, old bunk mate, my metaphoric rise within the ranks is mostly due to my secondary title, that being Absorber of the Unworthy. I grow stronger with each consumption; stronger, hungrier, increasingly focused to the task at hand,' Forty-Six beamed as the tentacles shot forward like ravenous maggots on a decomposing carcass, penetrating the other's hard outer shell with shocking ease.

As its flesh was ripped asunder and its innards greedily consumed, the servant of evil formerly referred to as Demon in Residence number Fifty-Seven found itself swept into a painless, guiltless realm, overcome by static waves that embraced its detached soul with hands filled with gentle forgiveness and a persona that exhumed unparalleled goodness and understanding.

DIR-Forty-Six stood over the mutilated husk of a former ally and grimaced as the chest wound began to automatically sew itself shut, the bloated feeder tentacles having already tucked themselves away deep within.

The Demon stared long and hard at the deflated skull of his former cohort, the sunken face of which held an expression that evoked a twinge equal parts disgust and fear. The expression revealed was not of eternal agony, as one might expect, but of joyous relief. Relief in the discovery of a new master, one which offered a new beginning for all who accepted its presence and believed in its ancient, biblical teachings.

"Damn. A new angel added to his cursed ranks," The Demon grumbled, rubbing its bloated midsection as it turned to enter the nearest tunnel,

230

wishing at the moment that regurgitation was an option.

Turning back for a final look at the shredded remains, The Demon felt the gnawing burn at its chest intensify.

"We'll meet again, old friend, in the final battle. The ultimate resolution. Then, my friend, we will see whose master will permanently grasp the keys to the kingdom."

Somewhere within the infinite reaches of another dimension, one filled not with despair and strife but with eternal hope and immeasurable love, a newly ordained servant of the Lord nodded in complete agreement.

***

"Dare I say it...the devil made them do it?" I blurt in order to break the silence as the screen fades to black.

"I've said it before and I'll repeat it to emphasize the point. Best special effects I've ever seen. Did you see the FX make-up job on those two? If I didn't know better, I'd say Hollywood had nothing to do with ..." Legs begins, trailing off as the Chief enters the room wearing a decidedly somber expression.

Lieutenant Lava rushes past me and blocks his passage, her lithe, shapely body posed stiffly as if at attention. "What's up, boss? We nearing the moment of truth?" The Chief swallows hard, tugging at the collar of his camo jacket, and I instantly felt the blood cool in my veins. Corporal Chatty stands up as well, ringing his hands nervously. "Swarm's noticeably diminished in the

231

last ten minutes or so. Not sure what it means, or where exactly they flocked to." "Maybe they were just....distracted temporarily," I croak, trying to sound sure of myself but failing horribly.

The Chief slides by Lieutenant Lava and takes a seat next to Airman Legs, who reaches over to lightly touch his left forearm, then tugs at it like a bothersome child begging for attention.

"There is only the...one way in, right boss-man? There isn't anything we've...missed, right?"

"One way in, one way out, Airman. Cool your jets, people. Doesn't mean a thing, at least not yet. It's just a strange development, that's all."

Inhaling deeply, the Chief slowly scans the room.

"Where's Sergeant Rock?"

"Generator check, Chief. You want me to..." I begin, feeling a sudden need to escape, if only for a few brief moments.

The Sarge practically bounds into the room before I could take the first step towards the exit. At that particular moment, I come dangerously close to whining aloud.

"Right here, Chief. Generator's juiced for another long stretch. What's goin' down? Ya all look like you're on the verge of a group barf-a-thon. Radar, you fart again?" The Sarge quips, buttoning up a thick cammie shirt over his barrel-shaped chest.

"Swarm's died down, Sarge.., ' Legs mutters, her face frighteningly drained of color, '..dramatically so."

"Speaker still playin' their favorite elevator music?"

The Chief interjects, his tone a level calmer than just moments before. As with any true leader worth their salt, he meant to quickly eradicate the wave of panic his original comment had given birth to within our ranks.

"Loud and clear. I've altered the tone a bit, just in case the masses had adjusted to the old and grown tiresome of it. Like Radar said, might just be an outside distraction of some kind. Building thunderstorm or the like. Monitor should tell us the story soon. Brain dog and Father Pete have their collective peepers pinned to the screen as we speak."

Everyone seemed to unwind in unison as the Chief leans back with the back of his head resting in his palms.

"Who else is ready for some grub? Airman Legs, you feel like a chow run?" he asks Legs with a lighthearted wink, and we all seem to deflate with a series of muted sighs.

Airman Legs nods cheerily, her cheeks suddenly flushed.

"Sounds like a novel idea, Chief Big Cheese. MRE's for everybody...on me," The Sarge exclaims, scooping up Kid Cadet with one tree-trunk sized arm and hoisting him airborne as if the kid weighed fifty pounds instead of eighty-five.

"What'll ya have, Junior Cadet? Turkey ala King or roast beef? I know it's a choice you'd rather not be forced to make, much less ingest, but such tests of bravery are mandatory for the future leaders of BUG STOMPERS, in-cor-peeeee-rated!"

Hearing the kid's raucous laughter was comparable to receiving an injection of 'joy' virus, wherein smiling was as infectious as the warm feeling flooding our collective chest cavities. Hearing Corporal Chatty giggle like a teenaged boy peeking at his first Playboy centerfold is easily the highlight of the last few months. We all feel as though we've dodged the proverbial bullet, no matter how temporary the relief. Maybe we aren't quite as prepped for the inevitable Moment of Truth as we thought.

Months of forced captivity without going hand to pincher with those slimy, overgrown houseflies have left us a bit rusty, in both a physical and mental sense. I'm afraid we've all lost the fearless edge we'd honed razor sharp in the days before entering the Hive's mountainside safe haven. The strongest human instinct is survival, self-preservation, even when faced with the slimmest of odds. Whether or not we regain our nerve, our 'eye of the tiger', remains to be seen. Personally, I've discovered I'm in no great hurry to re-enter the danger zone that looms near. I can see in my colleague's eyes, save Sergeant Rock, that the feeling is universally mutual.Funny, we always thought the world was going to end courtesy of a Middle-East conflict or via a Third-World country firing off a few well-aimed nukes. Actually, funny isn't the appropriate word. Tragic is a better fit for how modern society ended up biting the big one.

"I'll go grab us a handful of those packaged beauties, Chief," Legs beams, as if announcing she was off to the local grocery market across town.

"Ya need help with the bottled refreshment, my dear?" The Sarge chimes in with a wide, toothy grin.

"Private Radar, please assist Airman Legs in procuring chow. Sergeant Rock, since you are now officially back in uniform, how about accompanying me to the Boom-boom room?" the Chief interrupts while rising from the couch. "Got'cha, Chief," the Sarge replies, turning to Lieutenant Lava, who has since joined Corporal Chatty and Kid Cadet on the couch. "Lava, you guys hang loose. We'll meet back here in a few and chow down while viewin' another mystery flick."

The lieutenant flips him a playful salute and wraps her arms around Chatty's sizeable shoulders. Despite having shared not one but two rousing, electrically charged sexual liaisons with Tia within the past three hours, the pangs of jealously instantly reemerge.

"Affirmative, Sergeant Rock-Head, Sir! Corporal Blabblermouth here and I will busy ourselves changing disks, talking world politics and babysitting the future king."

As I follow the other three into the dank, dusky scented hallway, a feeling of dread envelops my being like a tidal wave formed from quick-drying cement. The smothering shroud of death shadows us ever closer now, I fear. Without shame, my remaining wish is to experience Tia's magical touch one final time before our time as the ruling species of a dying planet officially ends.

The roast beef from my 'meal ready to eat' would be more appropriately labeled 'roast jerky', but I still prefer it over the elastic, gummy textured Turkey ala King.

No one speaks as the next to last disk is inserted

and the wide screen flickers to life. A sweeping sense of foreboding fills the air like raw humidity, a cloak of apprehension that fuels our inner fears and transforms even the most vocal among the group into brooding mutes. The closet thing I can compare it to, despite never having experienced such a phenomenon, is a sports team minutes before departing the locker room for a big game. All thoughts turn inward; the mind's eye trained on possible scenarios to come.

As the lights click off, I feel Tia's warm palm clasp my own. The moistness our flesh shares is born from the horrific finality of what lies ahead...

Chapter Ten
Boils

Jerry shivered involuntarily as the steely-eyed technician casually punctured the inside of his right elbow with the loaded syringe. The thin sheet he lay upon did little to warm the cool metallic table beneath, and he secretly pondered why medical testing rooms always seemed to feel like the inside of a walk-in freezer.

"This solution helps enhance the imagery. You might feel temporarily flushed and detect a slight scent of alcohol. This is perfectly normal," the young techie explained, the forced calmness of his tone grating on Jerry's already frazzled nerves. Despite the cool outer demeanor, Jerry had noticed slight tremors in the man's rubber-gloved hands as the syringe dosage had been administered.

"How long will this take?" Jerry asked impatiently, leaning his head up just enough to catch a warped glance of the reddish colored, consistently throbbing growth just below his breastbone.

"Less than fifteen minutes, sir. Try to limit your movements once you enter the chamber. I will place foam earplugs in your ears to dull the scanner's hum, all right?" Jerry grunted acknowledgement as the flesh of his face and forehead reddened with sudden warmth.

"Major? Are you in here?" Jerry blurted just as the techie had leaned over to insert the first plug, the patient's sudden outburst causing him to openly flinch and back away as if a bee stung.

"Colonel, Mister Howe, Colonel Travis, and yes, I'm right here," the impossibly husky voice replied from somewhere behind Jerry's position. It was the deep, gravelly tone of a lifelong smoker, each word pronounced in a cantankerous, deliberate southern drawl that Jerry instantly pegged as frighteningly insincere.

"Where is Kay-...where is my wife and son, Colonel? Are they being...tested as well? I tried phoning them from my doctor's office...that is, before you and your damned Storm-troopers practically kidnapped me."

The pause was deafening in the brutality of its silence. Jerry's pulse pounded at his temples like twin jackhammers attempting to penetrate solid marble.

"Your family is fine, Mister Howe. They're just outside in fact. We transpo-...we drove them over for support purposes only. We...knew they'd be concerned about your status as the testing progressed."

The techie inserted the first earplug, much to Jerry's chagrin, then backed away like a stunned prizefighter as Jerry rolled onto his side in a clumsy lurch.

"Sir, just s-stay calm. The test is quick and painless..."

"Why all the secrecy, Colonel? Why couldn't my own doctor set this up? I've been seeing him about this....problem for almost two weeks. Why drive me forty-five miles to a government medical facility to run tests any local ER can accomplish? I get the feeling I'm not being told something here,

Colonel. Do me a big favor and soothe my nerves, will you? Toss a few more well-worn cliches my way, at least. I crave peace of mind, Colonel, whether your facts are manufactured or based in reality. Convince me my growing paranoia is unfounded...please."

The pause was thankfully shorter in duration than the last, and Jerry could almost visualize the Colonel's smirk.

"Simply a precaution, Mister Howe. Like we mentioned earlier, there was an accidental biological weapons spill near the area where you and your family camped last month. The...um...skin irritation you've experienced might possibly be a side effect of being exposed to one such weapon. Your family is one of many being administered th-.."

"Skin irritation? Colonel, with all due respect, calling this...thing...a skin irritation is kind of like comparing a mashed pimple to an active volcano, wouldn't you agree? Does one normally receive a C-Scan for an apple-sized zit, sir?"

The Colonel cleared his throat noisily, coughing harshly for an encore.

"As I stated, Mr. Howe, simply a precaution. The particular weapon we suspect can cause internal blistering to one's lungs and kidneys. We must establish the condition in order to properly treat it, you understand."

After a moment of tense silence, the young techie inserted the second earplug and instructed Jerry to lay back and relax, his voice once again borderline robotic.

"Please remain as still as possible, Mr. Howe,"

came the final instruction just before Jerry was slid into the narrow confines of a circular tube just wide enough to accommodate his considerable bulk.

Studying the flickering lights above his head as the space around him filled with buzzing noises of various decibel levels, Jerry fought to control his frenzied thoughts, instead attempting to focus solely on the events of two weeks before, when the origins of a baffling medical mystery still unsolved began to slowly surface.

As the insistent humming began to fall into a systematic rhythm, Jerry swore he felt the festering boil at the center of his chest kick and wriggle like a restless baby within its mother's womb.

***

Two to three days after returning from Cedar Creek Park, where the family had taken its annual three-day camping trip, Jerry had first noticed the irritating itch at his breastbone. The next day, while showering, he had run his hand across the same spot, wincing as the pain and throbbing became increasingly pronounced. At first, the pea-sized welt had resembled a tiny shaving bump, red around its circular edges with a lighter shade at its center.

Jerry had mentioned it to Kayla the next morning at breakfast, immediately after Jake had departed for his summer job as a grocer bagger. Upon viewing, Kayla had simply dismissed it as a pimple, suggesting one of Jerry's chest hairs had ingrown. It wasn't until a full week later, the once miniscule irritant now roughly the size of a grape and consistently throbbing like a rotted tooth, that Jerry recalled the incident at Cedar Creek Lake some ten days prior.

At the time, the scent of stagnation at the creek's edge had barely raised an eyebrow, as had the grouping of oaks and pines at the western edge of the lake that looked to have been seared almost in half, their ravaged tops protruding from the water like groping fingers.

He faintly recalled a slick, oily feel to the water as they had enjoyed a late afternoon dip on the eve of departing the park, Kayla quipping something to the effect of the three of them being 'oiled up fish ready to fry.' As they dried off on the bank, he remembered Jake had spoken of the water's less than aromatic stench, saying it smelled like 'sweaty gym socks.'

They had left the park at around 6:00 AM the next morning, hoping to avoid rush hour along the two hour trek towards home. Just minutes past the park's main entrance, they had met the convoy of Hum-V's decorated with military insignia, followed closely by a series of unmarked white van's and two similarly generic tow-trucks.

"We declare war with the squirrels?" Jake had joked, while Jerry and Kayla had shot each other puzzled glances.

"Just the games soldiers play, I'm sure, Jake-O," Jerry had replied while studying the passing hordes in his rearview.

On day eleven following the trip, Jerry caved in and called Doctor Jenkins, the family sawbones for the past fifteen years. Within that span, Jerry could have counted his office visits on both hands with a few fingers to spare. In fact, in eliminating the

241

occasional flu symptom or prostate check visits, Jerry had met with Doctor Jenkins only once in the past decade, and that had been for a full-blown physical when he'd turned the big-four-oh two years hence.

Doc Jenkins, a rather thin, pale looking man in his mid-fifties to early sixties who always seem to smell of Aqua-Velva aftershave, took a quick look at the welt and nodded knowingly.

"Boil. You eating enough fruit, Jerry?"

"Um..I'll ingest the occasional banana, Doc. If memory serves, I did manage to gnaw on an orange or two last spring."

The Doctor backed away with a distinctly dour expression.

"I take it that means no, Jerry?"

"Well, you know how it is, Doc. I'm in sales...most of my meals are on the run. Can't exactly be stopping to evaluate each morsel on the plate," Jerry replied rather meekly, refusing to meet the doc's searing gaze.

"You might begin to do so more often, Jerry, as these types of staph infections are often clues to a less than satisfactory diet on the patient's part. Is your work environment kept fairly clean?"

"I hose down the old cubicle at least once a week, although I do spend the majority of my day tooling around in the Buick," Jerry said, holding up one hand in a 'Scout's Honor' gesture.

"Good. People's work areas are ideal breeding grounds. Ensure you 'hose down' the Buick every so often as well. "

Leaning down to inspect the boil a final time,

the doctor grunted as he noted the noticeably darker ring encircling it.

"Going to put you on a daily iron supplement, as well as a thousand-milligram Vitamin C regimen. In the meantime, just allow it to run its course. I'll prescribe a topical anti-biotic that you'll need to apply twice daily and cover with gauze. "

Minutes later, as he pulled his tee shirt over his head, Jerry felt the boil throb and burn with unmatched intensity, as if personally objecting to the upcoming treatments.

"Down, boy. Bitch and moan all ya want, but your days are definitely numbered."

***

Three days later, Jerry re-entered Doc Jenkins office in a less upbeat mood, the bags beneath his eyes as pronounced as his slightly slumping posture.

"Damn it, Doc, this thing is keeping me up all night. It's worse than any toothache I've ever had. First it burns like somebody coated it with battery acid, then it throbs like a fresh gash. Can't you milk it or something? I don't care at this point. I just want some quick relief," he grumbled, laying shirtless on his back while the Doctor bent down for a closer inspection.

"It is definitely inflamed, but doesn't yet seem ready to drain despite the burning symptoms. I must say it's larger than most I've seen, and I've seen quite a few. Have you attempted to drain it?" he asked, running a gloved finger atop the mysterious black-shaded perimeter of the boil.

Jerry nodded, his face pinched in discomfort.

"Tried just this morning, Doc. No dice,

243

obviously. Now it's so sensitive, a stout breeze almost doubles me over."

"I take it you wouldn't disapprove of lancing at this point?"

Rolling his eyes comically, Jerry's smile was more of a strained wince.

"By all means, Doctor Jenkins, carve away."

Doctor Jenkins had departed a moment later to retrieve his nurse and the proper instruments for the task, leaving Jerry lying prone with the less-than-soothing sounds of Muzac filling his ears.

When the Doctor returned a full ten minutes later, he had been accompanied by Colonel Travis and two hulking, stone-faced, evidently lower-ranking cronies.

Jerry clearly recalled the look of dazed bewilderment that his family practitioner displayed upon Colonel Travis' insistence that Jerry accompany them to the base.

Thinking back on the moment with a deeper level of intensity, Jerry detected something more in Doc Jenkin's expression. It was the hapless, 'I have no control' look associated with a victim of brutish intimidation, government style.

Doctor Jenkins had wanted to step in to protect his patient's rights, Jerry understood. He had simply been outranked.

***

Just as the humming racket abruptly ceased, Jerry managed to reach up and pull the plugs from his ears, executing an impromptu Houdini-maneuver just to bend his arms. The snippets of conversation he heard only added to the overall enigma

244

enveloping the entire scenario.

"Colonel Sir, the....has arrived to....spect the vessel....full chem suits and...initial reports are......radiation levels are nil....creek area is cordoned off in....eight mile radius...all civilians ordered...remain inside...ty limits."

".....well. Clear images as of yet? ....have to determine...suitable...quarantine isn't enough, Major..." "..other families have been...posed of. How are...to ...explain to...families, Colonel?" "...nal interest is at stake, Maj.....all other consi....expendable at this point." Jerry's mind and pulse raced even as the aching in his chest intensified ten-fold.

Oh my god. It must be some kind of...plague caused by the chemical spill. I heard that bastard Travis say quarantine. More than likely have every town from here to Cedar Creek blocked off. What the hell now? I have to find out about Kayla and Jakey.

The buzzing again commenced, but only in short bursts, once again allowing Jerry to at least partially eavesdrop on the conversation, which seemed to be gaining volume dramatically.

"....incubation period is....clear, Colonel. ...answer from the ...tagon?" "....minate possible infected persons....treme prejudice...vidence of organism..." "...talking about thousands....cents, Colonel. Who...hell taking responsib...inhumane undertaking?"

"....your duty, Major. Clear?"

".....Sir."

"Is Howe....carrier, Major?"

245

"....near the liver and...the lungs. ...absorb into the skin...less than a minute..."

"......you, Major. We'll take...from here. You...more patients to scan."

The cylinder began to unexpectedly roll forward less than thirty seconds later, and Jerry felt his scalp begin to tingle as he gradually emerged into the open.

The two guards that had accompanied him to the base with Colonel Travis were again present, each armed with rifles and wearing black rubber gloves and glass face shields. The Colonel himself centered the two, his arms folded across his broad, heavily decorated chest. The Colonel's forced grin was no longer intact, instead replaced by a stern, tight-lipped sneer that instantly turned Jerry's knees to elastic.

"Come with us, please, Mister Howe. Your treatment awaits."

The techie stepped gingerly forward and handed Jerry an ankle-length white smock, the young man's eyes refusing to meet his own.

"Treatment? Exactly what am I being treated for, Colonel?" he asked, his tone shrill and coated in panic.

"Please heed my instruction, Mr. Howe. We have...many others who require scanning. I'll fill you in once we reach the treatment room."

On an uncontrollable whim, Jerry leaped from the table, waiving his arms madly and yelping aloud. Amid the sudden exertion, his entire chest felt on the verge of eruption.

The reaction within the confined space told him

246

all he needed to know about the seriousness of his 'condition'.

While the Colonel had remained unmoved, his eyes had widened in shocked surprise, his squared jaw dropping open like a cabinet with a shattered hinge.

The armed guards had slung their rifles forward and into firing position in almost perfect unison, their knees slightly bent into a semi-crouch.

The young techie had practically swan-dived behind the scanner; only the heels of his dress black shoes were visible from Jerry's vantage point.

"Pray tell, Colonel, why battle-tested, well-armed warriors such as yourselves could be so easily spooked by an overweight insurance salesman with flat feet and practically no muscle tone," Jerry muttered nervously even as he leaned back against the table like a weary boxer on the verge of collapse.

The Colonel had, amazingly, regained his composure in a matter of seconds. His steely glare was back in place, his overall expression utterly void of even the smallest measure of human emotion.

"Mister Howe, these delays can be costly. Rest assured, you will be filled in on all the pertinent details of your....situation as treatments are instituted." Sweeping his right arm towards the door in a 'lead the way, please' gesture, the Colonel nonetheless backed away an extra step as Jerry strolled cautiously by.

Down a narrow stone hallway that seemed surreally endless, Jerry caught a quick glimpse of the line of humanity awaiting the same test he had just endured. A 'cattle-call', his beloved grandpa used to call such formations. "Jerry my boy, you'll spend roughly half your wakin' life standin' in cattle-calls, and the other half wonderin' why you even bothered," Grand-pappy Howe once said while carefully navigating them through a noontime Fort Worth traffic jam.

Whether an hallucinatory image produced by his overtaxed subconscious or a true vision of stark reality, Jerry could have sworn Kayla and Jake's faces had been among the huddled masses, all of whom were donned in the same ivory-colored, lab-rat smock/sheet covering as his own. It had reminded him of every Nazi Concentration Camp movie he'd ever seen. Lambs to the slaughter without a clue to the grisly fate awaiting them.

"Tell me the truth, Colonel, is it more or less than say....a really nasty case of athletes' foot? Ring worm, perhaps?" Jerry quipped, cupping his hands beneath his armpits to halt their constant shaking.

The Colonel's response was stilted silence as he kept two strides ahead of Jerry, who was being flanked by the armed cronies.

"Tell me everything's gonna be all right, Colonel. Tell me it's nothing serious. Tell me I'll be eating dinner with my family within the warm confines of my own home this very night, Colonel. Tell me the vacation we planned this summer is still on. See, I've always dreamed of seeing the Grand Canyon, Colonel. Tell me that dream can and will still be realized, Colonel."

The small service elevator they crowded into smelled of recently sprayed disinfectant. One of the armed sentries reached around Jerry and pressed a button marked 'UG-RS', then quickly backed away, as if flinching back from a horrible smell.

"Where exactly are we headed, Colonel? Top Secret lab? Am I on the dissection schedule?" Jerry rattled, gently covering the festering bump at his breastbone with his left hand. His breath was becoming increasing labored, despite the lack of physical exertion.

Standing directly in front of the elevator's cold steel double-doors, the Colonel cleared his throat noisily as their descent began.

"Mister Howe, I do believe you've viewed far too many 'X-File' episodes. You are being taken for what folks in the nuclear business refer to as 'a crevice cleansing'. It is a common procedure for those exposed to unsafe levels of radiation or potentially harmful chemical products. Nothing more than a gentle hosing of your body to cleanse the pores. Following that, you will be prescribed a series of antibiotics and anti-inflammatory tablets."

Now reaching inside the smock and massaging the enormous boil with the palms of both hands, Jerry started to reply just as the elevator doors separated and ultra-bright hallway lights flooded the elevator.

Seconds later, a tall, thin man with a long, bushy beard and breath that reeked of peppermint led Jerry to the threshold of a spacious room strangely void of equipment or furniture, although marked outlines of such were embedded into the cold tile flooring. His lab coat swinging about like a bull-fighter's cape, the man placed a gloved hand on Jerry's right shoulder, then glanced wordlessly over at the Colonel. The Colonel nodded solemnly.

"I know this must be difficult, Mister Howe, but try to relax. Myself, along with Doctor Peterson there, will instruct you from outside the room through the speaker system."

Jerry entered the room with a gentle nudging from the taller man, who walked him forward like an orderly assisting a heavily drugged patient.

The Doctor departed without having spoken soon after positioning Jerry at the center of the room, facing a slightly tinted glass window. As the thick metal door closed with a low clicking sound, Jerry felt the burning sensation at his chest not only intensify, but also spread to his upper and lower abdomen. It was as if someone had lit a torch inside his gut and was slowly crawling through and inspecting every inch of his intestine.

"Mister Howe…Jerry, please remove the gown and lay it on the floor next to your feet," the Colonel's voice boomed from overhead.

Jerry pulled the smock free and tossed it aside, his trembling lips suddenly a bright shade of purple.

"C-Colonel, my c-chest and s-stomach are….are really hurting now…I mean…something's r-really wrong, I'm afra-…"

"Calm down, Mister Howe. The cleansing will commence soon. Now, remove your underwear and discard it as well, then do the same with the sandals you're wearing," came a voice utterly alien to Jerry, but one he quickly matched to the Doctor that Travis had mentioned. The tall guy with the fresh breath and the lab cape. 'Doctor Batman', Jerry thought crazily.

250

Just as Jerry bent down to remove his jockeys, the head of the massive boil split as if sliced by a heated scalpel, drenching his naked abdomen and exposed groin in a thick, yellow/crimson coating of pus and blood. Grasping the seeping, hollowed-out wound with both hands as if seized within the clutches of a sudden heart attack, Jerry's eyes grew horrifically wide as he stared through the glass at his observers.

"Wh-what the h-hell is h..happening to me, you s-son of a b-b-bit..?"

As he fell back and rolled roughly onto his left side, Jerry felt the jagged protrusion prick the flesh of his right palm. Shifting onto his back, he lifted his fluid coated palms and peeked at the wound with great caution, squinting like a man staring directly into the noonday sun. The waves of howling, choking laughter that followed were born of pure lunacy; the desperate, animalistic moans of a hopelessly cracked mind.

"The scout hatched earlier than expected, Colonel," the Doctor whispered while scribbling frantically onto a large clipboard, his eyes darting spastically between it and the glass wall.

"Damned things must use telepathy of some kind. Last scout must have warned the others somehow. We may need to....skip the scanning session with the others, Doctor."

"Skip the... y-you mean exterminate a-all of them?" the doctor replied, almost dropping the clipboard near the Colonel's exquisitely shined steel-toed boots.

"It's obvious that anyone who came into contact

251

with that lake water ingested the little shits, doctor. Howe there makes it five for five. Pentagon order arrived a half-hour ago, signed by the Secretary of Defense and endorsed by the President. I have full discretion. I see no reason to endanger National Security at this point. We're dealing with a highly contagious, highly aggressive enemy. I'm going to order the others be immediately sedated and subsequently disposed of. I feel the boils are proof enough of fatal contamination."

Waiving his free arm like a maniacal band conductor, the doctor's tone became desperately shrill.

"Colonel, after decades of waiting for such an occurrence, we finally have the opportunity to study an alien species first hand. How can you possibly order their termination so quickly, so…casually? If we can learn to control the spread of -…"

The Colonel's decidedly callous, unblinking gaze never wavered as he studied the gruesome scenario less than a half-dozen feet away through a foot-thick section of unbreakable glass.

"We have their ship in quarantine, Doctor. A team of seals pulled it from the bottom of Cedar Lake five days ago. Not a single dent was found on the damned thing despite the line of oaks and pines it cut through like a giant axe blade upon descent. Perhaps we'll learn all we need about the species from their vessel of choice. Even the most minute possibility of a plague or hostile takeover cannot be ignored. Not after….well, this morning's incident with the elderly man and his wife."

"What about freezing them? Can't we at

least..." the doctor pleaded before the Colonel cut him off with a raised hand.

"This is neither the place nor time for experimentation. The risk factor is far too high. I will not watch another human die in the manner of that elderly couple this morning, Peterson. Lying to these people concerning their...condition is abominable enough. The scouts are hatching too quickly. They must somehow feel...realize their eventual fate and whatever survival instinct they have is kicking in at warp speed."

Leaning forward, a thick bead of sweat rolling down his jaw as his lips neared the second of two microphones, the Colonel hesitated only momentarily before giving the order.

"This is Travis. Initiate incineration process immediately."

Hanging his head in utter disgust, the doctor groaned aloud.

"My God..I cannot believe we're...doing this."

The Colonel backed away a step, wiping his face with an open palm.

"Somebody has to, Peterson. I want the others medicated and ...disposed of in groups of five. You've got ample video footage of the extractions, correct?"

"I-I suppose. Not sure why we even bothered if none of the species are to be kept alive. Opportunity of a lifetime torched like so many fire-ants..."

Turning on the other man like a predatory animal trapped within the throngs of an unrelenting bloodlust, the colonel's words were nonetheless whispered in a cool, unemotional tone.

"Take a good look, Peterson...,' he said, calmly pointing into the room fronting them, '...you really want to sit through more footage like this? If so, I'd seriously consider checking myself into the nearest psychiatric unit for immediate evaluation."

The doctor slowly raised his head and openly winced just as muted screams penetrated the surrounding walls.

Jerry lay on his back, his hands submerged to the wrist into his own mutilated abdomen, which had been flayed open as if by a swinging pendulum blade.

The black masses poured from his gut like lava from an erupting volcano, dribbling forward onto the tiled floor in massive waves of pumping legs that seemed to march to some unheard cadence. Jerry was pulling out handfuls from his open torso and tossing them aside, a mask of pure agony stretched across his ashen face. Low gurgling noises escaped his lips, then were subsequently choked off as a new batch exited his mouth in thick globs. Jerry began to cough and spit in an attempt to clear his throat from the countless invaders now spewing forth from his grotesquely stretched nostrils and from both ears.

The room's four walls ignited in yellow flame just as Jerry's cranium began to noticeably bulge, his neck bloated to twice its normal size.

He managed a final pathetic cry just as his skull split open at the forehead, the skin peeled back in jagged strips to allow a fist-sized glut of slick blackness to push its way to the fiery surface.

Just seconds before the entire room filled with yellow/blue flame, a single entity leaped onto the glass wall and hung there, causing both the Colonel and Doctor Peterson to leap back in shocked surprise. The Colonel barely refrained from yelping aloud as the doctor's clipboard landed directly between his boots with a loud clap.

It resembled a strange hybrid of two distinctly different earth species, possessing the oily slick torso and limbs of a salamander coupled with the head of a Preying Mantis. It's tiny, whip-like tail stood erect, then began lashing about as the searing heat intensified. It's narrow, tubular neck twisted from side to side as it seemed to study its captors through the glass barrier.

The entity melted away like butter tossed into a bonfire as the whooshing inferno swallowed it whole.

"Call in the cleaners, doctor. Let's get the remainder of this nightmare behind us as quickly as possible, then begin worrying about the possible ramifications," the Colonel said sternly, watching the doctor as he reached to retrieve his dropped clipboard.

"Possib-?" the doctor muttered, leaning up with an expression of pure disgust as he tucked the clipboard underneath his left arm.

"Most will view this as murder, Colonel Travis, plain and simple. Half-a-million hard-earned taxpayer's greenbacks sacrificed to construct a specialized incinerator to be used against their own kind. On the other hand, the scientific community will be up in arms over the shameless slaughter of an extraterrestrial species. Pick your poison, Colonel. We're all in for one hell of a professional and public roast, don't' you agree?"

Leaning towards the other man with his head slightly cocked to one side, Colonel Travis studied the physician like a gallery critic gawking at an especially puzzling display of abstract art.

"You know as well as I, Doctor, that the public at large will never gain knowledge of what we do here today. Fortunately, they will also never realize how close they were to a very probable extinction. May I ask you something, Doctor Peterson?"

The doctor eyed him curiously, then he glanced back into the room ahead to the scattered pile of black ash that had once been a life/house/auto insurance salesman named Jerry Dean Howe.

"Yes, Colonel?"

Stepping back until he was mere inches from the first of the two armed sentries, the Colonel slid his hands behind his back in a 'parade rest' pose.

"Didn't you have physical, that is to say, flesh to flesh contact with the elderly man...uh, Mr. Watts, I believe his name was...when he was first being examined?"

"Well, I...yes. Yes, at the time we didn't realize the species...um, existed, and I performed a series of routine tests to include...,' the doctor swallowed hard, hugging the clipboard to his chest like a protective shield, '...what precisely are you getting at, Colonel?"

Colonel Travis' only response was the slight tilting of his head to the right.

"Colonel, it's been established that only those in contact with the lake water itself were infected. If it were an airborne or similar contaminant, I'm afraid we'd all have to take our turn inside the oven, agreed?"

"Not all, doctor. Just those unfortunate enough to carry the mark," The Colonel replied, his right arm swinging out from behind his back in a blur of dress blue and glittering steel.

The single shot centered the doctor's forehead with a hole the size, width and shape of a quarter. Peterson's head flung back from the sudden impact like a boxer from a hard right hook, then toppled forward as if shoved from the rear. His lifeless body crumpled to the tile, the rear of his skull a mangled puree of bone, flesh and bloodied gray hair.

"Sergeant," the Colonel said flatly while leaning over the doctor's still form. The second of the two sentries stepped cautiously forward and halted only when the Colonel held up the thirty-eight revolver palms-up.

"Holster your weapon and step forward, Sergeant Mills." The Sergeant did so, leaning over until he could clearly visualize what the Colonel was so obviously displaying. "You're my witness, Sergeant Mills. I spotted it when he reached down for the clipboard."

"Sir, what does it mean? I thought they said contamination by the lake water only," the Sergeant asked nervously, just as the other sentry joined them by the doctor's corpse.

"I do believe a re-evaluation is in order, Sergeant. A very...thorough re-evaluation," the Colonel grimly concluded, peering downward at the victim's exposed neck, where the relatively small but clearly defined boil protruded in a mound of irritated redness, its perimeter outlined in an almost perfectly circular ring.

***

It was around midnight of the same evening, while steering his newly purchased Ford Expedition through a series of sharp, hilly curves along the highway leading to his mountainside abode, that Colonel Eugene Travis first noticed the bothersome itch on the outside of his left forearm.

Pulling over onto a short stretch of wide shoulder, the Colonel removed his dress blue jacket and rolled up his shirt to the elbow. The bump itself had hardly begun to swell, but the ring's shadowed outline was horrifically evident, as if it had literally been drawn on with a lead pencil.

After a brief introspection, he calmly pulled back onto the deserted stretch of the two-lane, sighing deeply as he began to increase the vehicle's speed despite the sharp curb that loomed in the distance.

The vehicle ripped effortlessly through the ancient, badly rusted guardrail, its fiery descent soon doused by the crystal clear, cool creek waters that would become its eternal tomb.

***

Weeks later, a local fisherman spotted the Expedition's dented hood floating near a steep clay bank. Eventually able to wrestle the driver's door free after a long struggle, a horrendously bloated body was discovered within the cab. A body donned in tattered Air Force blue. A body ravaged by deep, wide crevices all along the torso and left arm. Crevices that looked to have been blown out from the inside of the dead man's corpse.

Days later, a local fisherman checked into a nearby hospital complaining of an itchy, inflamed bump that simply refused to heal on its own.

***

Corporal Chatty's husky groan accompanies the lights that assault our pupils as the screen fades to static.

"Hmm, Killer bugs. ..ain't i-ro-ny a real pisser?..." he mumbles in full dead pan mode, causing the Sarge to execute a picture perfect spit-take that sends the entire room into uncontrolled hysterics.

"Just what the doc ordered alright. At least that version resembled lizards more than your basic horsefly," the Chief manages to say a moment later while wiping fresh tears from the corners of his eyes.

Private Legs giggled between words, shaking her head as if to loosen cobwebs from the tight ball tied into her hair.

"Once again...the special effects were...unbelievable. The CGI team responsible for these little masterpieces should have won an Oscar."

"No argument there, Legs. Funny though, I still hadn't spotted a single actor in these things who looks even vaguely familiar. I was a pretty decent couch potato in my day. You'd think one of 'em would at least ring a bell," The Sarge replies, still grinning as he continues to observe Chatty's comically blank expression.

Easily dodging Lava's half-hearted attempts to trip me up, I pull the DVD from the player and turn back towards the others with my arms raised as if to silence a group of rowdy spectators.

"Down to the last disk, guys. Shall we indulge or take a break? Chief?"

The Chief pushes himself up from the couch, stifling a yawn.

"I'll go check with Brain Dog on the latest, then we'll crank her up. Anyone else want another bottled water?"

Private Legs raises a hand and begins to reply just as Father Pete sprints into the room at full bore, his face flushed red and his breathing harsh and labored. I saw the Sarge leap to his feet in one fluid movement, transforming from slacker to combat-prepped warrior complete within the single blink of an eye.

"Chief, y-you might want to see this…" Father Pete spat between gasps, already backing through the entrance, his eyes unnaturally wide and horribly bloodshot.

We depart in single file at double-time march, the Chief and Sarge leading the way, just as it was meant to be in times of crisis. I wait for all but Kid Cadet to front me, then lead him along like a protective father with his hand curled within my own.

Brain Dog is hovering over the monitor like a vulture over a fresh kill as we clear the circular hall and near the Com center.

"Dog? What's the…." The Chief begins, then grows instantly silent as Brain Dog backs away and allows us the full view provided by the seventeen-inch black and white screen.

We form a semi-circle around the console, our mouths hanging open like loose shutters. I look away quickly, then refocus on the monitor, as if to dramatically alter what was being transmitted.

"Mother of God....," whispers the Chief through trembling lips.

"Ho-leee shit," mutters Corporal Chatty, blinking rapidly.

"Behold the motherlode, up close and fuckin' personal......," The Sarge practically beams, the warmonger side of him shining through without a hint of shame.

"I-It's...it's...unbelievable...," Airman Legs whimpers, batting her eyelashes at warp speed.

"It..it actually worked...damned if it didn't...work," Lieutenant Lava mutters in an uneven mix of fear and awestruck wonder.

"Bingo," I manage to blurt, my throat suddenly filled with sand and my lips glued to my teeth in a frozen sneer. Unconsciously, I wrap my arms around Lieutenant...Tia's waist and pull her close. Her willingness to back further into my waiting grasp instantly soothes my shattered nerves.

"Lord help us in our t-time of need," Father Pete whispers, and I can barely refrain from replying with a heartfelt 'amen'.

261

Chapter Eleven
Passports To Hell....

It is undeniably the creature we had hoped to seduce into showing itself by first announcing and then continually advertising our very presence within the mountain. It is an entity many within the scientific community had hinted didn't exist at all, while others with similar credentials had stated just the opposite. We as a group had been split on the subject, although all had agreed that an attempt at mass-destruction in regards to our enemy would not be complete without first giving the mythological beast a chance to rear its head within the blast perimeter. Simply put, if such a specimen did exist, the extinction of the Cyclors could not be guaranteed unless it was among those terminated.

Now we knew without a doubt.

The latter group of eggheads had hit the nail on the proverbial head.

That is, unless the surviving members of 'BUG STOMPERS, INC' were experiencing a group hallucination.

It was indeed either the queen, or the Cyclor version of a seven-forty seven.

It's scaly bulk filled the entire monitor, frenzied groupings of Cyclor hanging onto its moistened underbelly like tiny leeches as it gradually circled the mountainside.

"Damned thing is the size of two C-one-thirty's tacked together," The Sarge says, his awestruck grin still pasted firmly in place.

"No tellin' how long or how far it flew to get here. And all just for little ol' us. Don't it make ya feel all warm and queasy inside?"

Father Pete lurches forward, causing The Sarge and Private Brain Dog to flinch back as if dodging live fire.

"But...if there is a queen, why does it...need us as hosts?"

"Speculation was that the queen could only produce a limited amount of offspring, and that the process was agonizingly long. For a full-blown planetary invasion, they needed hosts to speed up a mass buildup. Over time, the queen develops a...a taste for the hosts that's akin to a junkie craving a hot needle," I answer a bit timidly, feeling the group size me up like a history teacher posed at a blank blackboard.

"Like I said, it was pure speculation by some CNN egghead. On the other hand, why would Queen Shit herself show up to sniff us out unless she feels a veritable treasure of useable human flesh awaits?"

Corporal Chatty leans back with his arms crossed and a pained frown painted across his rugged mug.

"Big ol' bitch must think there's a hive full of us stuffed inside this rock. Like an army of fire ants just waiting to be sucked up and slurped down."

I see Airman Legs' eyes leave the monitor for the first time, briefly scanning Chatty from head to toe as if he was the alien species.

"Thanks for the picture, Chat. Dammmmmn, Did you see the pumpkin on that bad boy? Big as a freakin' Volkswagen and spinnin' like a windmill.

Had to be the head, right?" Brain Dog queries, his voice as jittery as his constantly moving hands, which gesture madly even as he awaits an answer.

Airman Legs tone is just the opposite, a mechanical droning that instantly sends a shiver sailing up my spine even as my heart literally skips a beat.

"Who gives a shit about its goddamned head? Did you see the p-pinc-pitcher..t-the fucking claws? Must have been at l-least t-three on each side, beneath the wings...thick as semi-trailers...."

The Chief shoots her a worried look, then quickly turns to Sergeant Rock, who is still in the grip of monitor hypnosis.

"Sergeant, you and Radar get down to the armory and retrieve the BJ-Launchers," he says as calmly as if he'd just ordered steak and 'taters from a local pub, then whirls about and grasps Private Legs firmly on each of her badly trembling shoulders.

"All but Lieutenant Lava need to don headgear and vests pronto, then meet at the conference room for weapons handout. Clocks ticking down to the two-minute warning we've prepped nine months for, people. You all know the drill. We're gonna do this, by God, and we're gonna do it up right,' he continues, his steely eyes never wavering from Leg's own until he visualizes her snap-to with a series of rapid blinks, '..Lava, take Kid Cadet and boogie on down to the holding area near the e-pods. I'll have your gear brought down. Otherwise, just sit tight and await further instructions."

Taking a final glance at the majestic behemoth

that was presently swirling just a few hundred feet above our heads, I begin to feel my initial fear ebb, mutating into a familiar burning that radiates within my chest and at the back of my skull. Like twin injections of adrenaline, the rush fills my senses and overwhelms all that came before. After nine months of inactivity, I find it is truly like swimming or making love. It does indeed come back to you.

I chase after Sergeant Rock with sprinter speed, almost passing him within the narrow hallway as our shoulders line up like pistons churning perfectly in sync.

We load the metal cart without speaking, packing its inverted shelves with enough 'bug juice' launchers, 'Raid Balloons' and what the Sarge dubbed 'PP's', or 'Pesticide Pistols' to terminate a small army of the little bastards. Problem is, and it's a topic that remains mercifully silent between us, is that it isn't just a small army we're about to face down. It's a damned large one, with a fifty-ton monstrosity roughly the size of Oklahoma leading the charge. Time and experience had taught us a hard lesson concerning the Cyclors weaknesses in regards to commercial insect poisons. It literally took gallons of the home-garden variety to make even one of the little bastards sneeze. Only the strongest manufactured, the industrial brew, had the immediate, lethal effect we desired. A Terminex warehouse on the outskirts of Dallas had provided us the brew, while a Super Toys-R-Us outside El Paso had provided the accompanying weaponry. Before entering the 'Hives' stony confines, we had found ample opportunity to test our newly assembled arsenal in real-world drills, including aforementioned 'shit-storm' battle just outside Las Cruces.

The Sarge and Brain Dog had taken various 'Super Soaker' water-rifles and pistols, some of which already had firing distance capability of one-hundred feet or more, and hopped them up with air-pumps and tubular wiring until they would pin down and disintegrate a 'Clor' at a range of up to two-hundred feet.

"Shit it and get it, Radar. We got enough PP's?" The Sarge finally asks, his face coating in thick beads of sweat as he scans the cart.

"One for each hand the group owns, Sarge. You got the piss bombs?"

The Sarge paused, placed his hands on his sides and sighed.

"Damn. Almost forget 'em. They're in cold storage."

He glared at me gravely, and we nodded in unison.

"I'll grab 'em, Sarge."

"Cradle 'em like Nitroglycerin, Radar. I'll meet ya at the C room."

"Check. See you in a few."

The Sarge looks over at me and winks, then reaches over and claps my shoulder.

"Time to stomp some bugs, pal. Time to stomp a shit-load of 'em."

Although I can't personally visualize it, I realize my grin must be a hideous site to behold.

"Big time, Sarge."

It takes me less than a minute to dash down the

corridor and retrieve the two metal cylinders from cold storage. Funny as the notion had been six months ago, the element of humor had long since vanished. Collecting pee samples to fill two gallon-sized metallic test tubes for the purpose of drawing the Cyclor Queen into the elevator shaft had seemed a bit ludicrous upon its inception. All save the idea's originator, that being the Chief, had secretly snickered, mostly due to the fact that none of us actually believed a queen even existed. The Chief deduced that such a beast would be drawn to bodily fluids, especially those produced by the host's kidneys, and would follow such a pungent scent into the bowels of hell if necessary, to feed upon its source. Now that the shit was officially going down, who the hell were the rest of us to argue such a point?

As I jog back up the corridor, the coolness of the cylinders pressed snugly against my chest, the echoes of a familiar voice suddenly slows my progress.

I halt just outside the entrance to the rec room, eventually drawn inside as the voice beckons.

The cylinders drop to my sides, one for each gloved hand, as I step inside the darkened room and the screen's dim imagery entrances me.

Someone once said that reality is a state of mind. I had never understood such a statement, not completely anyway, until the moment when I witnessed the fate of my very own soul being played out upon a large screen TV like some grainy black and white documentary.

The final of the mystery DVD's plays to a

startled, shell-shocked audience of one. The image is bathed in darkness, but ultimately reveals a battered, bloodied version of myself, clothes torn and shredded as I seem to be bleeding from a thousand wounds simultaneously. Wiping blood-crusted eyes with bare forearms that look to have been peeled with a straight razor, I glare upward from the shadowy abyss and scream out in obvious desperation. Not surprisingly, it is Tia's name I bellow, my voice cracking not from fear but from heartfelt sadness. A sadness born from losing the one person in your life you cannot fathom living without.

Just before the ringing echoes of someone calling my name reverberate within the Hive's cool stone hallways, I see a flittering shadow obliterate the scant circle of light that had revealed my video alter ego. The muffled cry that followed was one I would have never identified as my own; one I would have never thought myself capable of creating. For it was the pathetic groan of a lost soul drowning in an ocean of self-pity.

Someone…thing had taken me, and I had been only too willing to allow the fatal abduction.

I have to perform an impromptu break-dance to keep from dropping both cylinders. Once I do manage to regain control, I look up to see not only the TV blank and powerless, but the DVD player's power button also unlit with the disk itself still ejected.

The Sarge yells my name every few seconds, his tone more irritated with each refrain. Leaping from the rec room like a tailback breaking through a narrow hole in the defensive line, I don't even attempt to dwell on the nightmarish dreamscape just departed. The message it attempted to convey is far too horrifying to contemplate, even in the face of a certain death I now willingly sprint towards.

I make the final turn to see Private Legs standing outside the conference room, vest and helmet in place, diligently checking the fluid level of her Super-Soaker rifle. What the Chief refers to as our 'cyanide pills' hangs from their utility belts; small fragment grenades to utilize in lieu of becoming a 'Clor host in case of capture before the final explosion turns the Hive to rubble. I scoot past them into the room, where Brain Dog, The Sarge, and the Chief are huddled in front of the electronic board that displays a digital blue print of the Hive's inner workings. I scan the room only momentarily, then remember that Tia has taken up position at the e-pods with Kid Cadet. My heart instantly sinks in her absence, a gnawing loneliness that turns my knee joints to mush as I reach over to place the cylinders atop the room's lone oak table.

"Damn son, you stop for coffee and a donut?" The Sarge jokingly scolds me, turning around with his finger still pointing at the digital board, "Piss bombs intact?"

"The yellow juice of enticement is locked and loaded, Sarge."

The Chief and Brain Dog also turn to give the gray-colored cylinders a quick inspection, then look back to the white-light outline of the Hive's inner perimeter just as Legs joins me as an enthralled spectator.

"Where's Chatty and the Father?" I ask Legs in a much calmer tone than I thought myself capable.

Her haunted eyes lock on my own, and I can almost visualize the reaper's reflection within the slightly dilated pupils, his crimson-stained blade poised to strike me down.

"On monitor. Sarge took them gear already."

Even with gripping the P-Rifle in a veritable death grip, the shaking of her hands and arms is painfully obvious.

"You okay?" I ask a bit more sternly than intended, reaching behind her for a vest and helmet of my own.

"Peachy keen, Radar, and yourself?" Legs responds with a tight smile, just a hint of her normally sassiness intact.

"What can I say? A trained killer preparing to do what he does best."

The Sarge shushes us, but not before we trade nervous but genuinely sincere grins. The last such unspoken communication Airman Legs and I will ever share.

Moments before the Chief whirls about to begin the mission briefing, I realize how utterly hollow I feel without Tia standing near. I grab a soaker rifle and sling it over one shoulder while holstering a pistol. Strapping the fragment grenade to my belt, I notice the slight tremor of my fingers.

The Chief clears his throat to speak just as I finish piling Tia's gear together. The Sarge walks to the back of the room to radio Chatty on his walkie-talkie.

"Listen up, people. Radar, take Lava her gear

once I'm done here, then haul ass back to the point, got it?"

Feeling relief flush over me in warm, gentle waves, I nod without revealing a clue to my inner joy at the announcement. My admiration for the Chief has increased two-fold by this simple act of self-less generosity. The man isn't stupid. Somehow, he knows my true feelings regarding Tia, despite my never having revealed them to anyone inside the group.

"Two-minute warning's down to approximately thirty seconds. First up, Brain Dog is going to rig the Pee Bombs inside the entrance elevator. They'll be set to go off just moments before the main explosion. Once the chain of K-three's are ignited, the mountaintop is gonna peel off like the tip of an apple, opening up the elevator shaft like a beer tab. The shaft is thirty feet in diameter and just over four miles deep to our location. Corporal Chatty, the Father and Private Radar will form the first line of defense while the rest of us retreat and I remote control the pods to whatever safe-haven awaits. Once the elevator doors collapse under the bastard's weight, Chatty, Pete and Radar will fall back and join Airman Legs and the Sarge at barricade one near the conference room. Stout as it is, the iron paneling won't hold 'em more than a few minutes at best. Once they crease it, everyone will fall back and join Brain Dog and myself in the detonation room. By that time, the Hive outta be packed with bugs. Hopefully, big Mama will be crammed in amongst the masses or at least within blast range. Speaking of which…," the Chief raised a finger and

271

paused, looking over at the Sarge, who had just lowered his walkie-talkie.

"Chatty says the Queen is still hoverin', but that her glidin' speed has slowed dramatically. Ya think the big bitch is gonna try and land?"

The Chief faces front and shrugs.

"Doubt it. Be like a commercial airline trying to sit down on top of a basketball. Wish it was gonna be that easy. All right, where was I?"

"Team huddles inside the detonation room," I answer, and hear Legs grunt an acknowledgement beside me. The conference room reeks with levels of apprehension and fear I never realized could exist within such a small band of individuals. The details of the pact we made all those months ago is like the faded remnants of a long-forgotten dream. Made up of three simple but distinct points, it was created and agreed upon unanimously by a group of individuals gripped in a steel vice of deep depression and mental fatigue. A rag tag group of wasteland warriors whose will to carry on 'the good fight' had ebbed to its lowest possible level following a hellish road trip that had hopelessly decimated their shrinking ranks.

The pact was, as follows:

Point One: Take out as many of the enemy as possible in one fell swoop, hence the explosives set to open the Hive's rocky tip like a scalpel through soft tissue.

Point Two: Being as the Hive contains a single escape route, a two person pod constructed to transport its VIP inhabitants (Wing Commanders, visiting Senators, etc.) to a mysterious 'safe zone' in case of conventional or nuclear attack, Point One

272

would obviously serve as a 'suicide mission' to the majority of the team. Understood and duly agreed upon, as was the two team members chosen to carry on the legacy of the human race by entering said pods upon Point One's initiation.

Point Three: Lieutenant Lava would accompany Kid Cadet inside the pods. Lava being a bit younger than Airman Legs, it was only logical. Kid Cadet would be Adam to her Eve once he came of age. Earth Two would then commence with the eventual siring of their offspring.

So there it was in a nutshell. A cut and dry package for all involved. The pact had been made law two weeks after we had entered the Hive's cold embrace, when hopes for a future filled with images other than those consisting of starvation, dehydration and constant bug attacks teetered somewhere between slim and none. Nine months later and facing the law's activation, however, no one could blame us for having reservations, albeit silent ones.

I myself would willingly cut off my own foot to take Kid Cadet's place in the second pod. The pure hatred I feel for that boy does shame me somewhat, but it doesn't alter the cold-hard fact.

Private Brain Dog, Corporal Chatty, and Airman Legs, if asked under the effects of sodium pentothal, would state a similar case for themselves, I'm certain. Father Pete is, I'm sure, scared shitless as well, but in his particular case I'm unsure as to whether it would alter the ultimate sacrifice we all agreed to make.

Difference between me and the others is simply

this: It's not solely my own hide I wish to save. I love Tia, and would be willing to spend the next forty years living inside a tin can swarming with 'Clors as long as we shared the experience together.

Flat lot of good such self-inflicted pain is doing me now. Time to play the good soldier a final time. Curtain's coming down on this apocalyptic stage play, once and for all, it seems. In many ways, I understand this is long overdue, but that doesn't make it any easier. As Father Pete has preached many times in the past year and a half, there's a reason a handful of misfits such as BUG STOMPERS, INC. were allowed to tool around the country in a bus while the rest of the Planet was systematically consumed like canned meat from a grocery shelf. We were meant to accomplish something special in regards to the abomination that had done the damage. We were drawn to the Hive to perish, for certain, but also to punch the restart button on a planet that had been begging for a drastic makeover for decades if not centuries. It was the Alamo played out on a dramatically larger scale, with the Chief in the role of Colonel Travis, Sergeant Rock stepping in the boots of Davy Crockett, and yours truly playing the part of Jim Bowie. General Santa Ana, AKA the Cyclor Queen, had his/her troops at the cusp of certain victory, but it would not be without a steep price to pay....we hoped.

Alas, as the time fast approaches that we greet, unwillingly or not, our own mortality, I have to believe that Father Pete has a very valid point all the way around. Just wish there was an ark we could construct and sail away in before the carnage begins.

"Once we close off the detonation room, we wait for as long as the seal holds before Brain Dog pushes the plunger, so to speak. Now..." the Chief broke eye contact with us and stares downward at his meticulously shinned combat boots.

"...understand that the Hive's self-destruct mechanism isn't guaranteed to ignite at this point. Brain Dog assures me it will, and that the code he downloaded from the mainframe will indeed ignite the caps and blow this mother a mile high.." the Chief pauses as Brain Dog takes a slight bow, '..just as he assures me that the pod's release code can and will be operated through the small remote he practically super-glued together a few months back. Let's just...hope and pray that Private McGiver here is correct on both counts. If not...well, there's a reason those nut shakers are attached to your utility belts, people. Do not hesitate to pull the pin if capture is the only other option. Is everyone geared up?"

"We're stoked beyond reasonable sanity, boss," The Sarge barks, bouncing a fist off his vest in dramatic fashion while carefully eyeballing the rest of us. We nod in unison, our motions unnaturally mechanical. I can feel the adrenaline pumping in my chest and the raw, electric tingling at my groin.

"Radar, transport the gear to Tia and the Kid. Tell 'em the rest of BUG STOMPERS, INC. wish 'em the best in whatever future lays ahead," the Chief whispers, his voice cracking with an emotional tint I had never before seen displayed.

"I'll do it, Chief," I manage, reaching for the

275

gear just to avoid openly balling aloud.

"Let's move, troops. Chatty and the Priest are probably feeling a bit lonely right about now," he concludes while jogging from the room with Legs and Brain Dog hot on his heels.

Sergeant Rock pauses at the room entrance and turns to me, the barrel of his Super-Soaker banging hard against the side of his helmet, the words 'BUG KILLER' scribbled across the center with a black Sharpie.

"I know it's a temptation, Barry, but don't procrastinate back there. We need ya, you little jackass. Tell Tia and the kid we loved 'em, okay?"

"You got it, Sarge," I reply, this time unable to completely halt the barely audible sob that escapes the back of my throat.

Never one to be overly sentimental, the Sarge steps over and wraps his anaconda-sized arms around my shoulders. I barely manage to hang onto Tia's gear as he gives me a brief, intense squeeze.

"Just in case I don't get a chance to say so once the bug feces slams the fan, Radar, you're a damned good Joe."

"Same to you, ya big palooka," I croak, playfully head-butting him just as he breaks away and proceeds to rumble down the hall like a wild bull.

Racing down the opposite side towards the e-pods, I hardly feel my boots making contact with the smooth concrete below. Funny how sublimely free one feels as the reaper's grip takes hold. Funny in the most ironically tragic of ways.

As I round the final curve leading to the e-pod's, Tia is crouched down in a blocking stance with Kid Cadet peeking around her left side.

"Radar's Rent-A-Squirt-Gun calling. Good credit, bad credit, no credit, no freakin' problem."

Tia snatches the rifle and hooks it around her shoulder, then hands a pistol to the Kid before holstering one for herself, all the while doing her best to avoid eye contact.

"What's the word? We in full-blown shit-kicker mode or what?" she finally says through lips so tightly pursed they could have been literally sewn together.

"Looks like. Queen's still circling, but at a slower pace. Brain Dog is rigging up the Pee-Bombs and explosives as we speak. You two ready for blast off?"

If I had the power to rewind my tongue, I'd have done so. As it was, my fumbling apology for such an utterly crappy choice of words never materializes. Tia leaps up and into my arms, pinning my shoulders in a vice as her face burrows into my neck. The perfumy scent of her hair instantly intoxicates, and I take the opportunity to softly kiss the top of her head.

"This shit isn't right, Barry, you k-know? Just…not right," she whimpers, her words muffled as her lips press into my upper chest. For the first time in over eighteen months, I witness a Chink in her emotional armor. Months ago I had accepted that her 'tough-as-nails but still decidedly feminine' act was more the rule than the exception. Everyone within the group has their way to cope; a 'performance' mood that keeps the midnight crazies

277

away. My own is to clam up and hunker down within my own muted mindset until the swirling clouds of insanity at least partially dissipate. I had seriously thought that Tia, our Lieutenant Lava with her quick-fire temper and take-no-prisoners persona, hadn't possessed the mentality to break down in front of others, no matter how dire the situation. We had shared many battlegrounds together, standing back to back and side by side within a veritable funnel cloud of mayhem. We had simultaneously witnessed countless abductions and deaths within the ranks. We had shared both body and mind to relieve the stress of simply surviving in a world turned upside down by an enemy that seemed infinite in both numbers and relentlessness. But until now, Tia had never truly revealed all of herself to me. It only made my yearning to hold and protect her even stronger.

"It never was, Tia," I reply, pushing her forward so that I might stare into those luminescent, sparkling brown eyes.

"On the other hand, if not for those goddamned overgrown pests, I never would have met you or got to know you," I feel the hitch in my throat and fight to control the whining sob that threatens to accompany it. Never was much of a crier, at least not that I can recall. Made of sterner stuff, as they say. Stoic macho man of action, that's me. At least, it was until the last half-hour, when the spirit of Richard Simmons began taking over my soul.

"Or love you."

A single tear races down her left cheek, and I gently wipe it away and then gently kiss the same spot.

"Hell, I almost want to say I owe the bastards one."

Tia hikes onto her tiptoes and kisses my lips, then the stubble on my chin. She backs away and clears the moistness from the edges of her beautifully slanted eyes.

"Ditto," she replies with a sniff. With that single word response, all else can now remain comfortably unspoken between us.

Kid Cadet leans against the e-pod's open panel, restlessly shuffling his feet from side to side.

"Take care of my girl, Kid. You hear?"

He glares up at me, this embattled child who has experienced enough death and destruction for a thousand lifetimes and nods shyly, then smiles and displays a double 'thumbs up' gesture.

"We'll take care of each other, Private Radar," he says matter-of-factly, and I can't help but admire the courage, no matter how manufactured. Haven't met many adults outside the STOMPERS with half the testicular fortitude this kid seems to own.

I lean down and kiss Tia a final time, taking in the whole of her scent, the softness of her lips and the moistness of her tongue.

"We'll meet again...in a better place," I whisper, then whirl around and sprint down the hall as fast as my trembling legs will allow, diligently fighting the urge to turn back around for a final visual.

I get approximately halfway from the e-pods to the control room, covering the hundred yard distance until I'm just passing the rec room, when two sharp, distinct sounds ring out, and my feet react as if suddenly submerged in quicksand.

The first is a slow, steady rumbling one might associate with an earthquake or heavy ground shift. I look down to see a narrow crack form in the concrete beneath my boots, spreading up the hall like a spider's web. Leaning against the nearest wall, I crouch and brace my legs just as the shrieking echoes of metal being ripped and torn asunder fill the hall.

"They…they've already blown the mountain?" I babble to myself, unconsciously pulling a pistol free from my holster while flipping the rifle forward onto the opposite shoulder.

I suck in a deep breath and rise as the rumblings finally cease, then barrel forward into the next curve.

The screams come next, intertwined with piercing shrieks that aren't remotely human.

I think of Tia's caress, then of the unbreakable bond that ties me to these people for the duration of whatever afterlife awaits.

I willingly dive into the fray, twin barrels gushing forth streams of bug-flesh-eating poisons as the walls turn a dark shade of crimson around me.

***

Leaning forward until the tip of his brown-checkered tie rests atop the clipboard at his lap, the man cocks an eyebrow inquisitively. Sitting a few feet away, his black dress shoes hanging loosely from the gurney he sets upon, the younger of the two men blinks rapidly while awaiting a response. "Please continue, Mr. Rhodes. How does…did this conclude? Or, can you recall the details?"

The younger man wipes a hand through his

close-cropped hair and sighs in apparent frustration, then reaches up and rubs his prominent nose with the palm of one hand.

"I've noticed your not scribbling on the pad anymore, Doctor. You're not losing interest, are you? I mean, I sincerely hope I'm not boring you here."

"Not at all, Mr. Rhodes. Do not misconstrue my inactivity with the ballpoint as disinterest. It is not an essential tool, simply a visual aid to refresh my memory on specific details I wish to expound on later. Proceed, please..."

Caressing his rail thin arms as if chilled, Stephen Rhodes glanced nervously at the wall-clock positioned directly behind and over the doctor's head. He noted, for no particular reason, that it read 10:18 AM.

"Yeah, I better wrap this up before the details you wish to hear begin to fade away. They always do, you know. They're clear as crystal in short bursts, then begin to dissipate like nightmares at mid-morning."

"Vivid at the outset, then unfocused and bleared, is that correct?" the Doctor asked, leaning back until his head rests on the stucco wall, a coif of hair bent airborne like an insect's probing feeler.

"Do me a favor and don't go there. They're not dreams, doc. Don't you think I'd know the difference after all this time?" Rhodes replied with a deep frown, scratching his chin vigorously as his eyes darted about the room like a man checking the airspace for impending attack.

"My apologies, Mr. Rhodes. Go ahead..."

281

"Well, to say things didn't quite work out as planned is quite the understatement, doc...at least, it sure seemed so..." Rhodes said, his arms hanging limp with the hands resting between his thighs. His eyes no longer twitched or scanned about in obvious apprehension, but seemed dull and glazed over, as if he had fallen into a deep trance.

Enthralled despite the apparent certainty of the patient's delusional state, the doctor nodded while listening, then flipped to a fresh page on the clipboard and began to scribble.

"...seems that by the time The Sarge got up to the control room, the Chief had instructed Private Brain Dog to blow the mountain. A few minutes before while watching the monitor, Corporal Chatty had seen the queen come in for a landing at the tip, and the Chief figured it might be the only opportunity we'd have to blow her away. By the time I turned the corner and did a combat roll into the control room, The Chief, Sergeant Rock, Brain Dog and Private Legs were hauling butt in the other direction. If I hadn't done the roll, The Sarge probably would have clothes-lined me rounding the corner. You see, Doc, the Queen wasn't the giant, floating imbecile we had assumed she was. Once the mountaintop did sheer away and open up the elevator shaft, as planned, neither she nor her swarms of Cyclor storm troopers flew into the gap. No, she had a handpicked crew of specialists chosen for just such a mission, especially trained and apparently bred for just such a task. Sentry scouts, if you will.

The Sarge had said they were three times the

size of a normal 'Clor, and had cut through the sealed shaft door, which was at least three inches thick and constructed of Titanium, like an axe blade through a vat of warm pudding.

Corporal Chatty and Father Pete had apparently engaged the first of them as it bore through and dove into the control room. I never got the gist of what exactly happened, but the spatters of fresh blood that coated my three comrades as we sprinted down that hall told me all I really wanted to know. As Brain Dog sprinted ahead to the detonation room, the rest of us pulled the metallic barrier into place at what had been labeled 'barricade number two.' I couldn't help but ponder why we even bothered once I got my first clear look at the sentry 'Clors. Ugly bastards sailed down the hallway like black gliders. Although their wingspan was hard to determine within the narrow hall space, their legs were twice the length and thickness of a normal Cyclor, and their pinchers looked like mutated paper-cutters.

We pulled the barrier in place just as they nailed it full-force. Private Legs had been on my left when the impact sent me flying forward in a rolling heap, my forearms nailing the Chief in the back of the knees just as The Sarge elbowed me between the shoulder blades and we toppled over like a house of camouflaged cards. I recall flipping over with my lungs burning from a sudden lack of oxygen, trying like hell to focus one of my pest-pistols on the thing as it tore through the barricade. It was already shoving its way through a gap with one pincher flexing while the other had Private Legs pinned to the inside of the metal wall like a lab specimen. The tip of its pincher had penetrated the two-inch thick slab upon initial contact, ripping into Leg's upper back and completely through her chest. The Sarge practically stepped onto and over me, firing his Super-Soaker from one side and a pesticide pistol from the other, soaking the thing's spiked head as it struggled to clear the widening gap. I....c-couldn't. Damn it. Try as I might, I couldn't take...my eyes off Leg's as she...swung back and forth like a goddamned wind chime from the thing's.... blood coating her chin...one of her eyes still propped open even though she was..l-long g-gone....that damned bug had speared her like a...like a...gutted f-fish."

Rhodes paused, raising a badly shaking hand and pressing it to the gaunt, pasty-white flesh of his face.

The doctor glanced up from the pad and peered over the thin wire-rim glasses adorning his slightly bulbous nose. The look of disgust he displayed instantly vanished upon the patient's sudden glance in his direction, replaced by a look of deep concern that was nothing short of frighteningly sincere.

"Take your time, Mr. Rhodes. Deep breaths might help. If you need to take a break..."

Staring up into the fluorescent lights above, Rhodes sucked in a lengthy, labored breath.

"No, dammit. I need...have to finish this now. I'm already forgetting details of why we chose to corner ourselves in that stone tomb in the first place. Faces are getting fuzzy, starting to fade."

The doctor retrieved his pen and repositioned the pad on his lap, then nodded without speaking further. Before resuming, Rhodes again noticed the wall-clock, which now read 9:46 AM. Feeling a bit perplexed, he closed his eyes and then reopened them several times, then gave the clock another glance. 10:26 AM. Breathing a bit easier, he swallowed several times before speaking, his voice noticeably horse.

"The second of the sentries had bent back a large chunk from one side of the barricade just as the Chief had stepped up and joined the Sarge in soaking the first. I was finally able to suck in some air and stand, and was stepping forward with my pest-revolver aimed at sentry number two when the Sarge reared back an arm and yelled at me to retreat back. As I lurched back a few feet, I understood the order. The first sentry was mere seconds from breaking through, and had shaken off the pesticide bombardment like water from a duck's back. The stuff we had in those soakers would have melted the scaly flesh off a regular 'Clor like battery acid poured onto raw meat. Obviously, we weren't dealing with the norm on many levels. I backed away, unable to turn my back on the carnage as the sentries broke free.

I watched the Chief, a man I had grown to admire and respect at a level that my own father had never reached, stand his ground as the first sentry sailed forward like a scaly black bullet and tore him literally in half at the waist. I s-swear to you, Doctor. I swear on any stack of bibles you want to lay beneath my hands that I watched that man unhinged...t-tore...torn in half like a fucking rag doll, a-and...he still...s-still was barking out orders. Lying there coated in...in gallons of his own blood, his..h-his legs still standing upright while hi...his lower half laid a dozen feet away, the halves tied...hung together by a string of in-intes...of gut. Yelling at the Sarge to get...to get me out of there and have Brain Dog light the place up. I mean, we were all gonna die, right? Did it matter if I died right there or in a goddamned explosion that was going to level a sixty-mile radius? Well, it obviously did matter to the Chief, Doctor. The man never stopped protecting his troops, e-even when he was a single breath away from death.

Next thing I recall, Sergeant Rock is catching up to me in three or four long strides and practically carrying me towards the detonation room. I tell you, Doc, that man was as bulky as a tank and twice as stout, but it was his sheer speed that always caught me off guard. We had a good twenty-five to thirty yard distance to cover, and be damned if that big bastard didn't outrun those overgrown roaches to the d-room.

Brain dog was standing at the entrance, a double-barreled Super-Soaker propped on his left shoulder. He and the Sarge had taped two of the large rifles together, and from a distance it looked like a WWII bazooka.

The Sarge raced past Brain Dog and tossed me inside. He then reached back and wrestled Brain Dog in as well, all the while trying to explain to Dog that their 'secret weapon' would be of little use. Regardless, Dog dragged the P-Bazooka inside with him, then the three of us pulled barricade number three into place. Originally we had figured to delay the final explosion by at least ten to fifteen minutes by utilizing the thickest of the three metallic doors at our disposal, a four inch thick wall of titanium that weighed in excess of two tons, and that had taken a full month to put into place with rigged pulleys and thick electrical wiring.

Even as the mammoth wall slid into place, overlapping the entrance by a foot on each side and by two at the top, The Sarge and I understood that we were buying ourselves two to three minutes at best. Besides, the original plan of cramming as many 'Clors and hopefully big bad mama herself into the Hive before shoving the plunger had already gone haplessly array once the sentries had crashed the party.

Brain Dog was trying desperately to grill the Sarge on what happened to the rest of the crew as we congregated at the center of what The Chief had originally called the 'Boom Boom Room'. Things begin to get decidedly..hazy from there, more than likely my subconscious pressing the automatic 'delete images' switch. Unfortunately, not all were."

Peering up from the pad, the doctor paused before stiffly rising to his feet, his knees popping sharply. He reached over and gently placed a hand on the patient's badly slumping shoulder.

"We can break for a while if this is becoming too difficult for you, Mr. Rhodes. We have coffee in the outer office if you'd..."

"Haven't you been listening to me, doctor?" Rhodes screamed, his horribly bloodshot eyes filled with fresh tears.

"It's now or never. Details are being purged

from my mind as we speak. I have to exorcise these demons while I'm still able!"

The doctor backed away with a sympathetic nod, then leaned against a nearby filing cabinet with pad and pen back in hand.

Whether consciously or by recent habit, Rhodes once again caught a quick glimpse of the wall clock now hanging to the doctor's left. Strangely, it read 10:06 AM. The small examination room seemed suddenly far too warm, as humid as a Florida beach after a summer cloud burst. Rhodes tugged at the collar of his moistened T-shirt, swallowed several times to clear his parched throat, and resumed.

"The clock there is going spastic, Doc," he felt obligated to mention, pointing at the wall ornament with a shaky finger.

"No matter. Time is of very little consequence here, Rhodes. Please, back to the subject at hand," he heard the doctor mutter as he continued to concentrate on the long-sheeted writing pad sitting atop his lap like a TV tray.

"Uh, yeah…right,' Rhodes replied, for the first time noticing the black tint of the older man's jagged, obviously well-chewed fingernails.

Must be the lighting. Just like that damned clock.

"Like I said, things get a bit..fuzzy from here. The barricade I had thought might last a minute or two had been somewhat overrated. The Sarge and I soaked the entrance with bug-juice while Brain Dog coded in the Hive's self-destruct sequence. I recall Brain Dog screaming the same three words at least a half- dozen times as the sentries sliced and shoved their way in. H-he kept saying "blow, motherfucker, blow" over and over, his tone growing more hysterical with each refrain. The Sarge had pulled a nine-millimeter Glock from his utility belt, along with a machete, all the while inquiring to Brain Dog as to exactly why the Hive hadn't yet blown sky high. I recall their frantic bantering back and forth, although the conversation's contents escape me. Something along the lines of "Brain Dog, you might wanna blow this fucker up now!" by the Sarge, and a "goddamned code is for shit, man! It ain't like I could have tested it before hand!" reply from Brain Dog. I'm..uh, p-pretty sure I wet my pants at that point.

Like a small child shivering in a dark, cold place, knowing he is mere seconds from experiencing something really, really unpleasant.

I can still see the Sarge bounding by me just as the first Sentry tore through and wriggled its way inside. He must have fired six shots from the Glock directly into that thing's armor-plated noggin and it didn't even slow its forward progress. I must have been backing away by then, 'cause the image of the Sarge kept getting smaller. Big, brave SOB let out a rebel yell that still rings in my ears on certain nights, then bolted forward towards the sentry, swinging that machete with both arms like a power hitter under a hanging curveball. For a moment, a split-second at best; the single blink of an eye, I seem to recall my chest swelling with hope as the sentry actually fell back from the onslaught. The Sarge had chopped a large chunk from the thing's longest feeler, and had dug a sizeable crevice in its chest before it…it pinchers ended all arguments about our chances for temporary survival. The first had swung at a downward arc, while the…second hooked upwards.

I saw a d-dog ran over by a semi when I was a kid. Least, I think I did. Maybe it was just a nightmare. Took my dad and older brother an hour to scrape the remains from the highway. Ended up burying a sixty-pound dog in a goddamned shoebox, doc. Still, my old blue-tick hound looked positively healthy and intact compared to the Sarge once those damned baseball-bat sized fishhooks got through with him. I saw his top half sail into one wall while his lower flipped into the air boots first, spewing blood in a wide circle like an unmanned fire hose. Do you realize how unbelievably strong they h-had to have been to cut a man down the size and strength of Ken McKay? Chopped that muscular SOB down like it was snapping a brittle twig? It truly boggles the mind, Doc. B-boggled the living hell out of mine, anyhow. At…at least the Sarge…did go quickly. I only hoped my own demise would be as swift.

The second sentry entered soon after, followed by a thick grouping of regular-sized 'Clors. I guess by then the sentries had sent a telepathic signal to big mama that all was clear, so possibly a small team was sent in on a 'capture and detain' mission in lieu of the sentries 'assassinate with extreme prejudice' tactics.

I had…backed into a far corner, still firing away with the Soakers as the bastards closed in on me. The regular 'Clors fell back on contact, but I was fast running out of fluid in both revolvers, and had the rifle which had long since dried up.

My mind began to go numb then, I believe, and I had gone mercifully deaf while watching Brain Dog kick and punch his way through a mass of them, that is until one of the sentries reached him. Brain Dog was yelling and cursing to beat the band while executing a series of finely-tuned side and front kicks on the big buzzing bastard, this I only know by reading his lips.Bruce Lee Vs. the Fly, I recall thinking crazily. Hell, maybe I even said it aloud. My, uh,.. sanity had to have been hanging on by the proverbial hang-nail about that time.

The thing then wrapped its pinchers and lower appendages around him in a caress that, at least from a distance, looked anything but deadly. It seemed almost….parental, at least until the thing began to squeeze and convulse, popping Brain Dog open like a squashed grape and tossing the pulped remains about the room like pet-food scraps.

I think I threw my revolvers at the little shits once the fluid ran dry, maybe even tossed a few straight jabs and left hooks of my own once they closed in with their velcro-like grips and pinned me beneath their scaly bulk. The smell of pesticide was damned near overwhelming, since most of the ones mugging me were soaked in it.

The next….t-thing….I..," Rhodes hesitated, his complexion chalky-white as his mouth hung agape with a single droplet of drool pooling at each corner. Steady, old man, steady. Almost there.

"...t-they took me. F-flew..I sailed through the narrow hallways, my boots hanging airborne between the two...the ones who had h-hooked me. I t-think....I saw Corporal Chatty near the elevator shaft just...j-just before I was flown to...the surface. It was...just his head...b-badly..horribly mutilated, b-but I swear I...it w-winked at me just before the darkness swallowed the light. Old Chat Man offering up a final goodbye in his usual non-verbal style. Saw a...detached leg near the shaft that I'm pretty s-sure belonged to Father Pete. May he r-rest in peace. Good, decent man.

I g-get the feeling I had pretty much dropped my last remaining mental marble by t-then, though. The rest might or... might not have been based in reality. Of that I'll never be sure. Once I was flown from the cold abyss of the shaft back into a sunlight my flesh hadn't felt in over one-hundred eighty days, nothing felt quite...authentic anymore. Maybe the bugs had sedated me somehow, I don't...know.

Sailing towards the massive underbelly of the queen, it was like...I myself had the power of flight. Like I was...almost willingly making the trek towards my own demise, my ultimate destiny. Why I..seemed to be specially chosen as some kind of 'gift' to the queen didn't seem to matter at the time. As scared as I had been just moments before, a strange euphoria had emerged.

Maybe all the victims of the 'Clors had felt the same wave of joyful exuberance upon capture and subsequent breeding. Again, I'll never know.

The underbelly seemed as big as a football field, the slick surface coated in thousands of tiny, scaly pods about the size of a regulation basketball.

As I neared, it became clear that the hide

292

covering the pods was translucent. As I was being brought in for a landing between two glutinous folds that had flung open above me like...hell, like strips of flypaper, the contents of the closet row of pods became very....very clear. Too f-fucking clear for my t-taste.

Heads, Doc. They were filled with human heads. I..I saw my father in one, my grandmother in another. My...pop's right eye was open, and his mouth was open..almost like he was trying to t-tell me something, scold me possibly.

I prayed for death...screamed for it, in f-fact. Darkness came soon enough, but not before....not before I...I saw her face. Those perfectly sculpted cheekbones and s-slightly slanted eyes. Hanging in the p-pod nearest my left shoulder as it was being pinned...hell....g-glued into place. Tia's eyes opened just as everything faded to...to nothing. Popped from their sockets like someone or..something had shoved them from the back of her skull. There was a level of...desperation I had never seen in another human being in her expression, revealing stark terror at the horrors we hadn't yet...experienced, I guess. Again, I...I'll...never know...what was real or what w-was manufactured by my own...insanity. Questions without logical answers. Such is my true fate, I'm afraid, for as long as I walk God's green earth, anyhow. The heads...the queen....the flight through the Hive's elevator shaft, who's to say any of that shit really happened? Who's to say I wasn't gutted right alongside what remained of the Sarge and Brain Dog, and that the rest is nothing more than a meticulously manufactured nightmare created for the sole purpose of driving me stark-raving batty?

Makes what transpired next an enigma wrapped tightly within a fucking question mark. I heard no explosion, but felt a wave of heat wash over me like a thermal tidal wave.

Hanging from the Queen's underbelly like a cave bat, I opened my eyes to a mushroom cloud of rising flames, shooting skyward like a yellow wrecking ball. I heard the Queen shriek, wailing like a million Klaxon horns. Seems old Brain Dog had done the deed after all. The Hives self-destruct system must have been set on a delayed timer of some sort. I...I think I smiled just before that funnel cloud of blue-flame humanity melded me to the Queen's gut like a piece of fleshy shrapnel. Smiled for The Chief. The Sarge. My comrades. Smiled especially for Tia. Again, reality or hallucination? Can't say for certain. I...truly hope it did...end in that manner. If so, at least I...we didn't perish in vain."

Rhodes allowed himself to fall back onto the gurney, his head smothered by his own palms.

"That's...it, Doctor. In one very disturbing nutshell. Speaking of nutshells, you've got to figure I qualify as such, correct?"

Without leaning up or opening his eyes, Rhodes heard the doctor push away from the desk, as well as a barely audible but continuous thumping noise as the man's thumb slapped the writing pad.

"As I stated to you earlier, Mr. Rhodes, I am not a psychologist, but an ears, nose and throat man. However, I have taken ample notes to pass on to Doctor Willingham, our resident counselor, and will set you an appointment to meet with him."

"But, you're clear on my personal theory?"

The doctor cleared his throat, coughed, and then resumed the thumb-thumping.

"That these...grave images you visualize are from...past lives? That you have brief flashes from former incarnations of...yourself in those lives? Lives that all ended in....horrifying death or irreversible madness. Is this the gist?" Rolling over onto his right side, Rhodes winced slightly as the smell of spoiled pork momentarily assaulted his flaring nostrils, then just as quickly faded away. Doc must have released an air biscuit. Hell, might even have been me...man, did that reek.

"I'm convinced it's either tied into reincarnation, or I'm living out these experiences simultaneously, on another plain or...dimension. Not that I'm an expert on such matters, but I have read a few books covering such subjects through the years.

The wife thinks I've tossed an oar. Been on my back for years about...treatment. I've...lost a few jobs over the years due to occasional...breakdowns. She's actually the reason I'm here. Personally, Doc, I was afraid you guys would hear this story and toss me into the nearest padded room."

"Not at all, Mr. Rhodes. We are here to listen, evaluate, and treat. Actually, there is a fairly large percentage of the population who firmly believe in reincarnation. As far as the alternate dimensional twins' theory, I'm sure cults of followers exist that swear by it. I mean, astral projection has its believers, as does ideals concerning alternate heaven and hells right here on earth."

Rhodes rolled back over onto his back and placed his hands behind his head, cocking his neck until the doctor came fully into view. Maybe it was fatigue or possibly the mental strain of telling the story had taken its toll, but he could have sworn the doctor's voice had changed somehow, grown deeper...edgier.

Good God, am I losing it? This keeps up and I'm asking for a sedative. A very stout sedative.

"What's your personal opinion, doctor...doctor, uh...I never did get your name..." he inquired, noticing that the doctor now had his back turned to him while continuing to write on the pad.

"Oh, I'm sorry. I'm Doctor White. Elliot W. White," came the reply, the tone no longer altered. Rhodes breathed an inexplicable sigh of relief as the doctor turned about, the ever-present writing pad left lying on the desktop behind him.

I'm exhausted, that's all. Who wouldn't be in a similar situation? Warm meal and a good night's sleep and I'll be good as new. Images have already faded to a murky mist, and at least my head isn't pounding quite as hard. Confession is good for the soul, someone once said.

"Since you have asked, Mr. Rhodes, I must tell you, however, that I cannot quite agree with either possible explanation."

Leaning onto his elbows, Rhodes felt his face grow flush with a mix of excitement and dread.

"Then...what? Please don't mention the word dream, doc, because these visions mostly come to me in broad daylight."

"Dreams are not as vivid, as chronologically organized, and certainly not repeated verbatim on a semi or annual basis. No, to state such an opinion would be both a medical and professional copout."

The doctor stepped slowly to the office's far right corner, and Rhodes caught a faint, brief whiff of the same rotten stench as earlier, seemingly following the man across the room like a stale fart.

Lord, doc. Forget how to bathe or what? Cat crawl up the old poop-shoot and croak?

"Don't keep me in suspense, Doctor White. Name your suspect, and I pray it doesn't point to a future for yours truly filled with loaded hypodermics and straight jackets, although my better half might readily agree with such a diagnosis."

"Nothing quite that drastic, Mr. Rhodes, although again I must reiterate that this is purely a medical, not psychological, opinion."

"No problem, Doc. At this point, I just want another opinion, period. I have my belief, which I've stated ad nauseam. My wife and kids basically consider me a cracked egg. And you?"

"Mr. Rhodes, I must honesty tell you..." the doctor announced, turning about slowly with his chin resting on the knuckles of his left hand, "...and this may come as a shock..." he continued, strolling over until he fronted Rhodes until the two men were less than two feet apart.

"...but I believe that, within the past few moments, I may have accurately diagnosed your condition."

Rhodes couldn't refrain from openly smirking at the comment and groaned aloud.

"Within the past few moments, doc? I must have given you one hell of a clue that I'm sadly oblivious to, huh?"

The doctor shrugged, then reached over to gently pat the younger man's shoulder in an apparent calming gesture. Rhodes winced from the extreme heat emanating from the man's palm, a low clicking sound escaping his throat just as the man quickly withdrew his hand.

"Just hear me out, Mr. Rhodes. It may sound strange, but I can now offer you definite answers on both the origin and cause of your...visions, but also a suitable treatment at the conclusion of my explanation. You game, or would you rather speak to another member of the medical staff?"

Sucking in a deep, labored breath, Rhodes shook his head vehemently. He could have sworn the temperature within the room had suddenly dropped twenty degrees as chill bumps coated his arms and neck.

"No, no please. I..I didn't mean to insult, that is, I .."

"Fine. No harm, no foul, Mr. Rhodes."

The doctor hugged the writing pad to his chest as he again leaned against the corner of the wide oak desk; the broad, over-exaggerated smile he revealed less soothing in nature than arrogantly smug.

"First off, Stephen, let's drop all future references to the little misses or your shared offspring, shall we? They'll be no speaking ill of the dead on my shift, understand?"

Rhodes began unconsciously rubbing the exposed flesh of both arms even as his mouth fell open like a disengaged chain from a sliding door lock.

"Speak of..the dead? What do you...?"

Leaning forward as if to whisper, the doctor's hideously insincere grin never wavered.

"Aw, come now, Stevie-boy, this falls under the doctor-patient relationship clause. I'm no squealer. Hell, I've got a ball-and-chain all my own, and three little ankle-biters to boot. I know how they can grate on your nerves. I thought about...dreamed about, actually...doing what you did on countless nights when the stress of supporting a family became stifling...overwhelming."

His Adams apple bobbing up and down as his lips began to tremble and squirm, Rhodes hugged himself ever harder as the doctor walked around the edge of the wide desk and took a seat, the pad still clutched to his chest like a protective talisman.

"I..uh...I'm not sure what you're referr.."

"Jesus crow, Steve-O, ya ain't much for confessions, are ya?" the doctor blurted, cocking his head severely to one side until it looked as though his neck had snapped to even allow such an unnaturally warped position.

"C-confession? I d-d-don't..."

"You d-d-d-don't what, Rhodes?" the doctor mocked, the smile now a frozen grimace, '...remember where you stashed the bodies? Possibly which carpentry implement was used on each? Ya have to be specific here, man. I can indeed read minds, but digging into that pudding-based brain tissue of yours is quite the challenge, I must admit."

Wriggling atop the gurney like a beached fish,

Rhodes discovered the task of pulling himself upright a near impossibility. With Herculean effort, he eventually sat up, his hands grasping each of the gurney's metallic edges in a virtual death-grip, the knuckles of each turning a bright shade of purple.

"Listen, you whacked out son of a b-bitch, if you t-think this is so goddamned funny, I…I think I'll take y-you up on that second opinion you m-mentioned," he managed to croak, his arms beginning to shake madly from supporting his upper body.

"D-did you drug me, you b-bastard? B-but how did you manage t-to..?"

The doctor raised a hand and shook it slowly from side to side, palms up.

Rhodes could swear the man's skin tone had suddenly grown at least two shades darker.

"Save the insanity plea for the courtroom, Steve-a-rino. This ain't Judge Judy or the People's Court. My job is not to convict, but to…well, more on that later. For now, let's stick to the job at hand, that being those pesky visions of yours. Your reincarnation theory is intriguing, though misguided, as is the alternate world/alternate lives option, which would be viewed as haplessly farfetched by any reasonable standard. In baseball terms, Stevie-Wonder, you tried to stretch a double to a triple, and were tossed out by a good six feet."

Rhodes' teeth chattered uncontrollably as his blue-tinted lips parted to speak, and he glanced downward just long enough to visualize the wide circle of urine that had frozen onto his dress pants' groin and inner thighs.

"Dam…dammit, I was..not..imag…imagining…t-this…those…visions…"

The doctor seemed to levitate from the chair, and Rhodes noted in horror that the man was now almost completely bald, only a single coif of matted grayish hair clinging to the very tip of his pumpkin-shaped dome. His entire body utterly paralyzed, Rhodes couldn't even manage a choked gag as the putrid stench of decomposing flesh filled his nostrils once the doctor squatted before him.

"Yes, yes, the images are very real, Stevie-weanie. Of that there is no doubt whatsoever. You're just a bit confused on the when's and why's, that's all. Ya see, pal, you kicked some pretty nasty happenings into motion with your actions earlier today. Toppled the dominos, yes Sir; overturned the old fruit cart. Not that my people didn't see it coming, you understand, otherwise you and I wouldn't be having this delightful exchange."

"Wh-whaaa-what ac-act-act..tions?" Rhodes babbled, creating a series of tiny spit bubbles at the corners of his writhing lips.

Squatting down into a full crouch, the doctor stared up into Rhodes' wide, spastically darting eyes and momentarily studied the man's frantic expression, then reached up and placed the back of his hand on the man's sweat-moistened left check, gently stroking the pasty flesh. If a scream had been a workable option, Rhodes would have certainly wailed aloud once the doctor's jagged, pit-black nails swam fully into view. Subsequently, the rancid stench pouring from the man's sickly, overripe pores

301

would have certainly evoked a series of projectile vomiting.

"Poor Steve-Wonder-Kid, you've blocked out the whole messy shebang, haven't ya? Snapped a mind-string somewhere between claw hammer and nail-gun, didn't ya? By all means, allow me to smack your minds-eye 'refresh' button and catch ya up on the highlights. This won't take but a jiffy."

Using the same hand he'd used to massage Rhodes' cheek, the doctor reached up and clamped his fingers across the smaller man's forehead, the thumb and pinkie pressing firmly into the man's throbbing temples.

"This won't hurt a bit, my man, at least not physically. My little 'Vulcan mind-meld' imitation has been known to pan-fry a few brain cells, however, so be forewarned. It's....show-time!"

Rhodes' head reeled back violently even as his body remained rigidly prone, as if receiving a potentially fatal jolt of electricity. Beneath the doctor's steadfast grip, his eyes rolled back into his head and his teeth gnashed together with a sharp crunch, instantly shattering several recently implanted crowns.

***

The images are initially received as fast-motion vignettes, none more than a split-second in duration and displayed in frenzied blurs, but also shown in order of occurrence as to allow continuity as a whole. They soon slow to real-time motion, like a videotape switched from fast-forward mode to regular play.

A man working in a basement or garage,

302

wearing a clear plastic protective mask as he leans over an electric circular saw. Wooden chips sail onto his dark wool shirt as he guides the slim board with his thumb and forefinger. A female, her face shadowed in the room's dim lighting, enters from a side door and stands behind the man. The woman is shouting, but the gist of her words are being drowned out by the saw's incessant whine. The woman slaps the man on his upper back, the bottom half of her face now clearly defined as her lips curl into an angry scowl. The man shuts off the saw and turns slowly to her, his shoulders visibly tense. They scream and rant simultaneously, although it is clear the woman easily dominates the proceedings, now waving her arms frantically. She calls the man 'a lunatic', a 'crazy bastard', and finally a 'fucking maniac'. She then repeats the same series of words several times, each refrain louder than the one before. 'If you won't attempt to get help, I'm taking Roger to live with my father' she blurts at least five times, the man now backed away with the look of a cowering canine, his head sagging, the protective glasses coated in wood dust.

'And tell them what exactly?' the man mutters in reply, backing up until his faded jeans push against a metal work bench cluttered with various tools, 'that visions are ruining my life? Visions of my many past lives, all of which end either in grisly death or irreversible madness? Visions that caused me to lose job after job? Caused my family to fear and....despise me? You want to see me institutionalized, is that it? Would that satisfy you? Changing my bedpan and spoon-feeding me Jell-O for the next forty years?

The woman backs away a step in response to the man's aggressive tone, her own now turned down a notch and noticeably less hostile.

'Stephen, this has gone on far too long, can't you see that? We're going to lose the house...everything we own practically. I can't see anyone ever hiring you again, not in this town anyway. Your condition has to be...treated, dealt with...somehow.'

The man reaches back while speaking, pulling a long-handled tool from the workbench but keeping it tucked cautiously at the pit of his back.

'Treated? Don't you get it? Or maybe it's just that you don't really give a rat's ass, is that it? They'll lock me away, shit for brains! As soon as I begin to rant about....m-mutated flies taking over the planet or... killer ghosts from Indian burial grounds. How 'bout cannibalistic elves or spending time inside a break room from hell, playing the part of a demon whose fallen from Satan's good graces? A half hour of that crap, and they're gonna whip out a truckload of dripping needles and light me up like Fourth of July fireworks!' he bellowed, reaching out with his free hand and poking the woman in her upper chest. The woman's lips curl in fear, positioning her hands palms up as if to ward off impending blows.

'Stephen...y-you're scaring m-me.."

'Hoping they'll put me on permanent mental disability, sweet cheeks? Collect a monthly check from the State Banana Bin 'cause Daddy's gone off the deep end....slipped a gear...snapped a

304

cog...misplaced the majority of his brain-marbles?'

Backing against the closed garage door, the woman reaches back to feel for the knob just as the man throttles her with his free hand, pinning her head to the door's scarred surface. She struggles in vain to pull his hand free from her throat, low gargling noises escaping her tightly pursed lips. The man pulls the claw hammer forward into the sparse lighting, and the woman's eyes grow huge.

'You don't live with 'em, you selfish, condescending bitch! You don't wake up drenched in sour sweat, barfing your lungs out with the faces still stuck in your mind. The faces of death. The faces of the damned. Faces that won't fade away...ever. Awake or asleep, night or day, there they are. Same old reruns, over and over. Over and over...again. You have...no right...to question...me. No one... has that right. NO ONE!!!'

As before, the pace of the images drastically alters as the speed of all movement increases two-fold. The hammer sails up, back, down and back up again in a frenzied blur, crimson fluid flying freely from the clawed end until the garage door is drenched. Each short-range blow is administered at precisely the same angle until the man is forced to crouch down over his battered victim in a half-squat. A brief glimpse, no more than a half-second, is given of the woman's horribly mutilated head and face as the man leans back and then straightens to back away. Her head has been hollowed out like a Halloween pumpkin, gray brain matter spilling from a softball-sized crater at the tip of her skull. Her eyes and nose no longer exist, their remains mixed among a throbbing red mass of ripped flesh and shattered bone that looks to have been thoroughly pureed.

As the imagery again slows, the man strolls calmly back to the metal table and begins to casually clean the claw hammer with a dark-tinted rag, viewing the task through protective glasses coated in thick droplets of blood and yellowish gore. The man discards the hammer a moment later, its oak handle still cradled within the maroon-stained rag.

He wipes the protective goggles with a separate cloth, clearing just enough of the woman's thickening bodily fluids from the lens to allow a semi-clear tunnel of vision. He reaches for a nearby hacksaw, but his probing fingers change routes at the last moment, instead gripping a slightly rusty-handled nail gun posed at the table's edge.

Fast-forward mode ensues once again, a frenzied but organized outline of kinetic movement falling neatly into place within a framework of primal malevolence.

The man departs the garage, nail-gun tucked at his side like a gunslinger from an old spaghetti western, his clothing and work boots smeared in spatter marks. His hair is matted to his skull in spots, leaving the remainder standing out in various-sized cowlicks around his tightly donned goggles.

The man enters the aged, two-story Spanish brick home and follows a winding set of carpeted stairs leading to the smallest of two upstairs bedrooms.

The young teen is wearing headphones, his back turned to the man as the door is gently pushed ajar.

The first nail enters the teen's neck just beneath his left earlobe. He falls from the chair, wriggling like a hooked fish at the end of a bamboo pole.

The man stares at the surrounding walls, adorned with posters of various rap musicians and pop idols. Turning his attention quickly back to the teen, he fires a second nail through the pleading boy's uplifted right palm. A third shot enters the young man's right eye and mercifully ends his pathetic struggle for survival.

The man is back inside the garage, two bloodied forms piled in the background like cordwood.

The man again reaches for the hacksaw.

The five large kitchen garbage bags fit snugly into the trunk of the Grand Prix.

The cinder blocks allow for the bag's quick descent into the lake's deep, murky maw.

The man showers with scalding hot water, studying in amazement as the blood of others flows from his flesh and down the waiting drain in cascading swirls.

The man sleeps deeply for the first time in months, a grisly parody of a smile glued to his face

307

like a mask sewn of pure insanity.

***

"Hel-looooo! Rise and shine, Stevie-boy! Show and tell is over, my man. Now it's time for the question and answer segment of our little program," the doctor quipped, lightly slapping Rhodes across the face with the back of a horribly gnarled hand that held the tint and stench of badly burnt beef.

"Wh-? Th-that...who..how did y-you...?"

The doctor stood gracefully, then bowed as if receiving a standing ovation only he could hear. He was completely bald, his complexion pale and his expression bland, utterly without emotion. Sporting generically styled, thick-framed glasses, he was noticeably thinner and a full two to three inches shorter than before. The face was no longer full, but sunken and gaunt, the jaw square and slightly jutted.

Rhodes blinked several times, then refocused his bleary orbs on the mutating being, standing a scant two feet away. A sickening wave of familiarity loomed as the whole of the man filled his dilated pupils. Rhodes noticed his own hands and arms were tingling as if ablaze, and secretly prayed he would soon regain at least a portion of their use.

"I'm a man of many talents, Stev-a-rino. Things will begin to...clear up for you momentarily. Any further inquiries before I provide the long-awaited epilogue to this Greek tragedy of yours? Let's wrap this up, Steve-O-Meter, we're both verrrry busy men."

In between another series of rapid blinks, Rhodes noticed thick patches of hair spring up behind and around the doctor's ears. As another half-minute passed, the doctor's lips magically thickened and his reddish eyebrows grew decidedly bushier.

"They...s-she...never understood the...h-hell I went through on a d-daily basis. She w-was going to h-have me...committed. I c-couldn't...w-wouldn't put up w-with that, you know?" Rhodes whimpered, feeling the blood flow slowly returning to his arms, hands and lower extremities. He leaned forward to study the doctor more carefully, squinting until his eyelids were floss-thin. He frowned as his nostrils began to flare wildly.

"Wh-who are y-you, a-anyway? I..you..look familiar to me now. W-what's that awful goddamn s-stench?"

"My real identity is not important, Steve old pal old fart. My decision to reveal myself as Doctor White was simply an attempt to put you more at ease as we conclude these rather tiresome, but necessary steps in prepping you for what's to come."

Rhodes allowed his feet, now inexplicably bare, to drop gradually to the cool tile floor as he slid forward in virtual slow-motion, utilizing all the speed of a heavily sedated three-toed sloth.

"F-for what's to...? Y-you're going to have me...sedated, aren't you? Sedated and...held for f-futher...further observation, is that right?"

The thing calling itself Doctor White howled, whipping his head back violently and revealing neck veins as thick as cable cords. Miraculously, his Clark Kent-styled glasses remained pinned to his nose despite the sudden, hectic movement.

"Son, you can't even begin to comprehend how

far removed from the reality of the situation you truly are. Damn fine use of a well-worn cliché though. I see you've spent ample time in front of the 'boob-tube' in your time."

The doctor took a single step forward, and Rhodes discovered his gag reflex had undoubtedly returned. Lurching back, he fell against the gurney with the finger of his left hand pinching his nostrils while his right waived the air frantically, as if to ward off scorching flames.

"Whoops. I apologize for the rather...stout body odor, old chum. I realize it's less than rosy, but then again, if you were able to visualize my form in its true incarnation, you'd understand."

"My...g-god...I...it's...horri...oh...gawd..." Rhodes mumbled between dry heaves, twisting to face the opposite direction.

"Actually, it's essentially the same scent your former wife and child will exhume in a day or so, give or take a maggot feast or three. Hokay...back to the subject at hand.."

Lying across the gurney like a seasick sailor after a week-long drinking binge, Rhodes felt the moist, extremely jagged flesh of the doctor's palm scrape his back in a gentle series of compassionate strokes.

"I...I didn't s-start out to ki...ki...hurt e-either of them, but...I w-won't be l-locked away...I refuse to...l-live as a...doped up slave. Might as well...be..."

"Dead? Hey, now we're getting somewhere. Actually, my belief is that you figured such a drastic measure as slaughtering your family might serve to erase the grisly images living within your subconscious. Subtract by addition, you might say. If so, good try but no Cuban cigar, Steve-o-meter. Don't quite work that way. What you have managed to do instead gets to the heart of the purpose of my little counseling session. Allow me to preach on it..."

His head slumping over the far side of the gurney as if awaiting execution by axe-blade, Rhodes only response was a garbled whine.

"You see, Stephen, the systematic butchering of your family has qualified you as...well, sort of a grand prize winner, or...um...I guess I should say loser, at least from your perspective. Murder as a damnable charge falls under several legalities I won't bother to bore you with, but the willful killing of one's own blood is looked upon as the gravest of all. Thus, the punishment for such a ruthless, vile, abominable act has been set to fit the crime itself, possibly even surpass it. Example...kill a homeless bum in a momentary fit of rage because he wiped a booger on your best vest; qualifies as a Class A sin.

Example two.....exterminating your best buddy after he's caught hiding the sausage with the better half and subsequently taking action with extreme prejudice. Such premeditated elimination is normally ruled a Class B.

But you, Steve-o-gram, you stepped up to the plate of unholy acts, eyed a hanging curve and ripped the grand slam of all grand-slams with two out in the bottom of the ninth! Cleared the stadium roof with room to spare, my man! Class C termination...thus, a Class C ruling has been rightfully doled out in your honor. This is where I slither...pardon me, I should say, step officially into

311

the mix."

Lifting his head until his chin rested on the edge of the gurney, Rhodes continued to keep his nostrils tightly pinched as he muttered wearily, his voice comically nasal.

"W-who are you, anyway? W-where's the r-real d-d-doctor, d-dammit?"

The doctor again laughed heartily, then scratched his bald head, which Rhodes noticed began to immediately peel like dried snake flesh, large circular flakes filling the sky like confetti from a street parade.

"Sorry, Steve-O, it's just that you sound amazingly like Porky Pig with your nose-holes constricted. I am merely a messenger, my man, here to pass on sentencing to those who have so horribly lost their way as surface dwellers and have been made immortal wards to the Dark Master. As for your other inquiry, I believe the official sawbones you seek has taken solace in the metal locker just behind you."

The metal locker consisted of a single narrow section, not over a foot wide, and sat between two well-stocked glass medicine cabinets. The words 'SOILED GOWNS ONLY' was stenciled across the locker's top. Just as his left arm began to rise and extend towards the locker's pull-down handle, Rhodes felt a bolt of pure electricity crawl up his spine and into the base of his skull. His trembling fingers grasped the handle and hung there like a fleshy attachment. Feeling the cobwebs that had entombed his brain finally begin to rend and tear away, Stephen Rhodes desired nothing more at that very moment than to allow his hand to fall away from the locker handle without viewing the content. Although uncertain of his fear's exact origin, he had little doubt of its authenticity.

"C'mon, Stephen. One downward pull and I promise all the mystery, the insufferable guessing and double-talk, ends. All the frustration and confusion will vanish from your mind like cheap wine down a drunkard's parched gullet," the doctor's voice echoed as if he now stood a great distance away and was speaking through cupped hands.

"Time to end the dance, Stephen. I think you already know the answer, its time to divulge the matching question."

Metal screeched briefly, and the locker door swung open as if shoved forcefully from the inside.

Stephen Rhodes right arm instantly released his nostrils and fell limp, the knuckles striking the hard floor with a low thump. His left arm wrenched back in a sudden jerk, the momentum of the sudden lurch sending him toppling from the gurney and into a wild, clumsily executed roll in the opposite direction of the locker.

"G...god...oh...d-d-damn...n-now I...oh...uh,...s-shit..." he babbled in a mostly incoherent whine, kicking the gurney forward while simultaneously pushing himself back.

"Coming back to you now, ain't it boy? Its allllllll coming back, am I right? Subconscious denial is a true bitch when the mental levee collapses in the face of cold, hard truth," the doctor blurted happily, and Rhodes could suddenly swear

313

the man was actually speaking inside his ear canal.

Propped within the cramped space until it appeared to actually be standing upright in a slight crouch, the body was immersed in a virtual sea of crimson from neck to feet. The man's slack, lifeless face was scrunched within his own armpit, his arms tucked over his head in a grotesque 'touchdown' signal, his tongue protruding from between tightly gritted teeth.

The gaping slash below his chin was no more than two inches in length, but had obviously penetrated an artery, as the lab coat he sported was literally drenched in his own slowly seeping life-source.

"I do believe he had mentioned something about 'prolonged treatment' in a nearby mental facility. From that second mouth you so creatively designed for him, I get the feeling you disagreed with his recommendation rather vehemently. The poor sap shouldn't have left that scalpel just lying about, especially if doling out such drastic measures to…let's just say, potentially unstable patients, am I right, Steve-Mc-Queen?"

Pushing himself upright with visibly trembling legs, Rhodes lips began to twitch uncontrollably.

"H-he h-had no…r-right to…I won't be locked up, damn it! I-I j-just w-w-won't!"

"Y-y-you d-d-don't h-h-have to worry about that, old son,' the doctor/thing mocked gleefully, '….on the contrary, you're about to experience more freedom than you ever thought possible!"

The doctor/thing cackled madly while suddenly executing an impromptu 'Curly dance' from old

Three Stooges' shorts, kicking his heels back while frantically flexing his elbows.

Like a bolt from the blue, Rhodes suddenly realized where he had seen the doctor before. His eyes darted madly around the room, hoping to spot a potential weapon to secure. The wall-clock's hands spun counter-clockwise in a frenzied blur, the dark brown wallpaper around it peeling forth in pointy strips, like thousands of flexing, grasping appendages.

The doctor/thing suddenly leapt in Rhodes path, essentially pinning his weakened frame to the wall.

"I know what you're thinking, Steve 'n Edie, and believe it when I say, you're in no danger from yours truly. Alas, the damage you fear has already been inflicted."

As the doctor/thing backed away a step, it gestured downward with a single glance.

Rhodes followed the thing's glare to the origin of interest, then slowly lifted his arms and turned his wrists inward until they were parked just inches from his frighteningly pale face.

"Seems ya weren't quite finished with the blade after the doctor's unplanned surgical technique. Shoved him in the locker and then proceeded to slice your own hide like a Christmas Roast. By the time I got here, this entire room looked like it'd been painted over in Cherry Syrup!"

"Get a-a-away from m-me, y-you c-crazy son of a b-b.." Rhodes shrieked, placing his blood-smeared palms on the doctor/thing's chest in a feeble attempt to hold it at bay. Despite his hands facing in the opposite direction, shredded strips of maroon-shaded

315

skin visibly hung from each wrist like soggy confetti.

"Steve old buddy, kindly allow m-m-me to f-f-f-finish my debriefing. Your whimpering, 'lost-in-space at what's transpiring here' act is beginning to carve into my last nerve," the doctor/thing growled, slapping Rhode's hands away roughly, then backing away several steps.

"Here's the deal, buddy-boy. It isn't about reincarnation, but premonition. You haven't already lived the lives that filled your nightmares, Steve old chum. Fact is, you have YET to live them. Brief glimpses into your own infernal future, they were. Or should I say, own futures, as in the plural sense?"

Rhodes began wiping his mutilated wrists onto the wall at his back, leaving thick, twisted streaks of crimson in their wake. His entire face began to twitch and distort, as if suffering a mild electric shock.

"F-fu..future? Fu-future l-lives? W-when? W-wh-where?"

The doctor/thing shook his head, his jaw dropping in mock disbelief.

"Son, you aren't the sharpest tack in the bag, are ya? Dimmest bulb I've run across in decades, I sincerely believe. Let me spell it out for you, dumb shit..." the doctor/thing spat angrily, leaping from the gurney as if to attack.

Rhodes winced back in shock at the thing's sudden intrusion, violently thumping his skull on the nearby wall.

"D-d-don't k-k-kill...m-me..." he whimpered, covering his face with hands that looked to have been shoved through a sausage grinder.

"Kill you?" the doctor/thing howled sarcastically, '...Why, Steve old paint, how could I possibly commit such an act on someone who is...pardon my crudeness... already as dead as a fucking hammer? Sorry, but medically speaking, if I may be so bold...that shit just ain't possible."

"D-d-d-dead...e-a-d...?" Rhodes babbled meekly as the space around him seemed to shift somehow, growing increasingly dark and bleary, as if he were on the verge of passing out.

"That's right...dead ed...deceased...the final croak...the last gasp....kicking the eternal bucket...no longer with pulse. The minute you carved those horizontal smiles into your wrists and the heart muscle ceased to flex, I was instantly transported to your side to begin processing your travel arrangements, as is my assigned task."

Closing his eyes momentarily, Rhodes placed his palms at both temples and pushed inward with what minute strength remained at the core of his battered soul.

"W-wa-wake u-up...just n-need to...w-wake..up. This is...j-just a-another d-damned...v-vis...vision...t-that's a-a-all...."

This time, he was absolutely certain that the doctor/thing's voice did indeed originate from inside the undeniably deep-fried recesses of his mind, although the voice utilized no longer resembled anything remotely human. Raspy and impossibly deep to the point of being incomprehensible, each syllable was coated in static waves born of pure malevolence.

317

"Such ludicrous denial tactics are utterly useless at this juncture, Rhodes, or should I address you by your impending identity, that being country gentleman Bobby Drake, steel plant worker and future breeder of man-eating hound pups from a dark, distant galaxy. After that, your itinerary leads you smack dab into an upscale loony-bin, where you'll experience multiple deaths within the ultra-paranoid persona of a grand-scale lunatic. Following that thrilling little adventure, we're off to the circus, so to speak, as you play the part of animal-rights activist to a viscous little creature that craves the taste of human flesh. From there, it's a veritable funhouse of horrors, from haunted Indian burial grounds to a Ghost Rider of the old west who collects souls like some collect stamps.

Wake up and sniff the sulfur, you murdering, soulless worm...this joyride is never-ending, infinite, as constant as the shifting of the cosmos themselves. You signed up for the cruise of the damned as soon as you played Cain to those supposedly closest to you. I'll be your cruise director as we chart a permanent course into treacherous waters filled to overflowing with death, dismemberment, and unparalleled mental and physical anguish. There's a flashing signpost up ahead, past the blazing pits of eternally charred souls and fleshy masks of agony forever unchanged; it marks the initial port of call for the one formerly known as Stephen Rhodes...thrust forward to begin anew, equally doomed and damned but oblivious to the fact..."

Mercifully, the voice fades like a child's cry within a monsoon as the landscape melds from solid to liquid; from rock formation to mudslide and back again. The small, trembling form opens a single eye, the lid of his second stuck shut as if glued. His tiny nostrils flare as he tries desperately to focus the single orb, filling with a strong mix of anti-septic and warm bodily fluids.

"Big, stout male he is, Mister Drake. Gonna be a whopper, from the looks of 'im," a man's voice bellows just as the being's second eye pops open and joins the first in a fevered attempt to match a picture to the hectic noises surrounding it.

"You two have a name picked out yet?" the same voice asks.

"Robert Wendell Drake. Being the doctor that just birthed 'im, you might as well be the first to call him Bobby," another man answers as a female voice sighs wearily in the background.

Just as the hand swings over and connects with his bare buttocks, still moist from afterbirth, the newborn sees clearly the trio of masked forms eagerly surrounding his shaky, naked frame, hanging upside down and held by the ankles.

The infant Bobby Drake shrieks aloud, and hears the room fill with joyous laughter and sighs of relief.

"You'll have a fine life, Robert Drake,' the physician exclaims, handing the newborn to his beaming father. The child continues to cry in banshee-like wails as a tiny voice only he can hear penetrates his underdeveloped mind, planting subliminal messages that speak of impending doom and internal damnation.

Years later, the child's first spoken word will

319

not be 'mama' or 'dada', but a haunting whisper his shocked mother could only readily identify as 'demon'.